COTTON'S LAW

A Sheriff Cotton Burke Western

Phil Dunlap

BERKLEY BOOKS, NEW YORK

THE BERKLEY PUBLISHING GROUP
Published by the Penguin Group
Penguin Group (USA) Inc.
375 Hudson Street, New York, New York 10014, USA
Penguin Group (Canada), 90 Eglinton Avenue East, Suite 700, Toronto, Ontario M4P 2Y3, Canada
(a division of Pearson Penguin Canada Inc.)
Penguin Books Ltd., 80 Strand, London WC2R 0RL, England
Penguin Group Ireland, 25 St. Stephen's Green, Dublin 2, Ireland (a division of Penguin Books Ltd.)
Penguin Group (Australia), 250 Camberwell Road, Camberwell, Victoria 3124, Australia
(a division of Pearson Australia Group Pty. Ltd.)
Penguin Books India Pvt. Ltd., 11 Community Centre, Panchsheel Park, New Delhi—110 017, India
Penguin Group (NZ), 67 Apollo Drive, Rosedale, Auckland 0632, New Zealand
(a division of Pearson New Zealand Ltd.)
Penguin Books (South Africa) (Pty.) Ltd., 24 Sturdee Avenue, Rosebank, Johannesburg 2196, South Africa

Penguin Books Ltd., Registered Offices: 80 Strand, London WC2R 0RL, England

COTTON'S LAW

A Berkley Book / published by arrangement with the author

PRINTING HISTORY
Berkley edition / January 2012

Cover illustration by Dennis Lyall.
Cover design by Diana Kolsky.
Interior text design by Tiffany Estreicher.

ISBN: 978-0-425-24576-7

BERKLEY®
Berkley Books are published by The Berkley Publishing Group,
a division of Penguin Group (USA) Inc.,
375 Hudson Street, New York, New York 10014.
BERKLEY® is a registered trademark of Penguin Group (USA) Inc.
The "B" design is a trademark of Penguin Group (USA) Inc.

PRINTED IN THE UNITED STATES OF AMERICA

10 9 8 7 6 5 4 3 2 1

Acknowledgments

No books are ever produced in a vacuum, nor can they be written properly without the input of professionals, friends, and family. Support is essential. I must thank my editor, Faith Black, whose excellence in her profession makes me a better writer, and the designers and illustrators at Berkley for creating great books. Thanks, also, to my critique partner, Tony Perona, a top-notch author in his own right, and to my wife, Judy, who never fails to gently let me know if I'm veering off course. And I give a tip of the old Stetson to the folks at the Western Writers of America, whose tireless efforts to promote the Western genre are an invaluable asset to anyone hoping to entertain and inform about such an important period of our history.

Good friends all. Thank you.

Chapter 1

Apache Springs, New Mexico Territory—1880

Contrary to popular belief, a dark, soundless night may not always be a comfort.

The roar of the big-bore rifle echoed off the rocks a scant two seconds after the bullet splintered the front door of the Apache Springs jail, barely missing Deputy Memphis Jack Stump's head as he leaned over to pick something up off the floor. The hunk of lead then slammed into the back wall, knocking a one-inch hole nearly all the way through.

"Sonofabitch!" Jack yelled as he crashed to the floor with a bone-jarring thud. His heart was pounding like a stamp mill. He scrambled to untangle himself from the overturned chair. Hugging the floor in an effort to stay low, he gingerly reached up to retrieve his Remington .44 from atop the desk where he had removed the cylinder for cleaning.

"Damned lucky I dropped that cleaning cloth," he muttered aloud, sweat breaking out on his forehead. He was also happy the door had been made of solid wood, with no glass to make the shooter's aim more certain. He'd been shot at before, but never when doing a simple task in a closed room. The shock of it had him both rattled and furious at the same time.

With hasty fingers, he slipped the cylinder back into the gun's frame, loaded it from his gun belt, and cocked it in readiness. Whatever might come next, he had no idea. Knowing that someone had just tried to kill him—and would want to know if he had succeeded—kept him on high alert. He waited. And waited. Dead silence. He scooted to the front of the office, carefully reached for the oil lantern on the wall, and blew out the flame. *The lamplight must have given him a perfect target*, Jack thought. *He only had to aim three feet right of the window and he would have had me cold.*

He crawled on his elbows to the door, in preparation to yank it open and make a swift exit to the cover of a solid oak deacon's bench sitting under the porch overhang. He figured it would give him a safe haven to determine where the shot had come from. Maybe even get lucky enough to return fire. But no shots followed. He listened for the telltale noise of a horse galloping away to assure the shooter's escape. Several more minutes passed. He heard only the emptiness of the night, that hush that falls over the land when something terrible has happened and nature itself has gone into hiding.

Unwilling to wait longer, he threw open the door and dashed outside, throwing himself behind the bench. Peeking over the top, he realized that the probable source of the shot was from somewhere among the house-size boulders a thousand feet east of town. There was a wide gap between the two buildings straight across the street, left vacant when a fire had destroyed the home of the town's first minister. It was never rebuilt.

After several minutes of searching the darkness for any sign of movement up in the rocks and any follow-up shot, Memphis Jack eased from his position behind the bench and moved farther back into the shadows. He didn't wish to give anyone a clear target as, hunched over, he made his way around the side of the building to the alley, then trotted several hundred feet in the dark to a place where he could safely race across the street. His aim was to get himself in position to rush the rocks. He maneuvered alongside the hardware store where the road turned slightly, which gave him natural cover for a sprint across to the side of the bank building. His eyes had finally adjusted to the darkness, and he could make out several clusters of crates and boxes of trash set out behind stores. No sign of a single person, however.

It was a few minutes after midnight on a Wednesday. He didn't really expect to find anyone wandering the streets, other than possibly a straggler from the town's only saloon sleeping off a drunk in a doorway. While he *hoped* to find someone who might have heard the shot and noticed where it had come from, he came away empty-handed. Directly in back of the saloon, a high wooden stockade fence enclosed an area of several hundred square feet. That fence gave Jack cover to make for the cluster of boulders that rose up the side of the mountain. He cursed as he stumbled over a bucket someone had left in his path. He flattened himself against the wall to await any response from the shooter, who must now know where he was. A minute, maybe two, passed before he dared move deeper into the darkness.

Memphis Jack broke into a hard run toward the nearest of the rocks from where he figured the shot had emanated. He dropped to a crouch as soon as he was certain he was protected sufficiently to scan his surroundings. Making his way around and between boulder after boulder, his Remington held forward and cocked, he swiveled his head in nearly constant motion hoping to catch a glimpse of movement that would give away the shooter's position. Glad for a sudden glimpse of light from a quarter moon peeking from behind a cloud, he slipped around the largest and highest rock, only to jump at the sound of something skittering away. By instinct, he fired toward the sound. He held his breath as he awaited an answering shot. Nothing. It was clear he was alone. He shook his head at the probability that he'd merely scared the hell out of a desert rat. But he was now convinced that whoever had taken a shot at him was long gone. He paused before heading back to the jail, turning every few steps to check his back trail.

When he got to the jail, he locked and barred the door behind him and relit the oil lamp. He set the swivel chair behind the desk upright and pulled his handkerchief from his pocket. He nervously wiped at his sweaty brow and sighed deeply. He stared at the hole in the door and then turned to the place in the back wall where the bullet had imbedded itself. He took out his pocketknife and stepped to the wall. He dug out the bullet and whistled.

If that sucker had hit me, it would have left a hole big enough to stuff a squirrel in, he thought. Shaking his head, he went to the desk, took hold of two corners, and gave it a hard tug. The massive walnut desk scooted noisily around to a ninety-degree angle from the way it had been. He pushed the chair around behind it and sat. Looking at the door, then at the rear wall, he could tell his chair was far enough back. Now, if anybody tried that shot with the expectation of hitting whoever might be sitting behind the desk, they'd be sorely disappointed. Unless, of course, their weapon could shoot around corners.

After pondering the situation for several minutes, Memphis Jack got up, pulled a shotgun from the rack, loaded it with buckshot, and tucked it under his arm. He blew out the lamp on the wall and locked the door behind him. He stayed close to the buildings as he made his way along the boardwalk toward the small house the town had provided for its sheriff. Jack and his consort, Melody, had been allowed to live in it until Sheriff Cotton Burke was healed up after his confrontation with the Cruz gang, during which he had been seriously wounded. Jack had stepped in and saved the sheriff from certain death by killing one of the outlaws before he could get to the wounded lawman and finish the job.

Jack was now heading to Melody's bed. His near brush with death had him wide awake, so he was taking no chances on giving the shooter another chance at him.

When he pushed open the door to the small clapboard house, hurriedly slipping inside, he was greeted by Melody, already in one of her well-known snits.

"Where have you been, Jack? I've been waiting up for over an hour."

"Sorry, Melody, I was otherwise occupied."

"What could have been more important to you than coming home to me?" She leaned on the doorway to the bedroom, pulling back her filmy robe to reveal her ample charms. Her invitation was clear as she subtly raised one eyebrow.

"Nothing much. Just wrestlin' with a question. That's all." Jack leaned the shotgun against the table and unbuckled his gun belt, letting it drop onto the nearest chair.

"A question? That's what kept you away? A damned question? What question was important enough that you let me sit here all alone twiddling my thumbs?"

"Just wondering why someone wanted to kill me, that's all." He plopped onto the couch and leaned back with a sigh.

"What! Someone tried to kill you? Who?"

"Don't know. I'll look into it in the morning."

"Then how do you know someone wanted you dead?"

"The bullet that tore through the door to the jail, missing me by inches. That's how."

"Damn! I'll bet it was someone aiming for that scoundrel Cotton Burke. I'd bet that's who it was. It's time we got the hell out of this dreadful collection of run-down buildings and folks with no backbone. What do you say, honey? You finally ready to pack up and git?"

"Uh-huh. We'll talk about it later. Time for bed, Melody." Jack yawned and fell onto the deep feather mattress. Twenty minutes later, he was still wide awake.

Chapter 2

Catron County Sheriff Cotton Burke slapped the reins across the rump of the dapple-gray gelding pulling the buckboard. Beside him sat Emily Wagner, owner of the Wagner ranch and the love of his life. Since he'd been staying at her ranch for the past four weeks recovering from a gunshot wound, his deputy, Memphis Jack, had been left in charge of keeping the peace in Apache Springs. But Cotton was completely healed now–or at least *he* thought so–and growing anxious to return to the job to which he'd been elected. Although Emily had tried in her gentle way to persuade him to remain on the ranch longer to be certain he'd not have a relapse, Cotton wasn't the type to sit around on the porch in the evening, listening to the crickets, and chatting idly about this and that. Notwithstanding, he was deeply conflicted about his situation as every minute he spent with Emily was like heaven on earth to him. Returning to the world of risking his life had been made more difficult by each day he spent at her ranch.

Emily's husband had been shot down and killed during a

bank robbery almost three years back, an innocent victim of the treachery of a ruthless gang headed by the notorious Virgil Cruz. Vanzano Cruz, Virgil's brother, had fallen to Cotton's deadly accuracy with a gun. Much later, Virgil had also met the same fate. With her husband dead, and the ranch now her responsibility, Emily had accepted the challenge when most folks figured she'd move back to St. Louis, where she'd lived before her marriage. But Emily wasn't a quitter. In addition to her beauty, Cotton was also attracted to her spunk. He'd been fascinated by her even before her husband died, and now he was free to let her know of his interest. But he'd been reticent to be too forward, desiring instead the easier road of letting things take care of themselves.

Defensive to the point of righteous indignation whenever someone broached the subject of the two of them getting together, he had tried to keep his feelings from spilling out, as, at the mere sight of her, his knees felt weak. His eyes told the story he felt compelled to keep to himself. The simple act of watching as she went about her daily routine caused his heart to beat faster and laid his soul open for anyone to see.

And her offer to nurse him back to health during his convalescence had eased his shyness, and he had slowly revealed his long-standing interest in her. Her answer to his revelation was "What took you so long?"

"Will you be okay driving back to the ranch alone?" he said, knowing full well she'd done it twice weekly ever since her husband's death. He'd always been protective of her, but now, beginning to verbalize his feelings better, he often let slip his concerns for her safety, especially after her abduction by the Cruz gang. She had more than once expressed disdain for a man who hovers over a woman like a prison warden. That comment always drew him back into his shell for a time. But only temporarily. His overall desire to see her never again experience such a frightening encounter led him to ignore her admonitions and forge ahead as her defender-in-waiting, whether she saw it as necessary or not.

"Yes, my overprotective love, I shall, as always, be just fine."

"Just makin' certain."

"After I drop you off at the jail, I'm going to the dry goods store for some things. Do you need anything?"

"Not that I'm aware of."

"Well, I'm going to get you a couple of new shirts, anyway. Since you have only two, the one with the frayed cuffs and the other with the stitched-up bullet hole. A pair of socks wouldn't hurt, either. Shall I pick you up at the jail in about two hours?"

Cotton scratched his head. He needed to get back to the job of being sheriff, but he didn't know how to tell her. He'd been thinking of moving back into his little house and sending Jack and Melody off to the hotel. He'd need to get the town council's permission for such an expenditure first, however. And he wasn't that all-fired certain of their response.

"Uh, no. I should go to the livery and pick up my horse, that is if she still recognizes me. I'll, uh, ride out later."

Emily had been aware that this day would come, but that didn't stop her from giving him a disappointed pout. She sat silently for a moment and then slapped the reins to move the horse on down the street. Cotton walked to the jail glancing back at her three or four times.

When he stepped up on the boardwalk, he saw the hole in the door. He put his hand on the butt of his Colt as he slowly stepped aside and eased open the door. He found Jack sitting at the rearranged desk, flipping through a stack of wanted dodgers. He looked up at Cotton's entrance.

"Whooee! If it ain't my old friend, Cotton Burke. You *are* a sight for sore eyes. I'm real happy you're able to sit up and take nourishment, pard. If you're lookin' to come back to work, I'll bet I can find a chore or two that won't stress you too much." Jack leaned back in the swivel chair, laced his fingers behind his head, and grinned from ear to ear.

"Why, yes, Deputy, I do believe I am able to do a few *small* jobs, provided they can be done from an easy chair. Like that one you're sittin' in."

"Good, very good. Glad you're back, in that case."

"Not happy enough to ride out to the Wagner place on occasion to make sure I was gettin' along okay. Twice, in four long weeks, wasn't it?"

"I been right busy here, keepin' the peace in this hell-hole you call Apache Springs, so I wasn't able to tear myself away all that often. You understand."

"Uh-huh. A certain whore named Melody comes to mind."

"Why, Cotton, you really *do* understand."

"What I *don't* understand is that hole in the door. You screw up cleanin' your hogleg, or were you too drunk to know what you were shootin' at?"

"Now, that hurts, Cotton, that really hurts. How could I do somethin' so reckless, especially since anything I do could end up tarnishin' *your* fine reputation? We wouldn't want that, now, would we?"

"Just give me a straight answer, Jack. Who put the hole in the damned door?"

Jack suddenly got serious. He sat forward, leaning on his elbows.

"I wish I knew. One thing for sure, it come too close to blowin' my brains all over this dismal office. You could easily be lookin' down on my cold corpse in front of the undertaker's."

"Damn! When did this happen?"

"Last night. It was almost midnight, and I was cleaning my gun. All of a sudden a bullet the size of a fist blew all the way through the office. It buried itself in the back wall. I didn't hear the shot for a couple of seconds after the damned thing went whizzin' by. I had just bent down to retrieve my cleanin' rag when it happened. I tried to find where the shot came from, but in the dark, that proved impossible."

Cotton looked at the hole in the back wall and, as Jack had, judged the trajectory to be from up in the rocks outside of town.

"Any chance it could have been an accident? Someone out blowin' off steam? Maybe a stray bullet?"

"Is that really what you think? A bullet fired from a long distance off makes a perfect path across this very desk right where I was sitting a second before, and it could have been an accident?"

"No, I reckon it couldn't. Someone fully intended to kill one of us. Maybe the question should be which one? And why?"

Jack quickly adopted an all-too-familiar attitude. "Since we're talkin' attempted murder, I don't reckon I considered that I might have been the target. Me bein' the friendly one an' all. *Damn!* What was it that made you think it might be someone other than you?"

"Don't be a smartass. It'd likely be best if I stay in town tonight. I need to tell Emily before she leaves. Then, you and I are going to take a ride out to those rocks and see if we can find something that might point us in the direction of an assassin." Jack was scratching his head as Cotton left to find Emily and give her the news. He knew she'd try to convince him to let his deputy handle things awhile longer, but he knew Cotton wouldn't do that. Even though he hated leaving her alone.

Cotton caught up to Emily as she came out of the general store. She had her arms loaded with packages wrapped in brown paper. His first concern was that she had done more than replace his two shirts and, as he'd seen her do before, gotten carried away with finding other things she considered his wardrobe woefully lacking in. He took the packages from her and loaded them in the buckboard.

"Did you find out that Jack is capable of taking care of the town without you?"

"Quite the contrary, Emily, I found out that someone tried to kill him, or possibly me, depending on who the shooter thought was in the jail last night."

"Mercy! What happened?"

"A shot was fired through the front door, barely missing Jack's thick skull. I'm going to have to try picking up the shooter's trail. Don't know when I'll get back to the ranch. If it's too late, I'll stay here in town."

Emily looked disappointed, but he could tell her concern was for the safety of both him and Jack. She knew he was doing what he had to do. She took his hand as he helped her into the seat. She reached over and pulled two of the brown paper–wrapped packages off the top of the pile and handed them to him.

"Okay. Here, take these so you will look halfway decent when you catch the vermin that would do such a thing. Stay safe." She bent down and gave him a kiss before settling back for the long ride home. He watched as she drove off, raising a small dust cloud behind the one-horse conveyance.

He went back into the jail, to find Jack making certain they had ammunition for a pair of shotguns and some extra bullets for their revolvers.

Chapter 3

The day had turned into another hot one. Clear skies with nary a hint of breeze. They tied their horses to a nearby cottonwood and began their trek up through the rocks. Weaving in and around the monstrous boulders, each took a different dusty trail, slowly, methodically searching for any signs of someone having been up there recently.

They'd been at it for nearly two hours when, near the top, where a smaller flat-topped rock jutted away from the rest, Cotton found what he was looking for.

"Jack, it looks like he might have been hunkered down behind this one. It'd be a perfect spot to steady a big-bore rifle."

Jack eased his way to the top beside Cotton. He nodded as he said, "You're right. There's a powder burn on the rock surface. He was waitin' for the right opportunity. Still don't tell us who it was, though."

Cotton bent down to check the ground, a mixture of fine sand and gravel worn away from some of the sandstone that also permeated the area. Boot prints with one heel showing more wear than the other indicated there'd been but a single shooter. He also found a couple of cigarillo butts stomped out in the dirt. The biggest clue, however, was the .50-caliber brass cartridge of a type commonly used in the Sharps buffalo rifle. Cotton held it up. Jack took it and turned it over and over.

"Bring anyone to mind, Jack?"

"Nope. I haven't seen anything like this since the buffalo hunters killed off all their prey and had to resort to bringing down jackrabbits."

"I'm going to backtrack this fella as far as I can."

"I'm right there with you, Sheriff."

They began following the boot prints up and over the first hill, then down a slight drop into a narrow gouge in the ground. Water had cut a swash that wandered through the rocks to finally end up joining the creek at the edge of Apache Springs. During the rainy season, water gushed between the rocks, wearing them down slowly over the centuries. The prints followed the water's course to where they found where the shooter had tied his horse.

"Left his mount here. The animal probably stood for a little more'n an hour, I'd say," Jack said, bending down to feel how deep into the ground the prints went. "This ground is pretty soft, and slightly wet. But the prints aren't deep, so I'd say he rode a smaller horse, maybe a pony."

Cotton nodded.

"Let's get on back. I'm thinkin' we need to enlist the aid of a professional at tracking."

"You're thinkin' Henry Coyote, aren't you?"

"Who else?"

"Course Henry rides a pony, you know. What if he's our man?"

"Now, why in hell would Henry Coyote want to take a shot at you?"

Jack thought about that for a moment. He squinted from the bright sun bouncing off the white rocks.

"Well, if he got me out of the way, you'd have to come

back to town and take up sheriffin' again. That way, you'd be too far to call on in case Emily had a need, and she'd be forced to rely on Henry, once again."

"Jack, sometimes I think that imagination of yours has slipped over the side of a steep cliff. The whole idea of Henry Coyote being our culprit is preposterous. Forget it."

"Just sayin' he's the only one around here that rides a pony."

"No, there's another."

"Who?"

"The man that took a shot at you."

Whitey Granville reined in in front of the shabby cabin deep in the piney forest above Cedar City, a nearly abandoned mining town that had seen a steep decline in population after the last mine failed. His pony was lathered from the long, hot ride. It was nearing sundown as he tied his mount to a crude rail. A water trough was near enough for the animal to get a drink while Whitey went inside.

Two oil lanterns lit the inside of the single room. There were no windows. A potbellied stove sat in the center of the space, with a small pile of splintered wood stacked nearby, just in case the nights turned chilly. A man leaned on a long, wide plank held up at either end by an empty whiskey barrel. In front of him sat a glass and a half-empty bottle.

"'Bout time, Whitey. What kept you?"

"Forty miles of hard ridin' and a bunch of Indians on the prowl. I had to lay low for a spell till they decided to move on south. Got another glass?"

The man took a glass from behind him and set it in front of Whitey, who quickly snatched up the bottle and poured the glass full to the rim with the pale brown liquid. He raised the glass and took the entire contents down in one gulp.

"Did you kill that bastard? The one I paid you five hundred dollars for?"

"Don't know fer sure. Couldn't wait around to find out.

If he was sittin' at the desk, as I'm certain he was, then my shot likely took his head clean off. He sure as hell didn't return fire."

"I'm not payin' you for guesses, you idiot. I need to be sure. Damn!"

"You could ride back into Apache Springs and see for yourself. Don't no one know you there, do they?" Whitey said.

The man stared at Whitey with anger growing in his eyes. He shot a hand across the makeshift bar and grabbed Whitey by the collar, yanking him halfway across the plank.

"You dumb sonofabitch! I didn't shell out my hard-earned greenbacks for the job to get done halfway. Now, you get back on that mount of yours and bring me proof that the man I sent you to kill is dead. You hear me? I'm headin' for Las Vegas. That's where you'll find me, at the Saloon #1. And don't fail me again or I'll kill *you*, instead."

"Y-yessir. N-no need for that. I-I'll just be on my way." Whitey's eyes were wide as he found himself being stared down by the very face of evil, a look that, gun or no gun, could take a man's life as easily as any hunk of lead. He dropped the glass, which shattered as it rolled off the tabletop and hit the stone floor. He was out the door and back in the saddle in about twenty seconds flat.

As the sun sank low on the horizon, a warm red glow washed across the little cabin and the tall, well-dressed man leaning in the doorway. A wry smile swept across his chiseled face. He liked the feeling he got putting the fear of a bullet in Whitey, and others before him, especially since he had never been known to carry a gun.

Cotton mounted up at the livery stable. Jack stood nearby.

"What do you want me to do while you're gone?" Jack asked.

"You might spend some time doin' what you do best. Go over to the saloon, down a couple whiskeys, and listen for anything that could be useful in findin' this coward."

"Ain't had much time for drinkin' lately, what with all the crime needin' tendin' to around here. Mighta forgot how."

"Try hard to remember," Cotton said as he spurred his mare to a trot straight out of town in the direction of the Wagner ranch.

Jack stomped off toward the jail, grumbling to himself about so-called friends that can't seem to ever let a man forget his past mistakes. Truth be told, Jack wasn't all that good at forgiving himself for that night in Gonzales ten years back when he got drunk and shot up the town, ending the life of an innocent man sitting too close to a second-story window. Cotton was the sheriff there, then, and Jack had been his deputy. After the incident, Cotton told Jack to get out of town and never come back or he'd be sure he was hanged for his stupidity. Not long after that—primarily because of Jack's bad behavior—Cotton was voted out of office, and he began to wander from New Mexico to Texas to Colorado to Arizona and back, hiring out his gun to towns that needed a man who wasn't afraid to shoot when it became necessary. And Cotton could surely shoot with the best of them. As soon as Cotton had left Gonzales, Jack had snuck back into town and stayed.

After coming to Apache Springs, ostensibly to help an aging sheriff cope with a gang of owlhoots bent on turning it into another Abilene or Dodge City, Cotton was asked to run for sheriff at the end of the old man's term. He did and won, much to his surprise. He'd finally found a place to settle down after running from the Gonzales affair, in which Jack played the major role. While nothing could seem to keep Jack from the gambling tables and the whiskey and Melody, he still carried the scar of destroying not only his own career as a lawman, but that of a friend, also. Now Cotton appeared to be giving him a second chance. He wasn't all that certain he was up to the task.

As he strolled into the saloon, he looked around, searching the myriad of faces, looking for anyone who could be the midnight shooter. He walked to the bar and ordered a beer.

Chapter 4

When Cotton rode into the yard at the Wagner ranch, Emily came running out to greet him. She had a dish towel in her hand and an apron tied around her slim waist. Her smile lit up the evening.

"Cotton, you're safe. I'm so relieved you changed your mind about staying in town. C'mon in and have some supper."

Cotton followed her inside. Three of her cowboys were seated around the table, savagely attacking some steaks and boiled potatoes. He took one of the empty seats. The cowboys muttered mouthful acknowledgments of his presence but shied away from any formal greeting that might take them away from their ravenous attack on the victuals. Emily placed a plate with a still-sizzling steak in front of him, along with a cup of coffee. She sat down next to him, gave him a nudge with her elbow, and shot him a coy grin. His face turned almost as red as the bowl of beets that sat across the table.

"So, did you catch the man who took a shot at Jack?" she asked.

"No. I'm afraid not. In fact, I came out tonight to ask if you could see yourself clear to lending me one of your hands for a few days."

"Certainly. Who do you want?" She looked around the table, expecting him to pick one of those in the room.

"Henry Coyote."

"Henry? Why Henry?"

"Best tracker I know. I need someone who can follow whatever trail this ambusher might have left. The man appears better at coverin' his route than I am at followin' it. So—"

"So, you need an Apache."

"Seems so."

"In the mornin' soon enough?"

"Just right."

A couple of the cowboys started coughing as if they'd choked on something. Cotton knew Emily had made no pretense of her relationship with the sheriff, but her ranch hands still found the affair a tad naughty.

Henry Coyote squatted on the front porch of the Wagner ranch house at dawn. When Cotton emerged, stretching and pulling up his suspenders, the Indian grunted a greeting, at least that's what Cotton interpreted it as. The two of them had been friends for some time, especially since it was Henry who killed the man guarding Emily after her kidnapping by the Cruz gang. And it was Henry who brought her to safety and helped set in motion the downfall of a vicious bunch of cutthroats.

"What sheriff need with Apache?"

"I need your expert tracking skills, my friend. Someone took a shot at Jack night before last while he was at his desk in the jail. Nearly killed him. I need to find whoever did that and bring him in to answer for it. You willin' to help out?"

"Always ready to help a friend. When we go?"

"Soon as you gather up your pony and that Spencer of yours. Meet you by the gate."

Henry was on his feet and bounding off the porch before Cotton could open the door to say good-bye to Emily.

Cotton and Henry pulled up in front of the jail, remaining on their mounts. Cotton called out to Jack but got no answer. He dismounted and went inside. There was no Jack to be found. Cotton's frown gave away his dark thoughts as to where he figured Jack was: still tangled up in Melody's sheets. He motioned for Henry to dismount and come inside while he went to find his deputy.

"Wait here, Henry. I'll be right back."

Cotton wasted no time making tracks for the house at the end of the street, just around the bend. When he got there, he knocked on the door, then turned the handle and went in. He called out to Jack, and again was greeted by silence. After a couple minutes, he heard a shuffling and a yawn coming from the area of the bedroom. When he peeped in the door, Melody screeched something about bad manners and being sheriff didn't give him the right to barge into a woman's bedroom without an invitation.

He backed out, embarrassed at her scolding. He waited in the living room, hat in hand.

"Sorry, Melody. I'm lookin' for Jack. He should be at the jail, but he isn't. I just came from there. Do you know where he is?"

Melody stepped from the bedroom, half-naked, making no attempt to keep her robe closed. Considering the occupation she'd been in for the past dozen years or so, he wasn't shocked by her lack of propriety. She walked to a chair and plopped down, reaching for a cigarillo that lay on the tiny end table. She stuck the thing in her mouth, struck a sulfur, and lit the end. She blew smoke his way as she scowled at him like a mother lion about to slap down one of her cubs.

"What makes you think I keep track of Jack all day and all night?"

"I didn't come here for a fight, Melody. I just want to know if you've seen Jack, and if so, where can I find him?"

She took a drag on her smoke, held it a moment, then blew another cloud into the room. She glanced away for a second before answering.

"He crawled out of bed early this morning. Said something about following up on a rumor he'd heard at the saloon. That's all I know. Now, you get the hell out of here and leave a lady to her—"

"Yeah, I know. I'm leaving. If you see Jack, tell him I'm lookin' for him." He let the door close only partially behind him. His long strides took him to the jail and the waiting Apache in only a couple minutes. When he walked in, he found Jack talking to Henry.

"Hey, Cotton, ol' friend. Where you been?"

"Very funny, Jack. I been spendin' the past several minutes getting berated by your whore."

"I figured."

"So, what's this rumor you've heard?"

"A fella that just got off the stage this mornin' let it slip—over a couple too many drinks, I might add—that there's a new bank goin' to open in the old stone Miners Union building. Says some wealthy dude from Fort Worth plans to attract a lot of the cattle money here by offering loans at a lower rate than the Apache Springs bank can compete with."

"That'd likely drive Darnell Givins out of business."

"That's what I figured. Could be that's why he's doin' it. Apparently there's some bad blood between the man and someone here in town. Could be Darnell, but the fella didn't give any name. I gather it goes back a spell, at least that's the word floatin' around."

"You hear a name for this character?"

"Yep, and you ain't goin' to like it." Jack raised one eyebrow and gave Cotton a look.

"Well, spit it out. I'm growin' older by the minute. At

this rate, I'll have gray hair before you get around to spillin' what you know." Cotton crossed his arms, giving Jack a squint suggesting his impatience.

"Bart Havens." Jack waited for Cotton to explode. That didn't happen, but the sheriff *did* begin rubbing his chin and frowning as he walked to the door and looked out.

"You're right about one thing, Jack. I don't like it."

"But there ain't a damned thing you can do about it, right? He does it all legal-like, don't he? Kinda like before?"

"Since he's probably lookin' to square things with me, I reckon we'll get a chance to find out."

Chapter 5

The last time Bart Havens and Cotton crossed paths, Havens had paid several lowlife gunmen to try running the lawman out of town. Two tried, both paying the ultimate sacrifice for their inadequate knowledge of Cotton Burke's skills with a Colt. The others skittered out of town like cockroaches before a fire. Cotton couldn't help wondering if it wasn't starting all over again. Until he found out differently, he would operate on the assumption that Havens was somehow involved in the attempt on Jack's life.

As Cotton and Henry rode up into the hills and the boulder field where Cotton and Jack had found evidence of the shooter the day before, Henry Coyote quickly locked on to subtle signs that had been overlooked by the sheriff and his deputy. Cotton saw a knowing look creep across the Apache's face.

"You already know something I don't, Henry. Ready to share your insights?"

"Don't know insights, but know plenty about man with big gun."

"Such as—"

"Small man, no higher than me. Not heavy, skin and bones. Need lay heavy gun on rock to steady. Give off smell of sickness, cough up blood. There, on rock."

"Consumption? A lunger?"

"Uh-huh." Henry bent down to trace the outline of the man's boot print. He stood and took the reins of his pony, leading him through the rocks farther uphill. Cotton followed right behind the wily Apache.

On the down slope of the smallest of the hills, they both mounted up, and with Henry taking the lead, they rode across the desert to the northeast. Cotton knew he had the best tracker in the area; all he had to do was settle in and let Henry find the shooter. Until then, his mind wandered to when he and Bart Havens had first crossed paths, and the treachery that followed. It didn't take him long to dredge up those tragic past events. He'd tried, and failed, to forget them. He still struggled with why he hadn't killed Havens when he'd had the chance.

After about three hours of seemingly aimless wandering, Henry pulled up and pointed to a far-off shanty sitting in a copse of trees atop a rise about a mile and a half away.

"He go there."

Cotton nodded but said nothing. He turned in the saddle and began picking through his saddlebags. He pulled out his field glasses. He raised them and sighted through the lenses, adjusting for distance and focus. He scanned the area around the shanty before finally speaking.

"I don't see any sign of anyone. But we'll approach carefully just the same. You ride out in a wide circle to the left. I'll do the same to the right. Give a call if you spot anything or anyone."

Henry said nothing as he kneed his pony to a walk to carry out the sheriff's plan. Cotton did the same, pulling his Winchester from its saddle scabbard just in case. If this shooter had a rifle that could shoot accurately at long distances, he might just be sighting down on the two of them at that very instant. By separating, he figured to cut the chances of both of them getting cut down.

The closer he got to the shanty, the more intensely Cotton scanned the area. About a hundred yards away, he dismounted, dropped the mare's reins, and proceeded on foot, staying as low as possible and using as much brush as he could find for added cover.

He pulled up twenty-five yards short of the ramshackle building, cocked the rifle, and carried it aimed forward and ready. He moved slowly, looking left and right, listening for any sign of life. He heard nothing but the buzz of bees around the yellow brittlebush scattered over the landscape, and the occasional screech of a circling hawk as it zeroed in on its kill. He decided to call out.

"Hello, the cabin. If there's anybody in there, now would be a good time to come out, before I give the place some ventilation, the lead kind."

Hearing no response, he figured he'd put a bullet through the door for good measure. It certainly wouldn't reduce the property value any. The roar of his Winchester elicited no response except a cloud of smoke. No sound came from within.

"Henry, you see anything?"

The Indian slipped from the back of the building, looking cautiously around the corner. He looked at Cotton sheepishly with his hands in the air.

"I see nothing but bullet that go by. Miss me by this much." Henry held up his hands to indicate a distance of about a foot. It was Cotton's turn to look sheepish.

"Sorry. I didn't realize you were out back. Shouldn't have squeezed off a shot in the first place."

"It okay. Maybe miss by more than I say." Henry broke into a wide grin.

They both walked to the door of the cabin. Cotton kicked it in and shoved inside, looking left and right. Henry pushed by him, sniffed the air, and grunted. They went back outside, where the odor of stale smoke and rotting wood wasn't so prevalent.

"Man with big gun come here. Meet other man who make smoke. Wear perfume, like white squaw."

This man amazes me more every time I'm with him, Cotton thought.

"Any idea how long ago they left?"

"No. But go different directions."

"Can you tell which way the shooter went?"

"Maybe back to Apache Springs."

"He might be trying to get another shot at Jack . . . or me. I'd better make tracks to assure that doesn't happen. With what you've told me about him, he should be easy to spot."

"What about other man?"

"You follow him as far as you can without attracting attention. Maybe we can get an idea of what he's up to if we know where he hangs out. Come back to town as soon as you know anything. But do not confront him or let him know you are following him."

Henry Coyote gave a nod, mounted up, and spun his pony around in the opposite direction of Apache Springs. Cotton watched as the Indian picked up the trail, locking on to it like a hound dog.

Cotton went straight to the jail as soon as he got back. Jack wasn't there, but he probably wouldn't be hard to find. Cotton crossed the street, stomped onto the boardwalk, and pushed through the swinging doors to the saloon. Along one side of the narrow room, at the end of the bar, leaned Jack. He was chatting with Melody, talking and laughing like they'd just met for the first time. When he saw Cotton, Jack broke off his conversation and walked toward the sheriff.

"What'd you find?"

"We tracked the shooter to a vacant shanty above Cedar City. He met up with some other owlhoot. They split up with each goin' in a different direction."

"How do you know all that?"

"I was with Henry Coyote, remember?"

"Oh, yeah. Dumb question."

"Yeah."

"Where do we go from here?" Jack said, ignoring the fact that Melody had gone to the back room with the bartender.

"We keep our eyes open for a skinny 'lunger' with a big gun."

"You sayin' he's got that consumption, like Doc Holliday?"

"That's what Henry says. Pretty uncanny what all the Indian picks up on."

"That's for sure."

"I figure the man was headed back this way for the same reason he came in the first place: to kill someone. I'm the likely target, given that Bart Havens could be involved, but that doesn't mean you couldn't attract some stray lead, so stay alert." Cotton turned and walked out of the saloon and down the street to the bank. He had an itch that needed scratching and he figured the bank president was just the person to see about it.

"You're thinkin' that rumor about Havens might be true?" Jack asked, as he followed Cotton through the batwings, then peeling off to go back inside.

"I've seen it before."

When he reached the Apache Springs Bank and Loan, Cotton saw Darnell Givins sitting at his desk, thumbing through a newspaper. He pushed through a low swinging gate and sat down in front of the president.

"Mornin', Sheriff. What can I do for you?" Givins said.

"Heard a rumor, and I wondered if maybe you'd heard the same."

"I try hard to ignore rumors, Sheriff. Usually nothing more than nonsense."

"If this one's true, it could spell trouble for you, me, and the whole town."

"Okay, I'm listening. What is it?"

"You ever heard of a man named Bart Havens?"

"The town killer? Who hasn't? What's this got to do with me?" Givins said, his face turning ashen.

"I hear he may be fixin' to start up some competition for your bank."

The stricken look that came over Givins was unmistakable. He drew his handkerchief from his coat pocket and began mopping his suddenly moistened brow. He obviously hadn't heard that particular rumor, and it wasn't sitting well.

"I pray you're wrong, Sheriff. I certainly do."

Chapter 6

"Where you goin', Melody?" Jack asked as he watched her gathering her belongings and stuffing them in several bags and a trunk.

"I'm taking a little trip back to Gonzales. Got some business I need to clear up. I plan to be back in a couple weeks. You can live without me for that long, can't you, honey?" She smiled coyly and planted a kiss on his cheek.

"I'll make do. What kind of business you got?"

"I'll tell you all about it when I get back."

"Sounds pretty secretive."

"No, no secret. Just don't want to put a hex on my deal, that's all. Don't fret. I promise I'll be back soon. Don't forget, I need you as much as you need me," she said, fastening the last strap on her trunk and scooting it across the floor to the door. "How about hauling that over to the stage office for me?"

Jack bent over to lift the trunk. His eyes got wide as he straightened up instantly.

"What the hell you got in there, gold bars?"

"No, just some of my—"

"Yeah, I know, your women's *necessities*. I'll have someone from the stage line bring a cart over." Jack left the house rubbing his sore back and muttering something about "women" and "necessities." He didn't understand either one.

As he was passing by the bank on his way to the stage office, Jack saw Cotton emerge with a serious look on his face.

"Hey, Cotton, what's got you lookin' like you was snakebit?"

"I told Givins about Bart Havens and the rumor about a new bank starting up. He's the one who looked snakebit. I couldn't get a straight answer out of him about what he would do if the rumor turned out to be true. I got the impression he couldn't cover the withdrawals if many folks made a switch to another bank."

"That's not something the folks around here would take well," Jack said. "A failed bank could make for some pretty temperamental outbursts, and that usually means someone gets hurt."

"You don't have to remind me. Let's get back to the jail." Cotton looked up and down the street as they made their way back to the sheriff's office.

Jack was chattering about something, but Cotton wasn't hearing any of it. He was lost in the past and his last encounter with Bart Havens. That experience had left him with a bad feeling about what Havens might be capable of should their paths ever cross again.

It all started about five years back, in another town, but with similar circumstances. The town was named Benbow Creek, named appropriately after the town's only Civil War hero, a colonel who died defending a hill nobody had ever heard of. The town had one bank. Bart Havens came in and started another bank, using tactics that were questionable, but never anything clearly illegal. After about a year, the town's original bank closed its doors, costing its stockholders everything they'd invested and then some.

Cotton was the town marshal in Benbow Creek, and while he could do nothing to stop the migration of depositors from one bank to the other, he *could* put a stop to a sudden increase in violent crime in town, seemingly always against those who'd chosen to back the original bank by keeping their deposits there. Over a period of six months, Cotton caught a half dozen gun-toting troublemakers in the act of setting fires, breaking into stores, or beating some storekeeper or businessman half to death in some dark alley. He was able to take two of them to trial, where they denied any ties to Bart Havens, even though everybody knew them to be habitual liars. The other four he was forced to shoot, two of whom died. He felt no regret, except that he was positive Bart Havens was behind every dastardly deed, and he set out to prove it. Before the dust settled, Havens had been run out of town, losing everything. And now Cotton could see the seeds of the same scenario all over again. He wasn't eager to watch a man like Havens get away with ruining a decent businessman and, in doing so, putting a lot of families in financial jeopardy if they didn't toe his line.

". . . and so, I'm not sure what I'll do with myself while she's gone. Got any ideas, Cotton?"

"Huh?"

"I said, got any ideas what I can do with myself while she's gone?" Jack squinted at Cotton like he'd lost his hearing.

"While who's gone? What the hell are you talking about?"

"Melody, that's who. She's goin' back to Gonzales to put together some sort of deal. Didn't really get the gist of the thing. Damn, Cotton, don't you never listen to anything I say?"

"Sorry, Jack, got some things on my mind right now. Like how to keep Apache Springs from blowin' away like a tumbleweed in a whirlwind when Bart Havens hits town."

"Maybe someone should go visit the bastard and give him some friendly advice before he arrives here."

"Who do you suggest?"

"I got nothin' to do until Melody returns. Think on it."

"I got no problem with you havin' a talk with that scalawag, but first we got to locate him. Henry Coyote should be back with information on where he's hangin' out in a day or two. As soon as we find him, I reckon that's when *I'll* have to figure on how to handle him. Since he's likely painted a bull's-eye on my back, anyway."

"You just let me know what you want me to do, talk him out of comin' to Apache Springs or shoot him. I'm willin' to do either. Suit your fancy."

"The way I'm feelin' right now, that could well be a toss-up. You two ever meet up?"

"Nope."

"So you don't even know what he looks like, right?"

"Nope."

Jack left to get help carrying Melody's belongings to the stage office. A devilish grin came over Cotton's face.

Chapter 7

Upon arriving by stage in Gonzales, the town she'd called home for the past several years, before having her lover rudely uprooted by Cotton Burke, Melody went straight to her hotel. She called all her girls together in the large, elegantly appointed lobby. She chased out any remaining customers and locked the front door, pulling down the shades on the windows at the same time. As the ladies settled onto the plush velvet couches and high-backed chairs, Melody leaned one arm on the registration counter and cleared her throat. She occasionally sipped from a glass of brandy brought by one of the girls.

"Well, ladies, as you know I've been up in Apache Springs with Jack. He's there because of that scoundrel Cotton Burke who kidnapped him right out of my bed. At first I was furious, but after watching things unfold in that collection of shanties and termite-infested haciendas, I think I've found a gold mine right under the noses of those backward fools."

"And I'm bettin' you want us to help you *work* that

mine, huh, Melody?" Texas Rose said with a suspicious sideways glance. "All at a big profit to you, right?"

"You always were quick to catch on, Rose. Just don't get too smart for your own welfare."

"Not me, Melody. I'm just a poor workin' girl, bound to do my mistress's bidding. Uh-huh."

"I don't need no yappy bitches workin' for me, Rose. If you'd rather strike out on your own, just say so. Otherwise, keep your mouth closed."

Rose looked around the room for indications that any of the others might have some of the same inclination to break away from a woman who always thought first of herself. Once, when one of the girls got sick, Melody had told her to either work or get out. The girl had worked because she needed the money, but she only lasted a week before she died. The fever had taken her. Melody didn't even attend the funeral.

If Rose was seeking confirmation of a willingness on the part of others to brave the storm and break out on their own, it wasn't evident in the blank expressions she saw. Most merely pulled their gowns closed, crossed their arms, or fiddled with their hair. All eyes were devoid of any interest in anything even resembling a revolution. So, after a few agonizing moments of introspection, Texas Rose—the wind now taken out of her sails—fell into line and acquiesced to Melody's wishes.

"Okay, I s'pose I'll stick it out. What's your plan?"

"That a girl, Rose. Now, everybody listen up, here's what I'm aimin' to do."

For the next hour, Melody outlined an elaborate plan to buy the only saloon in Apache Springs, expand it by adding more rooms out back, and make the small offices on the second floor into cribs for the girls. She would expand gambling by bringing in some of the new games of chance that were wildly popular in the bigger towns, like roulette and faro. And she planned to up the profit from the alcohol sales by watering down the bar stock with branch water while also offering high-priced Kentucky bourbons, Tennessee whiskeys, and French brandies. She related how she had also come across a source for some homegrown bathtub gin that several of the hill folk had expressed an interest in getting their hands on. When she finished, she glanced about as if she might entertain questions, but the stern look on her face suggested she'd better not hear any objections. She got only nods of agreement. She then broke into a satisfied smile.

"And I'm going to rename it 'Melody's Golden Palace of Pleasure.' Don't you just love it? It'll have a pressed tin ceiling like back East, and flowered wallpaper with all the trappings of a first-class bawdy house."

The ladies seated about the room exchanged glances ranging from "Who cares as long as it brings in the customers" to "Can her self-indulgences get any more grand?" Melody took the lack of formal comment to mean they approved.

"When does all this take place?" Rose asked.

"I'm going to have to find a buyer for this place, although I doubt that will be too difficult. I've been asked several times by various businessmen right here in Gonzales if I'd consider selling. Once I find the person with the right amount of money offered, we're on our way. I've already started putting together a deal in Apache Springs to purchase the saloon. I'd guess, at the most, two weeks and we're off to a whole new life. A very lucrative life, if I have anything to say about it."

"Ain't all this gonna be powerful expensive?" one of the girls asked.

"Shouldn't be a problem getting a healthy loan. I'll close on the deal once we get to Apache Springs, provided the seller is still interested."

"Did you give any consideration to maybe keeping this place going while you make sure the new one pays for itself?"

At first, Melody shot Texas Rose an angry glance, then, seeing that some intelligent reasoning had gone into the question, she glanced off into the distance to consider that idea. It was something she had not contemplated before. But it *did* made sense. If she could find someone she could trust not to steal her blind, since she'd not be in Gonzales to keep an eye on every transaction, there might be merit in Rose's plan.

"Come up to my room, Rose, and we'll talk further. Bring that bottle of brandy with you. This might take a while. The rest of you, open back up and go on with what you do best."

The girls got up and began roaming around. One of them opened the front doors and pushed open the drapes to allow folks wandering by to view the wares. One buxom blonde went outside to stand in the doorway, long legs spread apart, while she smoked a cigar and blew short puffs of bluish smoke in the air. She let her robe fall open slightly and put one hand on her hip. Her stance couldn't be mistaken for anything other than what it was: a not-so-subtle invitation to an evening of pleasure.

Meanwhile, Melody and Rose disappeared upstairs, a bottle of brandy and two glasses in hand.

Bart Havens sat glumly at a worn, cast-off desk in Las Vegas, New Mexico Territory, the only place where his past few attempts at residency hadn't resulted in him being ridden out of town on a rail. And the only reason he had been welcomed here was because he hadn't dared try his signature bank takeover scheme, since the only bank was owned by the wealthiest cattleman in three counties, and he had enough money to fight back. The entire population consisted of about two hundred, all of whom owed their livelihoods to that same cattleman in one way or another. Much to the chagrin of drovers pushing herds through for other markets, the largest number of inhabitants was overseen by a scraggly old man who spoke very little English, the lack of which amounted to no distraction to his charges: two thousand sheep.

Havens hated sheep, but at least they didn't seem to object to his negative attitude toward them. The sheepherder, who also owned a restaurant, was a generous man, one who saw to it that whoever sought a meal was treated—for a healthy sum, of course—to a daily ration of mutton stew. Havens cursed his circumstances as he awaited word from his henchman as to the outcome of his late evening foray into the outskirts of Apache Springs and the shot that should have proved the last moments of Bart's mortal enemy, Sheriff Cotton Burke. It wasn't that he didn't understand that Whitey had no choice but to flee after firing the bullet through the door of the jail, but he hadn't wished to wait for several days to know if Burke was dead. That was, after all, what he was paying for. His desire to see the sheriff displayed in a pine box for all to see overwhelmed any other considerations.

The sheriff needed to be out of the way in order for Bart to rape and pillage the town of Apache Springs, complete its downfall, and take his onetime banking partner, Darnell Givins, with it. A sly grin crossed his lips as he contemplated his return to the world of banking and the untold rewards that awaited a socially deviant businessman such as him. He drew a cigar from his inside coat pocket, lit it, and rolled it around between his fingers. He let his mind wander as he conjured up a scenario whereby he might end up in total control of several thousand acres of land and a substantial percentage of the town's real estate, too.

On a high, grassy hill overlooking the cluster of adobe and wooden buildings and outhouses, a keen-eyed Mescalero Apache watched for any activity below. He waited as an old Mexican closed a gate that separated the structures from a vast field of sheep. The only sounds he could hear were the cries of the herd and the clank of the gate latch. After a bit, a man stepped out the back of what appeared to be a saloon and wandered to an outhouse. He was well dressed in a pair of dark trousers with wide suspenders. He carried no gun. His collarless shirt was open several buttons. He was clean-shaven save for a mustache that curled down at the corners of his mouth.

The Apache hurried back to where his pony grazed. He had a satisfied grin. He hadn't needed to get any closer to smell the perfume.

Chapter 8

"You heard from Henry yet, Cotton?"

"Nope. He hasn't returned. Be patient."

"Got any idea where Bart Havens went after you ran him out of Benbow Creek?"

"Sorry, Jack, but the last place I heard he'd been seen had also asked him none-too-politely to get his crooked ass out of town and never come back or suffer the consequences. Seems to me the words 'necktie party' had been uttered. I think that might have been El Paso. His reputation has apparently spread." Cotton removed his hat, then scratched his head. "Be nice if he'd confined his exploits to Texas."

"If Henry don't get back pretty soon, I reckon I could start lookin' for him in El Paso. Ask around. Maybe someone can head me in the right direction," Jack said.

"We'll wait awhile longer. No sense gettin' ahead of ourselves. Henry will get here; it may be that Havens is trying to be real careful that word doesn't get out about what he's up to before he's ready. It does seem strange, however, that some stranger in the saloon would know Havens was plannin' something in Apache Springs. Very curious.

"Just remember, if I *do* let you loose, you can't just plug Havens. If we're to take this owlhoot down, it has to be done *legal*. Unless of course he draws on you, then it's every man for himself."

"If what I've heard is true, that ain't goin' to happen. They say he don't carry a gun, or so the story goes."

"I admit I never saw him with anything in his hand more deadly than a forged deed or an ace up his sleeve."

"Well, unless you need me, I think I'll go take a nap," Jack said. "Likely be up late coverin' our butts in case this dry-gulcher returns."

"I'll wake you if Henry gets back anytime soon."

The sun had set and the air was moist and heavy, with dark gray clouds being hoisted up over the mountains to the west like sacks of grain. A storm was brewing that would bring much needed moisture to the ranches. But only *if* it brought rain. That was never a certainty. Often, what at first appeared to be a blessing turned into a storm in name only, fetching nothing more than a thundering display of lightning that could spook a herd of cattle faster than a stick of dynamite, or turn a man leaning on a wire fence into a cinder. Of course, that much of a display of heavenly power also brought fires to dry timberlands and split trees down the middle. Cotton figured the storm would likely get to Apache Springs by midnight.

He was seated on the porch of the jail, leaning against the clapboard wall in a rickety ladder-back chair that had long ago seen its best days. It creaked every time he shifted his weight. He'd been sitting outside the stuffy office trying to get a breath of fresh air after a day that had seen no breeze, not even a hot one. The storm's onset was announced by a thunderous discharge, followed by flashes of cloud-to-ground lightning erupting like gunfire on the Fourth of July. Thousands of shafts of electricity lit up the sky, the ground, and all the buildings. If it hadn't been so potentially dangerous, he might have enjoyed the display.

That's when he saw it. In one nearby strike of lightning, he caught a flash, a glint off a barrel out in the distance, up in the rocks, right where he'd assumed someone had taken a shot at the jail two nights before. He had no time to think about it, puzzle it out, or come up with a plan of action. He dove for the porch planking just as a bullet splintered the chair back. A second later, the roar of the rifle caught up to the bullet's whine. It had missed the sheriff by inches.

Drawing his Colt, he rolled far enough to find minimal cover behind a water trough next to the boardwalk. He scrambled to his feet and made a dash for the alleyway and the deeper shadows between the buildings. As lightning continued to shower the landscape with brilliant flashes, his world danced back and forth between daylight and pitch-black every few seconds. He tried timing each movement, but that proved impossible, so he had to take a chance that the shooter was having as much trouble adjusting to the changing light conditions as he was. If that was the case, it might give him an opportunity to get to the other side of the street and down the opposite alleyway, where he could move more easily using shrubs, cactus, and brush—anything to cover his movements. He needed to get up into those rocks where the shooter was, or had been moments before. And he needed to get there quickly or lose his opportunity to capture the man who was trying to kill him. He doubted the man would be foolish enough to stay put for long hoping for another opportunity to send a bullet his way. This time, on target.

Cotton was in a dead run, dodging and ducking to make himself as difficult to hit as possible. He raced to get closer to the outcropping of boulders where he and Henry had found evidence of a man with a large-bore rifle having sat in wait to commit murder. A murder Cotton was certain had been ordered by his old nemesis: Bart Havens. He'd recognized Havens from the way Henry had described him at the shanty where he'd tracked the shooter. There was no doubt in his mind that Havens was simply waiting to hear that Sheriff Cotton Burke had been shot down by some unknown person, which would be his signal to arrive in Apache Springs all puffed up with supreme confidence and ready to take another unsuspecting town for a ride straight down into the pit of hell. Havens would certainly wish Sheriff Burke dead rather than have to face him once again. After their last encounter, Cotton knew Havens would stop at nothing to eliminate anyone or anything that might offer resistance to his skulduggery.

Cotton stopped to catch his breath and listen for any sound that might give away the shooter's position. He doubted he'd be lucky enough to find him, but there was always a chance, slim as it was. He eased up farther into the boulders, working his way cautiously around each one with the expectation of coming face-to-face with the "lunger" with a buffalo rifle. Halfway hoping he would. He stopped every few steps, straining for the sound of a pebble being dislodged by a careless step, or the unmistakable squeak of gun-belt leather as a man took a step.

Suddenly, a horse nickered in the distance, from the other side of the hill. Cotton stood up, cocked the Colt, and hurried his steps toward the sound. Gravel skittered about by his footfalls rattled across the downgrade like dry beans spilled from a bag. The man must be heading for his horse in hopes of an easy getaway, Cotton thought. Then, another sound, one he'd not expected. The distinctive sound of a hammer being cocked. The hammer of a single-shot rifle. A Sharps buffalo gun. A Sharps .50-caliber with a bore that could send a shot three-quarters of a mile with incredible accuracy. Cotton spun around in the direction of the sound and came face-to-face with a stringy man lifting the barrel of the rifle to bear. Cotton's two shots were fired so quickly that the echo sounded as one shot. The man's rifle flew from his hands and discharged into the dirt, blowing a crater a prairie dog could make a home in. The fallen man groaned once, then fell silent.

Cotton knelt down to get a closer look. The man was

dead. Both bullets had found their mark: one in his throat and the other in the middle of his forehead. He would be no use as a source of information about the man who'd sent him to commit such a devilish crime. The sheriff picked up the Sharps, grabbed the dead man by the back of his shirt collar, and began dragging him downhill, through the rocks and over cactus that could exact no greater toll on his body than had already been done.

Cotton dragged the corpse to the jail and let it drop in front of the door. He then marched straight to the undertaker's shop, knocked on the door, and waited for a light to come on. The door creaked open, and a squinty-eyed man peeked through the crack.

"Oh, it's you, Sheriff. Sorry, you caught me sound asleep."

"That's okay, John, it's late and I'm regretful of the necessity to disturb you, but I have a customer for you. He's on the planks in front of the jail. I'd have brought him here, but I was afraid it might be your wife answering the door, and I didn't want to expose her to the bloody mess I brung you. Come get him when you can."

John Burdsall thanked the sheriff for his thoughtfulness. He promised to be there straightaway, just as soon as he could slip into his britches. He closed the door as Cotton turned and began walking back to the jail.

"Looks like I missed all the action last night," Jack said as he dropped into the chair across form Cotton's desk. He yawned. "I saw that body leanin' against a board in front of the undertaker's. There were a couple fellas starin' at him. One of 'em said he thought it was Whitey Granville."

"You sure?"

"That's what I heard. You know anything about him?"

Cotton proceeded to relay everything that had happened to bring the shooter to his ultimate and ignominious end. He told Jack that it had only been by sheer luck he hadn't been killed. He also said he'd had no opportunity to question the man before he died.

"So, you're pretty sure you know who sent him, but—"

"Yep. That's the unfortunate part; if it was Whitey Granville, I can't tie him to Bart Havens now. I only have Henry's account of the fellow meeting with a man matching the description of Havens. That would never hold up in court. Too many convenient circumstances. So, all I have is a dead man who tried to kill me—or you, depending on your viewpoint."

"I prefer to think it was *you* he wanted all along. There's something unsettling about knowing someone wants to get you in his sights and never knowing when that bullet's going to come," Jack said.

"I know what you mean."

"Does Emily know how close you came to being the 'former' sheriff?"

"No, and I'd rather she heard it from me and not some idle talk floatin' around town."

"She'll not hear it from me. And not from Melody, either, in case that's what you were suggestin'."

"You catch on quick, Jack. I like that about you."

"Uh-huh. So, still no word from Henry?"

"I hear my name?" Henry Coyote slipped into the open doorway with the silence of the wind. Cotton and Jack were both startled by his sudden appearance.

"Uh, yeah, Henry. Jack was just asking if I'd heard from you. I was about to say I expected you to return anytime, but you—"

"Appear like spirit of puma?"

"Uh-huh, something like that. Did you find our man?"

"I find him."

Cotton sat, waiting for Henry to disclose the whereabouts of Bart Havens. It was easy for him to visualize the consummate swindler sitting back in a plush high-back chair at the best hotel in whatever town he'd last worked his deviltry in. Most likely, he'd be sipping a rare French wine and smoking a hand-rolled cigar from Cuba. It came as a surprise when Henry finally blurted out his whereabouts. "He sleep with sheep."

Chapter 9

Melody and Rose sat across from the president of the Bank of Gonzales. His desk was littered with deeds, loan applications, and settlements. Melody couldn't help hoping he was better organized than he appeared.

"Now, Miss Wakefield, what is it I can do for one of my best customers?"

"Since you are also one of *my* best customers, Horace, you can drop the 'Miss' crap and call me Melody."

"Yes, er, Melody."

"Now, Horace, I think you know how profitable my *hotel* is by the way my mortgage payments are always right on time. Never missed one. So, based on my perfect record, I want you to remortgage the hotel for a higher amount, with a cash advance toward a saloon I'm planning on purchasing in Apache Springs."

"Why don't you take out a loan against the saloon from the bank in Apache Springs?"

"Because I don't know the banker there, and I do know you . . . *and* your lovely wife."

"Now, wait a minute, Melody, if you're thinkin'—"

"Hold your britches, Horace, I'm not thinking anything, just reminding you that it's good business to keep all your assets within arm's reach. I want to know I'm being taken care of by someone I know *intimately*. You *do* understand what I'm saying, don't you, Horace?"

Banker Horace Seagraves knew exactly what she was saying. He tugged at his collar. He was no stranger to Melody's charms. Blackmail was a fact of life for a woman like Melody. It was her second best weapon. And, while he dared not let on that he didn't appreciate her trying to bully him into doing something he might not otherwise do, he knew he would, in the end, wither under her demanding ways. Truth be known, Horace Seagraves was a bowl of mush before a beautiful woman.

"Have you thought of maybe taking on a partner?"

"Don't want a partner. That'd be just another hand dippin' into my pocket. This little lady can take of herself. Don't you worry none."

"Okay, how much do you need? I'll have to start putting the new mortgage and the bundled loan together. Take me a couple days. That all right?"

"That'll be fine. I'll need ten thousand dollars. Just make it out to me and I'll deposit it in the Apache Springs bank until I get the deal put together with the relatives of the former owner. Oh, I almost forgot, Rose is going to be in charge of the hotel here while I'm gone. If you need anything, *anything at all*, she'll be happy to take care of you."

Rose gave him a licentious wink that turned his face a nice shade of pink.

Bart Havens slapped the worn deck of cards down on the table when he heard the door to the Las Vegas Saloon #1 open and a man saunter in. He looked up from his game of solitaire and grinned at the sight of the rider. Since he hadn't heard from Whitey, he'd sent another of his long-time henchmen to find him. His man was hopefully arriving with good news.

"Come on in and sit, friend. I'll order you a whiskey."

Sleeve Jackson, rangy and gaunt, with long, greasy black hair, was a cold-blooded killer. He carried two Smith & Wesson Schofield revolvers and a stiletto in a sheath tucked in his belt. He'd escaped being hanged on at least three occasions by virtue of a clever lawyer—courtesy of Bart Havens—and once by a daring jailbreak. He was no man to trifle with, although his reputation with a gun had been earned not with marksmanship but by his ability to backshoot most of his victims.

"Thank you, Mr. Havens, think I will at that."

Sleeve sat down, responding with a toothy grin as the bartender came to the table with a bottle and a glass. Bart poured the two glasses full, lifting his in a sign of a toast. He put the glass to his lips and drank it down with a single gulp.

"So, I hope you have good news for me. Did Whitey get the job done?"

"Nope. He just got hisself killed in the process. He's lyin' in a pine box leanin' against the wall of the undertaker's place. Had two holes in him no more'n six inches apart."

Bart scowled at the loss of one of his best men. "Damn! How'd it happen?"

"Only know what I heard. He missed the sheriff, and the sheriff came after him, found him, and when Whitey went to cock the Sharps, that lawman plugged him twice before he could even get his shot off. That Cotton Burke must be as fast as they say."

"Uh-huh. You may get a chance to find out." Bart's face was deeply lined as he fell silent, suddenly lost in thought. Clearly it was now imperative he adopt a different approach to ridding himself of his old nemesis. Havens scooted his chair back, got up, and walked outside. His face was as dark as the clouds gathering in the west.

A breeze had kicked up and was blowing dust and debris down the streets of Las Vegas, where Havens had set up an office in a back room of the saloon in order to escape the constant bleating of sheep. Sleeve's horse whinnied and crow-footed around the post to which he had been tied. Nervous about the approaching storm, several of the horses in the corral in back also added their slobbery comments. Havens stuck his thumbs in his braces and stretched them in and out nervously. This latest news was more than mildly bothersome. He'd set up in this dusty, ramshackle excuse for a town in the middle of nowhere for a reason. And that reason was to make sure Cotton Burke was dead before Havens rode confidently into Apache Springs to make another killing, the financial kind. He also needed to keep moving around to avoid having people get too familiar with some of the lowlifes with whom he had recently been associating.

All he could think about was the hatred he had for this man Burke, this gunslinger-turned-lawman, out to set things right. Burke was the man who'd run him out of a town he'd been on the verge of taking over, lock, stock, and barrel. Cost him a fortune to have to run like that, and in addition, it had put other towns on notice that Bart Havens was a crooked skunk who'd not stop before he'd stolen every last dime in the treasury and walked off with half the outstanding, unpaid deeds to thousands of acres of some of the best grazing land around. Now he could never show his face in Texas again.

He had been so close. Well, it was time for payback. Havens had had his eye on Apache Springs ever since hearing that Burke was the sheriff there, and by damned, he was going to take that town down along *with* its almighty sheriff.

Havens spun around and stormed back inside, slammed the rickety door, and yanked the whiskey bottle off the table. He lifted it to his lips and swigged it like it was mother's milk. When he slammed the bottle back down on the table, he looked like the devil himself come to claim his prize. Sleeve watched Havens's quixotic behavior indifferently. He'd seen it before. He took another sip from his own glass, then leaned back in the chair.

"What do you want me to do, Boss?"

"We're going to do things a little differently this time, Sleeve. It's time we stacked the deck on Burke. I want you to ride to El Paso and bring back four of the best gunmen you can find. Let 'em know there's money to be made and they can count on me to pay 'em well. Make sure none of them are squeamish about puttin' a bullet in a man, whether he needs it or not. Got that?"

"Yessir. I think I know just who to round up," Sleeve said with a wry grin. "You want I should bring 'em back here?"

"Yeah. If I'm not around when you get back, sit tight and wait for me. I'll be workin' on another part of my plan. Rodriguez and his wife will feed and take care of your horses. Now, get on your way."

Sleeve downed the last of his drink and slipped outside. The wind was whipping up a chill, and he pulled his jacket up tighter around his neck, untied his horse, and mounted up. Havens was standing in the open doorway as Sleeve gave him a mock salute and spun his horse around, spurring him in a trot toward El Paso. The look in Havens's eyes as he watched his hired killer ride off was dark, full to the brim with hatred.

Chapter 10

Cotton was standing at the open door staring out on the bustling street. A high-sided wagon pulled by six mules lumbered past loaded with wood from the mountains and headed for the sawmill. Two ladies chattered away as they walked by him, turned briefly to smile, then hurried back to their conversation with little or no break. Memphis Jack emerged from the saloon down the street and wobbled his way toward the jail. He stopped short when he saw Cotton watching him. He shook his head then continued on.

"You just come from your usual whiskey breakfast, Jack?"

"What's it to you, Cotton? You ain't my momma." He brushed by the sheriff and dropped into the swivel chair behind the desk. Cotton followed him in.

"No, Jack, I'm not your nursemaid, either. But I'd appreciate it if you'd stay sober long enough to handle anything resembling gunplay that might come along. I'd as soon you shoot the bad guys rather than a passerby."

"You just can't let it go, can you? A fella makes *one* damn mistake, and the high and mighty Cotton Burke has to keep rubbin' it until it festers."

"Let me remind you, Jack, someone tried to plug each one of us, and that ain't a trifling matter. I need you sharp, not constantly crawling out of a bottle. Got it?"

Jack stood up, yanked his Remington, and blasted a hole right next to the other hole in the door, no more than an inch away. He put the revolver back in his holster and sat back down, hard.

"Maybe I have lost my edge, Cotton. I meant to put that one right through the same hole."

Cotton scowled at Jack the way a father would a wayward son, even though their ages were no more than two years apart. He shook his head and went outside. He called back, "I'm going out to the Wagner ranch."

The ride to Emily's place took about two hours and wound through cottonwood- and oak-lined canyons and across a wide, grassy valley. Emily's deceased husband, Otis, had chosen well when first they'd come to Apache Springs seeking property to buy land and settle down with a moderate-size cattle operation. Otis had sent east for some of the English breeds with more meat on their bones, rather than the longhorns so plentiful in Texas. *Longhorns are stringy and tough; people want better beef*, he'd insisted. At first, other ranchers had scoffed at him, but he'd slowly won them over, and now the Wagner ranch could be counted on to supply restaurants and hotels throughout the region with juicy, tender cuts. His Herefords and Angus were growing in popularity, too, as breeding stock, and other ranchers were mixing their herds with diversity.

As Cotton rode through the gate, he saw several of the wranglers rounding up a handful of new calves, readying them for branding with the Wagner brand, a "W" sitting atop a wavy line. He saw Emily step out through the front door to watch. He urged his horse to the porch. He got down, tied the reins to a rail, and stepped up on the porch beside her.

"So, stranger, you lookin' to buy some cattle?" she said with a wink and a subtle grin. Her eyes flashed in the sunlight as she moved closer. He leaned down and kissed her.

"'Fraid the only thing I see when I look at one of those four-footed beasts is a thick, juicy steak sizzlin' in the pan."

"Hmm. Does that mean you would turn down an opportunity to become the head honcho on the Wagner ranch?"

"I figure the head honcho the ranch has right now is doin' a wonderful job. Wouldn't want to start a landslide by makin' unnecessary changes."

"I see. Well, I reckon I'll just have to reward you for that nice compliment by fryin' up one of those steaks you seem so bent on consuming." She smiled, took him by the arm, and drew him inside.

"I can't think of a better arrangement. You raise 'em, I'll eat 'em."

They both laughed.

When Sleeve Jackson rode into El Paso, he was struck by the activity on the streets. The town was bursting with horses and riders, wagons, buggies, and buckboards. Noise seemed to come from every corner, along with the occasional discharge of a weapon. Sleeve mumbled to himself that he'd better not find one of the men he was looking for lying facedown in the dusty street. If he didn't get back to Las Vegas with four of the best shooters in Texas, he'd have to face a very unhappy Bart Havens, and that didn't bode well.

Even though everyone knew Havens never carried a weapon, had never drawn on anyone, never killed anyone with a gun, knife, poison, or an axe, the man struck fear in the hearts of men who didn't normally back down from anyone or anything. Sleeve was at a loss to explain how that could be, but the facts seemed to speak for themselves. And who was he to argue with fact.

He reined in front of the first saloon he came to, the first of a dozen or more. He wasn't certain how many there were, just that he would have to start at one end of town and hit every saloon, gambling hall, and whorehouse in search of the four men he had in mind.

"Howdy, what can I get you?" the bartender asked as Sleeve walked up to the bar in the saloon called the Original El Paso Watering Hole, probably because it was, indeed, the most aged, run-down establishment a person happened on when entering town, at least from the west.

"A beer and some answers," Sleeve said.

"Beer's a dime, answers might come higher. You can ask, though," retorted the bartender.

"We'll start with the beer."

The bartender slipped down to the other end of the long, polished bar and held a glass under the spigot of a barrel. He returned a minute later to place the foamy-headed glass in front of the shootist. Sleeve flipped him ten cents.

"Now, about that information," Sleeve said.

"Yeah?"

"I'm lookin' for some fellas."

"You some sort of badge-toter?"

"Hell, no. Just lookin' up old pals, that's all."

"Gimme their names. I'll spread the word there's some fella in town wantin' to palaver. 'Bout the best I can do. This ain't a town where folks put a man on another's trail till he gets to know who the hell's askin'."

Sleeve was seething inside. He didn't like it one bit that this lowly purveyor of spirits had the nerve to presume he was there for some nefarious reason. It wasn't any of the bastard's business, anyway. He mulled over whether he was goin' to blurt out the names or turn around and stalk out. He was known to be fast with his gun, but with his *brains*, figuring out the best moves to make—well, not so great. He stared at the bartender for a full three minutes before the decision was made. He had no choice. He could be stubborn some other time. Now wasn't that time. Not with Bart Havens expecting him back in Las Vegas with four top gunmen. He needed to avoid getting sensitive or, worse yet, letting that nervous trigger finger get the best of him.

"Okay. Reckon I'll have to live with that. Name's Sleeve Jackson. I'm lookin' for Buck Kentner, Black Duck Slater, Comanche Dan Sobro, and Plink Granville. You seen any of 'em around lately?"

"Maybe one or two of 'em. I heard Black Duck was in Abilene, and Comanche Dan, well, he may or may not be dead."

"Dead?"

"Said maybe."

"So, where did he 'maybe' get dead?"

"Can't rightly say. I know it weren't here. The sheriff we got couldn't hit his own foot with a scattergun. Coulda happened down near the border. Maybe one of them others will recollect. I ain't never even seen the man."

"That leaves Buck and Plink."

"Yeah, I've seen them in the past week or so. I'll put out the word there's some fella lookin' for them. I assume you ain't lookin' to shoot 'em, are you?"

"No. I want to hire them. There's good money in it."

"Hell, why didn't you say so? There's Buck at that table in the far corner. He's the lonely fella suckin' on that bottle like it was his mommy's tit."

Sleeve tried to hide his disdain for the bartender. Any other time, he'd likely have blown the man into the next century. But for now, striking up a conversation with Buck Kentner was his first aim. As he approached the table, Buck glanced up with rheumy eyes, giving Sleeve the once-over.

"Buck Kentner?" Sleeve asked.

"Who wants to know?" Buck put the bottle down, nearly tipping it over. A last-second grab saved the contents from spilling. Sleeve was immediately impressed by Buck's ability to react quickly even in a drunken state.

"Name's Sleeve Jackson. And I may have a job for you, if you're willin' to give me a minute of your time."

"Pull up a chair and fill me in on this 'job' you're offerin'."

"You ever heard of a fella named Bart Havens?" Sleeve said.

"Who ain't? Some kinda banker prone to stealin' other folks' land, way I hear it."

"Close enough. He's plannin' another town takeover and he needs a few good guns to back his play."

"Who I gotta kill and how much does it pay?"

"Pay is one thousand dollars up front and another two thousand to the man who actually gets the job done. How's that sound?"

"Sounds good. Who's the target?"

"A sheriff by the name of Cotton Burke."

"Whoa. *The* Cotton Burke?"

"The one and only," Sleeve said, raising his eyebrows.

"Hellfire and damnation, I'd have to have twice that amount to tangle with Burke."

Chapter 11

"What's eatin' at you, Cotton? You've been moody ever since you got back. It can't be that fellow that tried to shoot you, since you put him in his grave. It's all over, isn't it?" Emily and Cotton were sitting on her porch swing. She leaned in close to him, her arms crossed to ward off an evening chill. The sun was just setting, and the horizon was blood red as nightfall began its march from the east.

"I'm afraid it has just started. I reckon it's best if you hear it now . . . from me. If the rumors are true, there's a rattler named Bart Havens who's intending on starting another bank. If he does, all hell will break loose in Apache Springs."

"Why? The town can probably support another bank, can't it?"

"Not the kind Havens intends. You see I know him from way back. He's done his treachery before, in other towns. Folks lose their land, cattle, homes, and savings. People usually die before he's done."

"Heavens. I didn't realize he could be such a threat. What are you going to do?"

"The trouble is, he doesn't do anything illegal himself. He has others do it for him. He just steps back and watches the bodies fall. One of those bodies *could* be me, or Jack. At least I'm certain that's his plan."

"Why would he want to kill you?"

"Because I'm what stands between him and another successful town takeover."

Emily's pretty face grew pensive. Her eyes flashed with anger at the thought of another man in her life possibly being gunned down. And she had no intention of allowing that to happen. She had men working for her, and they could all ride and shoot with the best of them. If she needed to marshal her own army to save the man she loved, so be it. Emily Wagner was tough-minded. Even after what she'd been through during the short time she'd been in the territory, she had few doubts that she and Cotton, together, could weather any storm. And by damn, she meant to do just that.

As they swung slowly back and forth to the squeaks of ropes being stretched from their weight, she watched Cotton out of the corner of her eye. *What is really going through his mind?* she wondered. Will I ever get close enough to him for us to plan and dream as one?

Jack was finishing his meal at the hotel when he heard his name being called. He continued to stab a piece of beef and slipped it into his mouth. He was still chewing when he looked up to see a woman he thought he'd never lay eyes on again. He almost choked. Delilah Jones was a dark-eyed beauty he'd met before returning to Gonzales and taking up with Melody. The shock on his face brought a smile to hers.

"Yes, Jack, it's me. Did you think I'd come to some ignominious end after you left town?"

Jack stood up, pulling out another chair at his table.

"I'm certainly glad you didn't, Delilah. Damn it's good to see you. Please join me."

She sat with a rustle of her satin skirts, resting a parasol on the edge of the table. She leaned forward, just to tease him with a hint of her soft, white bosom, then leaned on one elbow and stared directly into his eyes. He became so flustered he forgot to call a waiter over.

"If I'm to join you, I suspect I should order something so as not to give the impression of vagrancy. Don't you think?"

"I, uh, yes, yes, of course. How foolish of me. Waiter!"

"Sir?" the waiter said from across the nearly empty dining room.

"The lady will be joining me. Could you please bring a menu and a glass of wine?"

"Of course, sir." The waiter left briefly, returning in seconds with a bottle of wine and a menu scribbled on a piece of paper. Jack handed her the menu, such as it was, noticing that she raised her eyes questioningly at the misspellings that accompanied the evening's fare.

"The food's real good, even if the menu's a bit rough. I can recommend the beef stew."

Delilah nodded at Jack's choice and handed the menu back to the waiter. "I'll have what he suggested. Thank you.

"So, Jack, what are you up to these days? Still shooting up towns? Or just trying to drink them dry?"

A resentful look came over his face. He chewed his lip for a second as he thought out what words he dared let slip out of his mouth. His relationship with this woman had been stormy at times, but his jealousy of the attention she got from nearly every man who saw her was what finally led her to dissolve their plans for something more permanent. He was crushed by her rejection over what he figured was a trivial matter, a normal reaction of one man to another who might be viewed as a rival. Not that his relationship with Melody hadn't had its ups and downs, but he knew from the start she was a whore and had no illusions about anything like marriage coming into the picture.

"Neither, Delilah. I'm a duly appointed deputy sheriff, and I'll thank you to try forgetting the old Memphis Jack

Stump of the past. I'm a new man. You're looking at a man with a future."

"Deputy sheriff, are you? Well, it does appear you've taken a different road. But I seem to recollect you had been a deputy when we first met, and you'd had a bit of trouble where you came from."

"Uh, well, I did stumble over a little root in the road, I guess you'd say. But that's all changed now. Say, where are you stayin'? Will you be here long? Is there a man in your life?"

"Hold up, Jack. Let me catch my breath and answer one question at a time."

"Oh, sure. Sorry. I tend to get ahead of myself whenever I'm gazing at a beautiful woman."

Delilah lowered her eyes as if in deep thought, wondering whether to tell Jack everything, or just a taste of the truth. She seemed to decide on the latter. She hesitated before speaking.

"Well, there *was* a man in my life, but events changed that. I, uh, came farther west to, er, evaluate other, uh, opportunities."

"You say there was a man? What happened?"

"As it turned out, he had, uh, chosen an unfortunate line of work."

"What work did he do?"

"They say he was rustling cattle. I never believed a word of it. But they hanged him, anyway."

"The law must have had some pretty solid evidence to hang a man."

"It, well, it wasn't exactly the law that did him in. It was vigilantes. They said they caught him with a running iron, standing with several newly altered brands and freshly butchered beef."

"Oh, I see. I don't hold with vigilantes, myself, but if he was caught red-handed, er—"

"I know. Evidence like that is hard to defend."

"I'm sure sorry."

"Don't be. He didn't treat me that well after we were

together a while. Tried to get me to work one of the cribs and bring him the cash. I told him what he could do with his whores. I'd walked out by the time he was hanged. So, there you have my sordid story. What's yours?"

Her food arrived just as she took a sip of wine. Jack smiled at her. He struggled with whether to spill the whole story of his own dealings with a fallen angel. He decided that glossing over that part might be the best idea. Besides, as good as she looked right then, and with Melody gone for who knew how long, well maybe, just maybe . . .

"I was living in Gonzales when the sheriff here in Apache Springs came lookin' for me, not because I'd done somethin' illegal, but because he needed help with a serious problem. The town had fallen under the influence of a gang of bushwhackers bent on robbin' a train, and they kidnapped a widow lady to keep the sheriff off their ass, er, pardon my language." He gave her a guilty look as if he'd just dragged something smelly onto her carpet.

"Goodness, what happened to the poor woman?"

"Oh, it turned out she got rescued; we killed all the owlhoots, and Cotton, that's the sheriff, went to stay with Miss Emily while he healed up from an unfortunate bullet wound. I don't think he minded all that much, the movin' in with her part, that is. He was in love with her, anyway. Probably had been ever since her husband was shot for doin' nothin' more than comin' out of the barbershop at an inopportune time. That's when he made me a deputy, so he could fiddle away the hours in her company while I busted my, er, sorry again, backside keepin' the riffraff out of town."

Delilah covered her mouth with her napkin to stifle a laugh.

Chapter 12

While Sleeve Jackson and Buck Kentner stared at each other over a bottle of whiskey, Buck seemed particularly pensive. Sleeve had figured the amount of money he'd offered would not meet with resistance. He was obviously mistaken.

"Tell you what, Buck. If you keep it to yourself, *and* you're the one that gets the sonofabitch, I'll make sure there's a healthy bonus in it for you. But if you spread that around to the others, the deal's off."

"It better be damned healthy. Cotton Burke can shoot the head off a fly in midair. Leastways that's what I've heard."

"I'd have to say that's a bit of an exaggeration. Suffice to say, he's quick all right, but he's still just a man, not unlike others you've faced down. Now, you in or not?"

"Yeah, reckon I'm in. Besides, I'm damned near busted, anyway."

"Good. Now, do you know where I can find Plink Granville?"

"Aww, he's around somewhere. Probably down at the

Silver Strike. Leastways that's where he generally hangs out, proppin' his chin on the bar to keep from fallin' into the cuspidor. Man's a fallin' down drunk, you know. What do you want with a kid like that? He'd be just as likely to shoot himself as he would Burke."

"Maybe the information I have for him will convince him to sober up for a spell."

"Yeah, what information is that?"

"Cotton Burke killed his brother, Whitey, last week."

"Burke got Whitey Granville?"

"Yep. Shot him twice before Whitey could even pull the trigger on that Sharps."

Buck got a sick look on his face as he stared at his glass. Sleeve noticed a change in the gunslinger's demeanor at hearing the news. He wasn't certain he could keep Buck from bolting. But he had to try.

"I know it sounds like Cotton Burke is unbeatable, but he ain't. One of Virgil Cruz's men near killed him a month or so back. He'd be dead if it hadn't been for Memphis Jack Stump."

"Stump? Damn! Is he in on this thing, too? On Burke's side?"

"Likely, unless we can take him out."

"Any more money in the deal for takin' down the two of 'em?"

"I don't know. Depends on whether Bart Havens figures Memphis Jack for a threat."

"He does if he has any sense at all."

"So, Delilah, what are you doing in town? And how long do you figure on bein' here?"

"I'm not sure."

"Where are you stayin?"

"The hotel says they're full up tonight, but I can get a room tomorrow. Maybe I'll just sit up in the lobby tonight."

"Not while ol' Memphis Jack's got a bed that'll fit two just fine."

"You're suggestin' I spend the night with you?"

"That's about the size of it. What do you say?"

"You *do* remember what happened the last time we were together, don't you?"

"Uh, yeah, but as I recall it didn't have nothin' to do with a problem over the sleepin' arrangements."

"No, it had to do with me not wanting anything to do with a whiskey-soaked drunk. So, unless you're reformed, I think I'll just avail myself of one of those plush chairs in the lobby for the night. Thanks, anyway."

"I have," Jack said, "reformed, that is."

"I'm glad to hear it."

"So, you'll take me up on my offer after all?"

Delilah slowly broke into a smile. "One night."

"That's Plink over there, the one with his head on the table, snorin' away like a wounded grizzly. Don't look much like a shootist, does he?" Buck said, as the two of them pushed through the doors of the Silver Strike Saloon.

"No, I reckon he don't, at that." Sleeve sauntered up to where Plink Granville had chosen to sleep off a drunk, spilling whiskey all over the tabletop and lying in it. "Plink, wake up!"

After Sleeve hollered his name several times, Plink slowly lifted his head. His eyes were bloodshot. Spilled whiskey ran down his cheek.

"Leave me alone, you bastard. I'm busy."

"Yeah, I can see that, you drunken pig. Wake the hell up. I got some news and a proposition for you," Sleeve growled.

"What'd you call me?" Plink went for his gun and got it halfway out of the holster, when he realized he was staring down the barrel of Sleeve's Schofield. Sleeve gave Plink's chair leg a swift kick, dumping the surprised man onto the floor with a thud.

"I called you what you are: a drunken pig. Now, you goin' to listen or just keep wallowin' there under the table in the chawin' tobacco spit?"

Plink groaned and tried to get up. He fell back twice before Buck reached down and grabbed his shirtsleeve and yanked him to his feet. Plink grabbed hold of the table, leaned on it with both hands splayed flat in the foul-smelling spill, then stood blinking. He shook his head a couple of times. Sleeve called for the bartender to bring some coffee, hot and strong.

Sleeve and Buck sat across from Plink as he drank the coffee, although not without a fair amount of resistance did he do so. He called Sleeve some names that normally would have gotten him shot. Had the circumstances been different, there could have been no doubt he would have, at that moment, been laid out, pasty white and ready for burial.

It took almost an hour for Plink to regain a sense of what was going on, where he was, and who these men were who had so rudely forced him back from his stupor. His eyes, still bloodshot, wandered from Sleeve to Buck and back. Finally, Sleeve decided it was time to sober Plink up with the reality of his brother's death.

"Plink, I'm Sleeve Jackson, and, like I already said, I'm here with news and a proposition. You ready to listen?"

"Do I have a choice?"

"Not really. Anyway, here it is: Bart Havens needs some gunhands to help him take over a town. He's willin' to pay for it."

"How much?"

"One thousand up front, and another two thousand to the one who guns down the sheriff."

"A sheriff? What sheriff you talkin' about?"

"The sheriff of Apache Springs, Cotton Burke."

"Sorry. I may be a drunk, but I'm not plumb loony. Get yourself some other fool."

"Now hold on there, you dumb—" Buck growled.

Sleeve stopped Buck from going further. He knew that if Buck antagonized the young gunslinger to the point he'd draw on him, one of them would sure as hell die. He couldn't take that chance. If he was to come up with four killers for Havens, and do it in the time he'd been given, he couldn't take a chance on losing either one.

"Plink, there's one other reason to go along with this plan. Sheriff Cotton Burke shot and killed your brother last week."

"What? Whitey's dead?"

"Sorry to break it to you this way, but I reckon there ain't no good way to tell a fellow his kin has been murdered."

At the news, Plink Granville suddenly seemed to sober up.

"I'm in. When do we leave?"

"Tomorrow. On our way, I have to try locating Black Duck Slater and Comanche Dan Sobro. Either one of you know where they might be?"

"Black Duck was last seen wandering around Lincoln County, probably tryin' to cook up more trouble down there," Buck said. He waved the bartender over to bring him a beer.

"And Comanche Dan?"

"Somebody here dishonoring my fine reputation?" The rangy man coming through the door wore deerskin leggings, knee-high boots, and carried a Winchester rifle held like he figured to clear the house.

"Well, I'll be damned. You must be Comanche Dan!" Buck Kentner grumbled. "I reckon we heard wrong, he ain't dead."

Chapter 13

When Delilah drew open the drapes to let the sunlight in, her naked body cast an enticing shadow across the bed. That's when she noticed for the first time all the feminine accouterments lying about. She frowned as she picked up a hairbrush with long blond hairs caught in the bristles, then, tossing it aside, she continued her perusal of where she'd just spent the night, wrapped in Jack's arms. Jack was slowly coming awake when he spotted her dark expression.

"Jack, you sonofabitch, you didn't tell me you were married. Where the hell is your wife?"

Jack slipped out of bed and pulled on his pants and boots.

"I didn't tell you I was married because I ain't married. That's why." He went into the kitchen to put some coffee on to heat. He stuck several small pieces of wood in the belly of the cast iron stove, tossed in some paper and lit it.

"Then what are all these womanly touches lyin' around everywhere?" she said.

"I'm, uh, sharing the place with, uh, a workin' girl."

"You're *livin'* with a whore?"

"I guess you could put it that way; Cotton does."

Delilah broke out laughing. As if suddenly ashamed, Jack looked at the floor.

"What's so funny?" he asked, pouring water and coffee grounds into the pot.

"Hope this won't come as a big disappointment, Jack, but, after a fashion, you slept with another one last night."

"You? But I thought you, er, that is, didn't you say we couldn't get hitched because I drank too much? You didn't say nothin' about goin' into the business of sellin' your charms."

"At that time, I *was* true to you, Jack. When you left, I found I was flat broke and needin' to come up with money or get tossed out of my house. This nice man came along and offered me a deal. He said if I'd come work for him, and only him, he'd treat me nice and I'd have money left over at the end of the month. He's made no demands for sharing a bedroom. But, I guess you could still say I'm a whore, too. In a way, aren't we all?"

"He the only one you, uh, do business with?" Jack squinched up his eyes in a dark frown.

"Uh-huh. That's why I'm in town. I'm supposed to be sizing up the population hereabouts, so I can give him an idea about who is important and who isn't when he gets to town. I kinda act as his eyes and ears when he's setting up a deal."

"So, where is this '*nice*' man?"

"Oh, he'll be arrivin' soon. Guess he's got business elsewhere. We can stay together and keep doin' what we did last night until he does. If you'd like, that is."

Jack found himself in a quandary, at an awkward crossroads. He didn't know when Melody would return, but he knew damned well if she caught him in bed with Delilah, he was as good as dead. Her offer was tempting, however, and if they went ahead and got a room at the hotel, well, Melody might never be the wiser. He let a broad grin wipe away the frown.

"We'd have to get that hotel room, but the other part sounds fetchin'."

"Since my benefactor will be footing the bill, we'll have to keep a watch out for his arrival. Then, I'm sad to say you'll have to go back to your previous lady friend."

"Fair enough. Just who is this 'gentleman' I'm to keep an eye out for?"

"You've probably never heard of him. His name is Bart Havens."

Comanche Dan pulled a chair over to the whiskey-soaked table and sat. He leaned the rifle against the arm of his captain's chair, took out the makings, and rolled himself a smoke.

"So, how'd my name come up in conversation with you three?"

"Sleeve has a proposition for you. It's a good'un," Buck blurted out.

"Uh-huh," Dan said, blowing a smoke ring.

"You ever heard of Bart Havens?" Sleeve said.

"Heard he was a snivelin' rattler. That the one?"

"Probably, but a wealthy rattler. That's what's goin' to make the difference," Sleeve said.

"Okay, so what's the deal?"

"Havens is fixin' to take over a new town, and he needs some men good with shootin' irons to lend a hand. He'll pay a thousand dollars to each man, up front, and another two thousand to the one who actually plugs a certain man."

"Who is the target?"

"Cotton Burke."

Comanche Dan scowled at the mention of Cotton Burke. He didn't look pleased.

"What if it takes all of us? Any extra in it?"

"I never thought about that possibility. I'll have to ask

Havens. But I'm certain he'll want to make *some* accommodation. He hates Burke."

"What did Burke ever do to him?"

"Got Bart chased out of Benbow Creek. Cost him a fortune. Lost everything. Fact is, Havens can't show his face in Texas again 'cause of Burke. Man's got fair reason to want to get even. So, you interested?"

"I got nothin' against this Cotton Burke, but I *could* use an infusion of cash. I'm strapped. So, yeah, I'll throw in with you. Where we headed?"

"We're to meet Havens in Las Vegas, New Mexico. He'll lay out the plan. We'll leave at sunup."

Right after breakfast, Cotton walked out on the porch with Emily on his arm.

"You seem to be off somewhere else, 'stead of here with me. What's eatin' at you, Cotton?"

"Whitey Granville. The man I shot."

"He shot at you first, didn't he? Why should that bother you?"

"The part that bothers me is: I'd never met the man, had no qualms with him, and wouldn't have even known who he was if Jack hadn't come up with a fella passin' through town who recognized him lyin' in that pine box."

"You think somebody has it in for you? Or maybe Jack?"

"Uh-huh."

"How can you find out?"

"I'm not sure, but I have more than a passing feelin' that Bart Havens is already gettin' back to his old ways."

"Maybe Havens figures you might try to block his bank venture."

"If that's his thinkin', he'd be right. That's *exactly* my intent."

"But if he doesn't do anything illegal, how can you stop him?"

"My only chance is if I can *prove* Havens hired Granville to shoot me."

"How do you do that?"

"I'm not certain I can. But maybe Jack is the answer."

"Jack?"

Cotton stepped off the porch and headed for the corral to get his horse. Emily stood in the shade of the overhang watching him walk away, deep in thought. Cotton waved at her as he rode through the gate.

Melody and her two other working girls stepped off the stage in Apache Springs just after three in the afternoon. Dusty and tired, Melody told the other two to go down to the hotel and get a room. She would meet with them later, after she'd had time for a bath and a short nap. The trip had been exhausting. Melody told the stage driver to have someone take the girls' baggage to the hotel and hers to the little house at the end of the street.

She hadn't figured that Jack would be home in the middle of the afternoon, and she wasn't about to stop at the jail and risk running into Cotton Burke. So, walking in the door, she looked with disgust at the haphazard way Jack had left the blankets half off the bed and one pillow on the floor. As she straightened up before heating some water for a bath, she noticed something on the pillow that lay on the floor. There was a long, black hair plainly visible on it. She cursed loudly, spewing profanities about what a cheating, lowdown piece of garbage she'd hooked up with. She didn't calm down until she was soaking in the lukewarm water. Her ire returned only after hearing the front door open, and Jack's distinctive whistling. She reached over to the stand beside the copper tub and picked up her .41-caliber derringer, waiting for Jack to show himself. When he stuck his head in the bedroom, she pulled the trigger, missing him by inches.

He dove back into the front room, rolled away from the door, and drew his Remington.

"Come outta there, you sonofabitch," she screamed, "and face the music!"

"Melody? It's me, Jack. What the hell!"

"You know damned good and well what, you cheatin', lyin' rattlesnake. I go away for a few days and you drag some tramp into my bed. I oughta blow your privates off!"

"Now, hold on, Melody. What makes you think I did anything of the sort?"

"Long black hairs, that's what! And on my very own pillow, you, you—"

"Melody, you gotta let me explain. Just calm down and I—"

"It better be good, Jack, or you'll be hobblin' around like a castrated pig," she yelled at him as she stepped through the door, naked as a jaybird, pointing the derringer at his crotch.

"I got home late last night, after a few too many beers at the saloon, and while there, I met up with a cowboy I used to know. He had long, black hair, and I musta rubbed against him and picked up a hair or two that he'd shed. That's all. When I got home, I dropped into bed, clothes and all. And that's the truth."

Melody lowered the gun, chewing on her lip, not certain whether to believe him or not. Finally she tossed the weapon on the chair, and returned to her bath. She emerged a half hour later, calm and freshly perfumed and powdered. Jack gave a sigh of relief.

She walked across the room to a table where a bottle of brandy sat. She poured a couple of glasses, handed one to Jack, and then settled onto the couch, patting the seat next to her as an invitation to join her. He did without hesitation, partly because she seemed to have accepted his explanation, and partly because she was still naked. And Jack was still Jack.

"Jack, I went to Gonzales to remortgage the hotel. I've made a deal with One-Eyed Billy's next of kin to buy the saloon. I'm going to expand the offerings over there, too.

Whiskey, cold beer, brandy, and Kentucky bourbon, and some girls to help all the poor lonely men survive the hardships of a frontier existence." She gave him a self-satisfied grin as she sipped her drink.

Jack just stared at her as if she'd lost her mind.

Chapter 14

Sleeve and his three new recruits had decided to ride through Lincoln to see if they could add Black Duck Slater to their number. It had been a good decision. When they arrived, Slater was riding hell-bent for leather straight at them with a posse hot on his trail. When the posse saw Slater riding toward a bunch of armed men they didn't know, it gave them pause. The town marshal held up a hand to halt the posse. As Slater continued toward the four riders, each well-armed, giving no indication he feared them, the marshal turned the posse around and headed back to town. Lincoln County had already seen its fill of gunslingers and wasn't eager to engage any more of them without more backup, preferably in the form of a detachment of soldiers.

Slater rode up on Sleeve and his men in a cloud of dust. "Howdy, gents. Looks like you came along just in time to save me from some unsavory sorts wearin' badges. Good thing I recognized you, Buck."

"Happy to oblige. What had those folks so riled up?"

"That marshal was none too happy when I cleaned him

out at a poker game last night. Then, someone accused me of palmin' a king, and the marshal decided I'd look best decoratin' a tree."

"I don't suppose you actually were palmin' a king, were you?" Sleeve said with a frown.

"Hell, no. It was an ace." Black Duck snickered.

"Then it looks like it was a good thing we came along when we did," Sleeve said. "In more ways than one."

"Why's that?" Black Duck asked.

"I have a proposition for you. One that offers a one-thousand-dollar reward for helpin' us take over a town," Sleeve said.

"Okay, what's the catch?"

"No catch, Sleeve's tellin' it straight. That's what we're all doin' here," Buck said. "And that ain't all."

"There's more?"

"Another two thousand to the fella that actually plugs the sheriff."

"Who is this badge-toter I gotta plug?"

"Sheriff Cotton Burke, over in Apache Springs. Ever heard of him?"

"Uh-huh. And I have to admit, I ain't so all-fired eager to match bullets with him. However, in my present financial condition, I may have to alter my stance. Reckon I'm in. As long as the money is up front."

"It is," Sleeve said, "Havens has guaranteed it."

"Then, let's get to it," Black Duck said.

The five gunmen rode into Las Vegas, New Mexico Territory, mid-afternoon and headed straight for the hotel. As they dismounted and tied each of their mounts to the hitching rail, Bart Havens stepped out onto the wide porch. He lit a cigar and leaned on a porch pillar. The men walked toward him, with Sleeve leading the way.

"Mr. Havens, these are the men I promised to enlist for your, uh, venture in Apache Springs," Sleeve said, then introduced each of the men.

"Good work, Mr. Jackson. Step inside, boys, and we'll get down to business. I'll explain more over a bottle of whiskey. How's that sound?"

"Sounds fine, Mr. Havens," Sleeve said, motioning for the other four to follow him up the steps and inside.

The hotel had its own saloon separate from the dining room. Plink kept looking around like he'd never seen the inside of a decent hotel before. Buck kept pushing him ahead as if he were some recalcitrant child. They all sat at a table Havens pointed to. He ordered the bartender to bring a couple of bottles and some glasses. Having filled each of their glasses, Havens raised his and suggested a toast. Plink couldn't wait and swallowed his in one great gulp, accompanied by a look of disgust from Sleeve.

"To the success of the new Havens Bank and Loan of Apache Springs. You boys are the keys to helping build my new empire and bring down an old enemy. I drink to you."

They all swigged, and each glass was immediately refilled.

"I'm sure Sleeve has told you about the financial arrangements. Tomorrow morning, I'll withdraw five thousand dollars, one thousand for each of you. It's yours *if* you agree with my terms of employment."

"I also told them there'd be a two-thousand-dollar bonus for whoever brings Cotton Burke down, Mr. Havens. That was right, wasn't it?" Sleeve said.

"Yes, Mr. Jackson, that is correct. But that's not the end. My plans also call for needing men beyond my immediate requirement for the elimination of a troublesome lawman."

"Mr. Havens, you mind a couple questions?" Buck Kentner spoke up, his dark eyebrows hovering over his squinted eyes like roosting buzzards.

"Ask as you will, Mr. Kentner."

"What did this sheriff do to put a burr under your saddle, sir?"

"He got me driven from a town, *my* town! Damned near broke me. It was, however, my good fortune to come across another opportunity, on which I shall not elaborate at this time, but one that allowed me to reestablish my wealth. Now, with your help, I shall prosper beyond all I've ever gathered before. And Mr. Cotton Burke will have to be content to lie six feet under in Boot Hill, viewing my success in his eternal damnation!" Havens shouted. The depth of his need for revenge burned in his eyes, an almost demonlike manifestation.

Buck glanced over at Sleeve, then to Comanche Dan. Both had the same look on their faces, as if they'd just laid eyes on the devil himself.

"Get a good night's sleep, boys. I'll lay out the finer details of the plan first thing in the morning." Havens downed the rest of his whiskey, shoved his chair back, and strolled out of the saloon like a great weight had just been lifted from him.

As soon as he was out of sight, Buck turned to Sleeve Jackson and frowned.

"What the hell have you gotten us into, Sleeve? That hombre's jumped the tracks."

"He may seem to have wandered a bit off the beaten path, I agree, but the man's got a fortune stashed away, and he's bound to make a lot more. We can get hold of our share and then some if'n we're patient. Don't go gettin' spooked on me, boys. I got a plan of my own."

"You're plannin' to go against that hombre on your own?" Buck said.

"I don't figure to risk my life for no thousand dollars. I'm after the whole herd, not just one steer, if you get my meanin'."

"What's in it for us, Sleeve?" Buck continued. "Stickin' with you, that is."

"Equal shares. Right down the line. We get rid of the sheriff like Havens wants, then we sit back and watch him rake in more cash from these dumb yahoos than any of us has ever seen. That's when *my* plan goes into action. I got it all worked out. I'll let you in on it as soon as we get to Apache Springs. You with me?"

They all nodded, although Comanche Dan seemed less

enthusiastic than the others. Plink was hard to read because he was already well into another of his famous slobbering drunks. Sleeve couldn't tell if he was nodding his acceptance or about to fall into another stupor.

The next morning, Sleeve and his gunslingers wandered into the hotel's restaurant for breakfast. Havens was already there, a table set up and a fresh pot of coffee awaiting them.

"Good morning, gents," Havens said. "Sit and have whatever you'd like. Soon as you're finished, we'll go over my plan for Sheriff Burke."

"Since I've never met this Burke, nor have I had occasion to ride into Apache Springs, what do you know about the town? Is Burke the only law or is there also a marshal or a constable? How 'bout deputies?" Comanche Dan asked. He seemed particularly concerned about walking into an unknown situation without forehand knowledge. "And how about the army? Any of 'em stationed nearby? They close enough to send help if the sheriff should request them?"

"Fear not, Mr. Sobro. I have all that covered. There is no one except a sheriff, and possibly one deputy, from what I've gathered. The closest the army gets is a few buffalo soldiers at Fort Tularosa, and they're busy keeping that Chiricahua chief, Victorio, at bay. With your numbers and expertise, you should have no trouble overcoming whatever skills the sheriff might have with a firearm. In fact, his talents may be just a myth, made up by enthusiastic journalists trying to make a name for themselves," Havens said, playing down the fact that he knew just how much of a threat Cotton Burke could pose.

That seemed to dampen the urge for any of the others to query Havens further. He appeared pleased by their response as he put a spoonful of sugar in his coffee and sipped it. He looked around as if to be sure there were no more questions, then called the waiter over to bring whatever the men wanted.

As the men ate and drank coffee, Havens began to outline what he wanted each to do, how they were to arrive in town, and that they were not to openly communicate with one another, so as not to arouse the sheriff's suspicions.

"It must be made to look as if you each rode into Apache Springs separate, quite innocently, and not as a group of gunslingers looking for trouble. Stay out of fights, don't gamble, and keep your consumption of whiskey to a minimum. A drunken shootist is no longer a shootist, he's just a man who carries a gun and thinks himself capable of using it against any opponent. I can assure you that is not true. A drunk is a drunk, period. I need you sharp and ready should the opportunity come to face a common enemy. And make no mistake about it, gents, Burke is an enemy to each of you, as well as of me. My enterprise will depend on my remaining above the fray in order to gain the confidence of all those suckers I intend to fleece."

"How do you intend to go about that, sir, if I may ask?" Buck said.

"I shall simply offer loans at a much lower rate than the present bank offers, then I shall foreclose on those ranchers and mine owners who fail to meet my strict terms for repayment. The details will be buried in the contract in such a way as to discourage anyone but an experienced lawyer from understanding them. It's complicated, but it has worked many times before and it shall again. I can assure you of that."

"Is that what you'll be wanting us to stick around for? Forcing men off their land when they don't pay up on time?" Comanche Dan said.

"Mr. Sobro, you are a man of deep understanding," Havens said, "and I laud you for it."

"So, you say you want us to arrive separately in Apache Springs?" Buck asked.

"That is exactly what I wish."

"How do we make contact with you? And if we're to corner this sheriff, don't we need to palaver amongst ourselves?" Black Duck asked.

"Indeed, Mr. Duck. I already have carpenters working on outfitting the interior of my new bank. As soon as they're finished and I arrive in town, you'll be able to come to my office by way of a back door to an alley. It won't ever be locked. You can also meet there between yourselves."

"When do you want us there?" Buck asked.

"Right after breakfast, each of you may set a course for Apache Springs at your leisure. No hurry. Any questions?"

"Does it make any difference how soon we brace this sheriff?" Black Duck asked.

"Once I've given you the okay, none at all, Mr. Duck, none at all. Individually or as a group."

"So, we're to wait for you to give us the go-ahead?"

"Timing is essential for the whole thing to work. Certain recent events have caused me to revise my original plan. We can't get ahead of ourselves." Havens shied away from claiming that Whitey Granville's failure to kill the sheriff was the reason behind this alteration. Certainly not in front of Plink.

"You can count on us, Mr. Havens," Buck said.

"Good. Oh, Sleeve, keep your eyes out for a beautiful dark-haired woman named Delilah Jones. She is in Apache Springs at my, uh, personal request. She will be assisting me at the bank. Do not be seen talking to her, any of you. Her reputation must in no way be tarnished by familiarity with gunmen. No offense, gentlemen, but people do often make judgments based on the company others keep. Our customers must see us as highly respectable."

Chapter 15

The whole time Havens had been talking over his plans for assuming control of Apache Springs, and how the demise of Sheriff Burke should proceed, Plink Granville sat in sullen silence, nursing one drink after another. Suddenly coming into a thousand dollars to do something he would have gladly done free of charge, plus the extra fee to be paid upon completion of the job, appealed to him, but Havens's rules just made him angrier and angrier. He had no intention of following any convoluted plan laid out by some pompous, highfalutin ass. He had his own purpose and his own plan. He owed this Sheriff Burke payment on his personal debt, and he damned well intended to collect. His brother was lying cold in a grave as a direct result of Cotton Burke. And Bart Havens, too, when you got right down to it. Maybe after he collected the extra two thousand, he'd put a bullet in Havens for good measure. That would even things up considerably, he figured. All this, of course, he kept to himself.

Plink Granville had grown up in Mississippi in the

shadow of his older brother. He wasn't nearly as good a shot with a rifle as Whitey, but when it came to a sidearm, he could compete with most. Plink never finished his schooling. He found out early that reading and writing weren't something he was good at. As soon as he could, he quit attending the one-room schoolhouse and found a job cleaning floors in the town's only saloon after all the drunks had left.

Plink had killed three men, each of them almost too drunk to stand. His reputation had been built on a lie, but few knew of that well-hidden aspect of his fabled past. Only once had he come close to picking on the wrong man, a wrangler that wasn't nearly as drunk as he'd let on. When Plink pushed, the wrangler pushed back. Plink found himself in a tight spot. When the man went for his six-shooter, Plink dropped to the floor. The man's shot missed, allowing the wily Plink Granville to roll behind an overturned table and skedaddle out the side door. From then on, he avoided contact with that particular adversary. He soon left town and began wandering all over Texas, slowly falling into the very same trap so many men had: consuming too much liquid poison. But now he had an opportunity to put a thousand dollars in his pocket, to shoot down a highly regarded gunslinging sheriff, and avenge his brother all at once. His reputation as a shootist should jump up a notch.

Cotton had no sooner walked through the door to the jail than Jack was in his face with a concerned look and some noticeably uncharacteristic nervous fidgeting.

"Cotton, I, er got somethin' needs sayin."

"Yeah."

"Well, uh—"

"Spit it out, Jack."

"Okay. I, uh, figure it's about time you moved back into your little house. I'll be movin' on, so you can stop payin' for a hotel room," Jack said.

"Where you figure on movin' to, Jack? Your contract isn't up by a long shot."

"Well, uh, here's the situation. Melody is buying the saloon from One-Eyed Billy's heirs, turning it into, uh, a more profitable business, if you know what I'm sayin'. And, she's settin' aside a cozy room upstairs for the two of us."

"I heard a rumor to that effect, but I hadn't figured on you goin' back to livin' in a whorehouse. Of course, it *does* put you closer to the whiskey."

"Hmm, I hadn't thought of that angle. Thanks, Cotton."

"Just when do you figure on makin' this momentous change in address?"

"Melody hired a couple of carpenters to turn the place into a more desirable environment for, uh, entertainment. She's lookin' to gussy it up with drapes and a chandelier, and even some rugs here and there. They're startin' the renovation tomorrow. She figures to have it done in two weeks. Sounds good, don't it?"

"Sounds like just what it is, Jack. Trouble."

"What trouble? She'll be bringin' in more business to the town, and that helps everyone, don't it?"

"Where'd she come up with the money?"

"Said she borrowed it from the bank back in Gonzales. Put up her other establishment as collateral. She's turnin' into quite the entre—er, enter—"

"Never mind. I get the idea. I reckon she'll be bringing some of her other girls with her, huh?"

"Yep," Jack said, with a licentious leer.

"Like I said, *trouble*." Cotton just shook his head as he walked outside. Jack followed.

"She's not doin' anything illegal, Cotton. You know that. Just because you don't like her don't mean she's no good."

"I didn't mean to suggest she was. But you know as well as I do that trash attracts trash. When there are women *and* whiskey involved, men do stupid things. I hope you're up to keepin' your part of the bargain as a deputy. That's all I'm sayin'. Things could start to get real busy."

"You can count on me, Cotton. I'll not let you down . . . again. You got my word on it."

"I'll hold you to that, Jack."

"Oh, and Cotton, there's one more thing you probably ought to know."

"Yeah?"

"I probably should have told you earlier. An old friend of mine blew into town last week. Delilah Jones. She's a, er, a businesswoman. But Melody doesn't know about her. Yet. There'll be hell to pay when she finds out."

"Is this Delilah plannin' on settin' up some sort of business?"

"No. She's been sent here by Bart Havens to size up the town, uh, let him know about who the most likely prospects are for his bankin' business."

"You mean who'll be the easiest to fleece."

"Uh-huh. That's the way I see it," Jack said.

"You're right, Jack."

"Right about what?"

"There is goin' to be hell to pay."

Cotton had wrestled with how he should handle a situation he knew he could do little to control, short of posting Havens out of town. Posting a sign saying that Havens couldn't enter the town wasn't really a choice, though it was one that had flitted through his mind. Over a span of a few days, his awareness of a couple of rough-looking strangers arriving in town also had him edgy. One of them Jack had pointed out as the man who'd identified Whitey Granville. None were from any of the ranches nearby. It was time to talk to the mayor, although he wasn't sure he'd get very far with the stubborn, contrary politician. But he had to try.

He walked down the middle of the street toward the mayor's office shaking his head and grumbling to himself. His anger at the idea of Bart Havens coming into Apache Springs seemed to heighten his awareness of several pairs of eyes watching him carefully from different locations along the boardwalk. One man was sitting in a chair leaning back against the whipsaw-sided meat market. Another sat with his elbows on his knees on the steps to the hotel. Yet another eyed him over the batwing doors of the saloon with a beer in his hand. Each looked to be studying the sheriff as he strode down the dusty street, likely sizing him up for any sign of a telltale habit, a move that might give a hint of hesitation, any awkwardness that might translate into an advantage for one who sought to take his life.

A gunslinger who wished to stay alive couldn't take any chances on not knowing his opponent right down to the size of boot he wore.

Chapter 16

"Sheriff Burke, what's on your mind?" Mayor Orwell Plume said, looking as if the sheriff's entrance had interrupted a nap.

"There's trouble comin' and its name is Bart Havens. That's what's on my mind. And it's weighin' heavy."

"This something you can prove, or are you just being overly concerned? I assume you're referring to the fellow I've been told is planning to bring some competition to that stuffy banker, Givins? Just found out myself a week or so ago. But it doesn't seem to be anything worth getting in a lather over."

"You may not know his history. I have considerable experience with that rattler, and I've seen what his kind of business brings with it."

"As long as he operates within the law, there isn't much you or anybody else can do about it, is there?"

"Listen to me, Mayor, this man is the dirtiest kind of lowdown skunk. He'll cheat the socks off decent folks and laugh while he's doin' it. I've seen the kind of underhanded tricks he uses. I'm warnin' you, he's not here for the good of Apache Springs. He's here to line his pockets by the most devious means possible. That's all."

"Well, until he *does* step outside the law, we'll just have to sit back and watch the town grow. You might even benefit yourself."

"How do you figure, Mayor?"

"If the town gets big enough, we might be needin' a deputy U.S. marshal, instead of just a sheriff. You given any thought to the possibility of moving up?"

"When you see how quickly Havens can deplete a town's resources, you'll change your opinion soon enough. Gettin' your own marshal will be the *last* thing on your mind."

"You're a pessimist, Sheriff. You need to stop lookin' at every rock like there's a scorpion under it."

"Mayor, I know this man, and I assure you he's every bit as dangerous as any scorpion."

"What'd he do to get you so riled?" The mayor scowled at Cotton's continued insistence that Havens was certain to be bad for the town. "It sounds personal."

"For starters, he tried to have me killed back in Texas. When that didn't work, he tried to convince the town council I was bad for business. Fortunately, they saw him for what he was and they ran him out of town on a rail. Cost him most of his fortune, a mostly stolen fortune, I might add."

"So, if he's broke, how can he be settin' up a new bank here?"

"That's just what I aim to find out. And that's not all. I have a hunch he was behind that fellow who took shots at Jack and me."

"Sounds like you can't prove it, though," Plume said with a smirk.

Fuming, Cotton spun around and stormed out of the mayor's office before he was tempted to take a swing at the pompous jackass.

"Jack, I believe the town is slowly becoming infected with the gunslinger disease."

"Yeah, I've seen 'em, too. So far, I count five; mostly they're just hanging around and watching. Getting the lay of the land, I reckon."

"Yep."

"Havens won't be far behind." Jack walked over to pour himself a cup of coffee from the pot on the stove in the corner.

"Keep your eye on that Delilah you told me about. She may be nothing more than his eyes and ears for getting set up, but it can't hurt to be alert," Cotton said, pulling out a sheaf of wanted dodgers from his desk drawer. He plopped them on the middle of the desktop and began leafing through them.

"I already went through those and didn't spot any of the men I've seen," Jack said, standing at the open door, sipping coffee, and watching every movement up and down the street.

"I did, too, but I figured maybe once more would convince me I hadn't overlooked something."

"You goin' back out to the Wagner place tonight?"

"Uh-huh."

"You got anything you want me to be doin' till mornin'?"

"If you can get Delilah to give you a progress report on how Bart's newest banking scheme is coming, I'd appreciate knowin'."

"I figure I'd have to risk life and limb to keep Melody from knowin' what I'm up to, but I could slip out and go to Delilah's hotel room real late, maybe pry somethin' useful outta her." Jack set his empty coffee cup on the desk with a devilish grin.

Cotton just shook his head. "You do that."

Cotton slipped from his saddle and was greeted at the door by Emily. Her beautiful face showed concern, her usually sparkling eyes full of trouble. Cotton saw the frown even through the shadows of the porch. He pulled her close and felt her trembling.

"What is it, Emily? What's wrong?"

"A man came by today looking for you. A hard man with the look of a killer."

"Did he give a name, or say why he wanted to see me?"

"No."

"What do you suppose made him come here instead of going to town?"

"That's what worries me."

"Describe him."

"Well, he was about your height, slender, with long black hair that went to his shoulders. He wore a Colt like yours on his hip, and he carried a rifle in his saddle scabbard. He wore a vest with silver conchos."

"He wear a hat?"

"Yes. It was a broad-brimmed officer's hat. Confederate."

"Confederate? You sure?"

"Very. Otis had one just like it from the war. When he died, I burned it. My family came from Indiana."

"Thanks. You're not only beautiful, but you're also damned observant, Emily Wagner. Now, is there any chance of a steak somewhere inside with my name on it?"

"Uh, yes, of course. I'm sorry. I was so upset by that strange visitor, I forgot to ask you to get washed up for supper." She took his arm and pulled him inside. He tossed his hat on a chair and followed her into the dining room. Two of her hands were just finishing up when they entered.

"José, Ben, how are things in the cattle business?" Cotton said.

"Very good, Sheriff. Looks like you doin' okay, yourself," José said and grinned.

With hands on her hips, Emily shot them both a squinty-eyed frown. The two left the table so quickly one nearly knocked over his chair.

Chapter 17

In the morning, as Cotton was shaving, Emily slipped up behind him and wrapped her arms around his chest. He lowered the straight razor to avoid accidentally cutting his own throat in case she wanted to start the day with more than a hug. When she pulled away and turned her back to him, she sounded pensive as she said, "Cotton, I couldn't sleep all night. Kept tossing and turning, worrying about that man. Who was he and what did he want?"

"I'm not certain, but until I know, I'm not going to let it spook me. And you shouldn't, either. I'll be fine. But in case he does prove to be a threat, I want you to have Henry Coyote around at all times, except when I'm here, of course."

Emily rolled her eyes. "I don't think you realize how worried I am for you, Cotton Burke, but I'll do as you say."

She left as he continued scraping soap and whiskers off into the bowl of water.

* * *

Cotton pushed open the door to the jail to find Jack once again foraging through wanted dodgers. He had some of them spread across the desk, while others were piled in uneven stacks. Several had even found their way to the floor. Cotton stood staring at his distracted deputy, who apparently had either not taken notice of the sheriff's entry or was so lost in thought that he failed to see the looming shadow across his disarray.

"What are you looking for? We both looked through those and found nothing."

"I'm tryin' to put one of these pictures with another owlhoot that rode into town last night. I'm hopin' I can stick his worthless butt in one of those cells back there," Jack said, throwing a thumb over his shoulder. "Although, I'm not sure he's a gunman, anyway. May be just gettin' jittery."

"You aren't alone. I take it you've had no luck."

"You take it right." Jack sat back and threw up his hands. "But I know damned well those hombres are part of Havens's doin'. I just can't prove it. Yet."

"You'll be able to prove it about the time one of them throws down on one of us."

"Yeah, but then it might be too late. I count a number of 'em."

"Uh-huh." Cotton walked over to the stove and picked up the coffeepot, looked inside, then frowned at what he saw. Or didn't see. "I reckon you didn't have time to put some of those dark brown beans in the pot to brew some coffee."

"I reckon you reckon correct."

"I'm goin' down to the hotel for some breakfast. You stayin' here or taggin' along?" Cotton said with a grumble.

"Can't very well sit here alone while you stumble into one of those hard cases on the street and get your fool head shot off, can I?"

"Wouldn't be good for your continued employment prospects."

"That's what I figured. Course, you could sign me to a

long-term contract while still aboveground, then I might be talked into stickin' around awhile longer."

"Check with me after this Havens thing is over. If, that is, we're both still standin'."

Cotton pulled a shotgun from the rack and headed for the door. Jack pulled his hat off a wall peg, hiked up his holster, and followed suit. They both looked around to make sure they weren't walking into something neither one looked forward to. On the way down the boardwalk, neither of them spotted any of the three scruffy gunslingers they'd observed before.

"Hmmm. You suppose all the rattlers took notice of the peace and quiet and figured they were no match for us?" Jack said with a smirk as they mounted the steps to the hotel's dining room.

A wagon loaded with boards stopped in front of the saloon. From inside, the distinctive sounds of nails being pounded and boards being sawed made their presence known. Melody stood outside, hands on curvy hips, shouting orders like some wartime general. When she noticed Jack, she waved, then quickly returned to whipping her new enterprise into shape.

"Melody ought to consider bein' a drover, Jack. She could sure make those dogies stay in line," Cotton mused.

"She does have a way of gettin' things done. Won't be long before that place is bringin' in more business than this town has ever seen."

"Or more trouble."

"That, too."

"Could keep you up nights dealin' with womanizin' drunks with loaded guns, Jack. Nothin' you aren't already used to, I suppose."

"Gonzales wasn't all that tough a town. A couple of drunks now and again. That's all."

"And you were one of 'em, as I recall."

"That's all in the past, Sheriff, all in the past. But now Apache Springs could pose a different circumstance, 'specially since there seems to be an element bent on addin' to their reputation as shootists. And that star on your chest seems a likely target."

"And that's just the reason we both have to be alert to every gun-totin' rattler that crawls into town. And I do mean 'every.'"

"You see any of those that looked the type to be Havens's hires on the way down here?"

"Nope. That's what worries me. I would rather face two men straight-on than have to worry about a back-shooter," Cotton said, taking a seat in the lunchroom then leaning the shotgun against his leg.

A man with slicked-down hair and sliver of a mustache came to their table. As soon as they both ordered coffee, the man stopped at another table before retreating into the back room.

"I noticed some fellas comin' and goin' from that empty building the mayor said was goin' to be the location of Havens's bank. I'd say, another couple weeks and that bastard could come struttin' into town, all ready to start fleecin' the locals," Jack said.

"That's how he works; although, he normally doesn't have a small army of gun toters followin' him around. One, maybe two. I'm wonderin' if he's figurin' on changin' his tactics."

"Could be he figures you're too tough for a single pistolero. You ever think of that?" Jack said, as the coffee arrived along with some biscuits and jam.

Cotton picked up his cup with both hands and blew on the steamy brew. His look was serious, his demeanor calm but direct. He took a sip as his gaze suddenly became distant.

"Something on your mind, Cotton?"

"A rough-looking hombre stopped by the Wagner place yesterday. Scared Emily, by the sound of it. Said he was looking for me. Didn't say why."

"How'd he figure you might be out there?"

Cotton looked down at his cup. "I don't know. If he's one of Havens's men, he might have found out from your friend Delilah."

"I, uh, don't recall sayin' nothin' to her about your *sleepin'* arrangements. It isn't none of her business. Of course, I mighta let it slip that you two were, uh, close."

"What about Melody? She knows where to find me if I'm not in town."

"I'll ask. That is, if I can shake her loose for a few minutes of conversation while she's building that shrine to herself."

"Good luck."

Plink Granville sat in sullen silence, nursing glass after glass of watered-down rotgut whiskey, seemingly oblivious to all the hammering going on around him in Melody's saloon. Sleeve Jackson's constant harping about him drinking too much was becoming more than he could stomach. He felt that his hand was steady and up to the task, and he didn't need Sleeve doing the talking for a pompous jackass in a fancy suit telling him what to do and how to do it. He was slowly getting closer and closer to having had all he could take.

Chapter 18

Sleeve Jackson had slipped out of Apache Springs late at night on his way to look up Havens and give him a progress report on the bank. He'd been keeping an eye on the construction inside Havens's newest venture. He'd tried to keep a sharp lookout for the sheriff and his deputy, neither of whom had paid him much mind, and while he generally found favor with the overall plan, little things picked at him, like a cinch strap wasn't tight enough. Sleeve liked things neat, all lined up and ordered like a new deck of cards. He didn't like surprises. He wasn't certain, however, just how much of what he'd observed over the past three weeks he should pass on to his employer. First, during one of his clandestine evening roamings, lurking in the shadows like a window peeper, he'd spotted an apparent friendship between Delilah and the deputy, Memphis Jack Stump. He had no idea of what might be going on between them, if anything. Had she blabbed Bart's intention to kill the sheriff? Or was she simply working the trade he assumed she'd come from when Bart found her?

Then, he didn't like what he was hearing in the constant bleary-eyed blathering of Plink Granville, nor his inability to crawl out of the bottle of whiskey he carried with him everywhere he went. Plink was a loose cannon, and Sleeve knew that if the kid went off half-cocked, Sleeve would end up bearing the brunt of Havens's fury. It was beginning to look like he'd made a mistake in his choice of enlisting the brother of the man Cotton had shot in self-defense. If Bart figured Plink for a liability, he could make Sleeve's life a living hell. It had happened before.

As he rode, he thought about all the ways he might insulate himself from any possible misstep along the way to Havens's plan to disembowel the town of Apache Springs. And while he knew a little about Bart's hatred of Cotton Burke, he didn't completely understand the full scope of such hatred. It was much more than that, even, almost as if the devil himself was inside Havens, directing his every move. What Sleeve did understand, however, was the tenuous nature of his own relationship with his employer, and the consequences of any perceived failure. He wasn't in it just for the pleasure of killing the sheriff; he was in it for whatever money he could take away from Havens, thus ensuring his future, a future free of work and worry.

Although there had earlier been a half moon, clouds now began to obscure the trail, and the calm darkness surrounded him like a blanket. The trail was anything but a clear-cut, easy-to-follow set of wagon tracks, more like a deer path often edging too close to steep drop-offs. He could envision his horse stepping off the edge and dropping him hundreds of feet into a rocky chasm and a certain death. So, since there had been no specific day assigned for him to make his report, Sleeve decided to set up camp for the night in a copse of cottonwoods nestled along a stream. He'd no sooner gathered an armful of dead and broken limbs, gotten a small fire started to brew some coffee, into which he'd pour a significant amount of whiskey to settle his nerves, than he heard a sound of something crashing through the underbrush. He dropped his hand to his gun butt and backed against a boulder to await whatever was sure to emerge.

Suddenly, from the shadows stepped a man the size of a mountain, wearing a dark cotton shirt and a bandolier across his chest, filled with twelve-gauge shotgun shells. He carried the short-barreled instrument of death those shells were meant to feed, and it was aimed directly at Sleeve. A bushy beard covered the man's face like a tangle of creeping vines. Sleeve moved his hand away from his gun so as not to spook the intruder. He knew better than to try drawing against a shotgun aimed at his gut.

"Howdy, stranger," the man said with a big grin and a gravelly voice. "Got any grub in that bag hanging from your saddle?"

"Some."

"Then I believe I'd like to share a meal with you."

"I don't recall any invitation."

"This here's all the invitation I need. What's on the menu?" The man waved the shotgun in Sleeve's face. The look in his eyes didn't suggest ambivalence.

Sleeve was torn between the strong desire to try pulling his revolver before the man could pull the trigger, and acquiescing to his demands. When the man cocked both hammers, Sleeve made his decision, one in favor of his continued good health. At least for the time being.

"Look for yourself. I ain't runnin' no restaurant."

The man lowered the shotgun and strolled over to the burlap bag Sleeve had tied to his saddle horn. Before he left town, knowing the trip to Las Vegas would take at least two days, he'd stocked up on some coffee, beans, and a couple cans each of tomatoes and peaches. As the man lifted the bag from the saddle, he carefully kept the scattergun aimed back at Sleeve. He brought his purloined find over to the fire. He dropped it on the ground, whereupon one of the cans rolled out. His eyes were instantly diverted from Sleeve to the can's label, one which proclaimed it to be filled with peaches in syrup.

Sleeve saw his opportunity and started to draw his six-shooter, but the man was not to be denied his meal. He spun around, discharging one barrel into the ground a foot from Sleeve's left boot.

"Next one'll be mid-chest. Now, hand me that knife and we'll get to openin' this can full of heaven. Peaches is my favorite, you know."

Sleeve let out a low growl as he let his revolver slip back into the holster. He slipped his knife from its sheath and handed it to the man, handle first. "Anything else, Your Majesty?"

"You can unbuckle your gun belt with your left hand and let it drop on the ground, too. That's just so's we can get to know one another without bullets flyin' every which way," the man said. "And, you ain't told me your name. Folks eatin' together ought to get acquainted."

"Sleeve Jackson."

"Ahh, the gunslinger. Got yourself quite a reputation over Texas way. What'cha doin' in New Mexico?"

"It ain't none of your business."

"A might touchy, ain't ya? But then, I reckon I'm forgettin' my manners, too. Folks just call me J.J."

Sleeve's eyes grew wide and his jaw dropped. "Y-you ain't J.J. Bleeker, are you?"

"Uh-huh. You heard of me?"

"Who hasn't heard of J.J. Bleeker, the man killer? What are you doin' out thisaway?"

"Well, I got myself in a bit of trouble in Louisiana, and a posse and a troop of cavalry convinced me that the best way to keep my skin intact was to skedaddle."

"I hear tell you've killed a dozen men. That right?"

"More or less. Course that don't count soldiers. Or Injuns."

"What are you up to now?"

"Beggin' food off'n strangers in the woods, or hadn't you noticed?"

Sleeve's eyes lit up and his mind began racing. Sitting right in front of him might just be a chance to get off the hook for choosing Plink Granville. He didn't know J.J.

Bleeker, but he'd sure heard about him, and none of it flatterin'. The man was a stone cold killer. Not a man to trifle with. Sleeve knew he had to choose his next words carefully, but it seemed at the moment that fate had finally dealt him a winning hand.

"Hmm. How'd you like to make some *real* money doin' what you do best? You see I've got a sweet little deal brewin' over in Apache Springs. I think you might just fit in fine. It's a simple job of pullin' those triggers at the right time. There's a thousand dollars up front if you agree to the proposition."

J.J. squinted with suspicion as he said, "And what do I have to do for this money?"

"Just kill a sheriff."

J.J. burst out laughing.

"What's funny? This particular sheriff ain't goin' to be all that easy to kill."

"And what sheriff might that be?"

"Sheriff Cotton Burke."

"Never heard of 'im."

"Even better. He won't know who you are, either, especially when you stroll down the street, pretty as you please, and blow him to kingdom come with that cannon. Oh, and did I mention that if you are the one who gets Burke first, there's another two thousand in it for you?"

"Gets him *first*? Is there to be others gunnin' for this hombre besides me?"

"Uh, a couple. Includin' me, of course."

"If you got all those others backin' you up, what the hell do you need me for?"

"Insurance."

When J.J. Bleeker agreed to the proposal, Sleeve's desire heretofore to continue on to meet Bart Havens evaporated. Bringing his boss up-to-date on the bank's construction progress could wait a couple more days. He and Bleeker could just ride back to Apache Springs together and join the others in anticipation of Havens's arrival. Sleeve was almost joyous as he thought about shedding himself of the unreliable and drunken Plink Granville.

"How far is this Apache Springs?" Bleeker asked.

"We'll be there by sunup. Town sits in the middle of a wide valley, surrounded by mountains on all sides. Lots of ranches up in the higher elevations where the grazing is good and there's plenty of water. Town itself ain't much to look at, but it can boast of havin' all the things a man needs to survive: whiskey and women." Sleeve laughed at his own attempt at humor.

"The whiskey appeals, but most women don't take to me. Don't know why," J.J. said, quite innocently.

Sleeve knew exactly why, since he'd found it necessary to ride upwind of the giant ever since breaking camp, but he damned well wasn't fool enough to put it into words. Bleeker was clearly a man to be handled with kid gloves, and Sleeve Jackson was no man's fool.

Chapter 19

For two weeks Apache Springs had been as quiet as a prayer meeting. None of the gunslingers hanging around the town had shown even the slightest inclination to cause trouble. Except for one, that is—the kid with a nasty habit of half-pulling his six-shooter from its holster, then letting it drop back almost as if to show how limber his shooting hand was. Of course, Cotton also noticed how much whiskey the kid consumed. He figured the kid's capacity to maintain some semblance of civility toward others in the saloon night after night suggested he was in control of his personal demons, but he doubted it. Thus, he kept a watchful eye on the kid at every opportunity. He'd seen this type before: an aimless kid with nothing but an eager gun hand and a short fuse. If he expected *any* of the gunslingers hanging around Apache Springs to do something stupid, he figured this kid to be the one, even though Cotton had yet to learn his name.

Keeping watch over the influx of gunslingers the past weeks had brought him to two conclusions, but neither of them was worthy of hopeful thinking. First, evidence was growing that Bart Havens would soon be arriving, to the detriment of all around him, and, second, Cotton still didn't know the names of any of the potential threats he'd observed loitering about. It was for the latter reason that he sauntered into the saloon seeking whatever information he could glean from anyone drunk enough to blurt out anything they might know about the crooked banker and his deadly followers. As he entered, he saw Melody at the top of the new stairway leading to the cribs on the second floor, gazing down on the activity below like a queen surveying her subjects. She turned away when he looked up at her.

When Cotton walked up to the bar, he was greeted by the bartender, a man with almost no hair and a nose that appeared to have been broken several times. "What'll it be, Sheriff?"

"Draw me a beer, Arlo."

The sheriff looked over the evening's crop of drunks, cardplayers, and whoremongers. He had to admit Melody had spruced the place up nicely, and the crowd seemed appreciative. The woman did know how to please a man while at the same time making money, and lots of it. But with her fractious temper, he failed to see what Jack saw in her, other than a superb body, which Cotton, too, had enjoyed on occasion several years back. When his beer came, he asked Arlo if he had any idea who the youngster was sleeping off a drunk at a table in a far corner.

"Nasty fellow, that one. Says he's Plink Granville, as if anyone here ever heard of him. Fancies himself a shootist, I'll wager. Personally, I don't see how he could hit the floor with a rock as drunk as he is all the time . . . dawn to dusk."

The name "Granville" hit Cotton like a sucker punch. His theory that Havens was behind the sudden influx of gunslingers in town, here to do his dirty work, had just been confirmed. And his blood was beginning to boil. He drank his beer in two big gulps and stormed out the batwing doors, heading for the jail and a talk with his deputy.

* * *

Bart Havens had been confidently anticipating his arrival in Apache Springs. All of his hired assassins were already there, just in case Cotton Burke saw him get off the stage and decided to run him out of town immediately. He'd have plenty of protection. The coach rolled to a stop in front of the hotel. The driver called out that they'd reached their destination and everyone could climb out. He emphasized that he was a driver, not a doorman.

Havens saw Sleeve Jackson sitting in the shade of the porch overhang at the hotel, leaning back in a rocker. When Sleeve gave him a subtle nod, he figured it was safe to disembark the Butterfield coach. He stepped down, brushed his long black coat of its accumulated dust, and turned to ask the driver to send his luggage to the hotel. He had already arranged to have the best room available, the one that looked down on everything that happened along the main street.

When he stepped up the steps to the hotel, he felt uneasiness, as if hatred-filled eyes were drilling into his back. He turned to see Sheriff Burke across the street watching his every move. That hatred went both ways, he thought, as he strode through the hotel's double doors.

"I believe you have a room for me. Bart Havens is my name," he said to the man behind the check-in desk.

The clerk turned the register book around to let him sign in, handed him a pen, and laid a key beside the book.

"Nice to have you staying with us, Mr. Havens," the man said. "Your room is at the top of the stairs on your right. I hope you have a pleasant stay. Please let me know if there is anything you need."

"I shall require a bath, if you could arrange that. The trip was unusually dusty."

"Yessir. I'll have the boy heat some water for you right away. The tub is in the room at the far end of the hall. There are towels and soap already in the room. Oh, and I have a message for you from a lady."

Havens took the folded letter, grabbed his key, and started up the stairs. As he got to his room and put his key in the door, he heard footsteps behind him. He turned to see Sleeve Jackson hurrying up.

"Sleeve, I thought I told you we were not to be seen conversing," Havens whispered.

"You did, Mr. Havens, but I have something to tell you. It may be important. May I come in?"

Bart grudgingly stepped aside and ushered Sleeve into the room before him. He closed and locked the door.

"Now, what is this important news that couldn't wait until after dark?"

"A couple of things. The first is that I've hired another gunman to help with, uh, cleaning up the town. His name is J.J. Bleeker. He's camping outside of town."

"Is he reliable?"

"If that means dangerous, yessir, I believe he is that."

"And what is the second *important* matter?"

"That lady friend of yours you told me about, Delilah Jones, seems to have struck up a friendly association with Burke's deputy."

"Are you certain of this?"

"You said keep my eyes open."

"That I did. Thank you. I'll deal with *her* in my own time, and fill you in later as to the disposition of my further relationship with her. Now, it would be best if you left by the rear stairs. We mustn't be seen conversing again. Do you understand?"

"Yessir," Sleeve said. When he got outside, he headed for the saloon. The look that had come over Havens when he was informed about Delilah Jones made Sleeve uneasy. He never had any qualms about shooting a man for just cause, but hurting a woman was an entirely different matter. And he had a bad feeling about what Havens might do to her. The man's capacity for evil was well known. Sleeve was beginning to wish he'd kept his mouth shut. His dislike for Havens had grown even greater in the last few minutes. He needed time to further hone his own plan.

Chapter 20

Jack was trying to stifle a yawn. He leaned back in the chair at Cotton's desk as the sheriff walked in. Cotton's expression suggested to Jack that he'd better wake up fast. The deputy had wandered over to Delilah's room and spent the night because Melody told him she would be staying at the saloon making last-minute preparations for their own cozy little love nest. She wanted to surprise him. So, Jack being Jack, he took advantage of her absence to have one last fling with the comely Ms. Delilah Jones.

"Rough night, Jack?" Cotton said as he sat heavily on the edge of the desk.

"Uh-huh. By the look on your face, somethin' got you riled," Jack said, eager to change the subject.

"I finally got more than just a suspicion that Havens is behind those gunslingers arrivin' in town so conveniently. One of 'em is Whitey Granville's brother, Plink. And since Henry Coyote tracked Whitey to a rendezvous with Bart, it's more than likely the kid is here to do Bart's dirty work. Probably jumped at a chance to even the score."

"That's pretty convincin', Cotton, but what about the others?"

"I figure Havens's plan is to come at me from several sides, so he can be assured of success. He's one devious sonofabitch."

"You got a plan?"

"Yeah, to stay alive."

"Other than that?"

"I'm not certain the two of us can keep track of all the guns that've shown up in the past several days. We may need a little help."

"You got anyone in mind?"

"I figure the only reason any of these hombres would take up with Havens is money. That could be our answer."

"How's that?"

"We take his money away from him."

"How the hell do you figure to do that?" Jack said with a doubtful scowl.

"Cogitatin' on it."

When Cotton arrived back at the Wagner ranch, he found Emily at her desk staring bleary-eyed at a stack of papers. She looked up at his entrance and gave him a weak smile, then sighed. She put down her pencil and rubbed her eyes.

"You look worried about something. Anything I can do?" he said, dropping into an overstuffed chair.

"You can quit puttin' yourself out there so every gun-crazy killer can take a shot at you. That's what you can do," she said, leaning on one elbow and pointing at him.

"You're still concerned about that feller that dropped by lookin' for me, aren't you?"

"There was somethin' about him that shook me deep down. That man had the look of a killer, and if he was intent on seekin' you out, he didn't mean you good tidings. You're darned right I'm concerned. Scared to death is more like it."

"I'd like to know what he had in mind myself. You said he didn't make any threats, didn't you?"

"Yes. But do you know him? You didn't say anything after I told you he'd been here."

"Mighta heard *of* him, from your description, although we've never met."

"Well, am I right? Do you figure he's a killer?"

"No more'n me, I reckon."

"You? You are a good man—honorable, kind, and dependable. You're no killer. You sayin' he's on the side of the law? Or that you've been on the other side at some time?"

Cotton struggled to get up out of the deeply plush chair. Emily had seen it in a catalog and just had to own one. She'd sent all the way to St. Louis to have it shipped. He stretched and started for the dining room. "Any chance for some beans and biscuits left from supper?"

"I'm not moving till you answer my question, Cotton Burke."

Cotton stood expressionless as he allowed silence to fill the room. He looked into Emily's questioning eyes for but a moment before redirecting his steps toward the front door. He loved her more than life itself, and he couldn't lie to her. But his answer might change everything between them, and he couldn't face that possibility. *Why did I open my big mouth?* "You can't just walk away without answering me, mister, unless you want to sleep in the bunkhouse tonight," she scolded through clenched teeth. She stood up with hands on her hips and followed him through narrowed eyes. "Now, is he or is he *not* a killer? And is there some terrible thing in your past that you don't want me to know? Tell me!"

Emily was still fuming as Cotton left the room and gently closed the door behind him. Cotton went without any beans or biscuits that night, and slept in the bunkhouse. The next morning he saddled up and rode out before sunup.

The two hours it would take Cotton to get to town would be the first real chance he'd had to concentrate on the situation swirling around his old enemy, Bart Havens. He'd never talked to Emily about the many twists and turns his life had taken after he left Gonzales many years ago as a result of Jack's deadly drunken rampage. Those years had taken him places he'd rather not revisit, especially not if it meant Emily would find out that Cotton Burke hadn't always been such a law-abiding citizen. There had been dark moments when the law was forced to take a backseat to revenge. And he wasn't especially proud of those events.

As the trail slowly descended from the higher elevations where grassy valleys and tree-lined creeks were plentiful, he looked back over his shoulder, imagining Emily just crawling out of bed, wrapping her robe around her to ward off the early morning chill, only to realize that he wasn't there. It pained him to think what might have been going through her mind at that moment. He briefly reined in at a free-flowing creek to let his horse drink and nibble some of the tender grasses sprouting along the bank. He wasn't in a big hurry to return to town, where his troubles were just beginning.

Letting the mare wander as she wished, he sought the shade of two large oaks to wrestle with his thoughts of both Emily and Bart Havens. Two opposite sides of the coin of decision. One beautiful and good, one pure evil. He was suddenly at odds with himself. If he were to eliminate the Havens threat in the same manner in which he'd handled an equally despicable man, could he ever face Emily again? He was lost in a wave of contradictions when he was suddenly aware of a presence. The man in the Confederate hat with the conchos on his vest stood quietly staring at him from the other side of the creek, no more than twenty feet away. The man's thumbs were stuck in his belt and he signaled no move that might suggest a threat.

"Howdy," the man said.

"Howdy," Cotton answered. His curiosity about the man's identity was intensified as they stood there, two serious men, neither appearing unfamiliar with the firearms that accompanied him.

"I have a fire over here with some coffee brewin'. Care to join me?" The man was casual in his manner and had an easy smile. He kept his hands well away from his pistol.

Cotton could detect no ill intent, so he splashed across the stream and up the bank on the other side. If this conversation was headed the way he figured it might be, the friendly atmosphere between them *could* erupt into gunfire at any moment, a situation he hoped to defuse should it occur. It was clear just from looking at him that this hombre knew his way around a six-shooter. While a suspicious nature ran deep with the sheriff, he intended to avoid any confrontation. He eased down on a fallen log at an angle to the man, keeping his gun hand free just in case. The man poured a cup of coffee and handed it to Cotton, who took it in his left hand. The man then poured himself one and leaned against a tree, blowing on and then sipping the steaming brew.

"So, you're the famous Cotton Burke, eh?" the man said.

"Didn't know I was famous, but I *do* answer to the name of Burke. Who's askin' and how'd you know my name?"

"You can sit easy, Sheriff. I'm not here to provoke you or nothin'. But you're right in askin'. I *am* here for a reason."

"And that reason is?"

"In due time, Sheriff. First, I'd like to know if you recall a shooting in Fort Worth about five years ago. Ever hear of a fellow by the name of 'Lucky Bill' Sanborn, got himself gunned down over a gal?"

"I remember, and since you're askin', you must know damned well I do. Get to the point."

"I been sent to track down the man who shot Sanborn and take him back for trial."

"That could be harder than you imagine."

"That's what I figured."

"Exactly how much do you know about Sanborn and what got him killed?"

"Damned little," said the stranger.

Cotton held out his cup for the man to pour him some

more. That coffee was the only breakfast he'd had and his stomach was beginning to protest.

"Well then, if you're interested, I'll lay it out for you," Cotton offered.

"I am. Go on."

"Lucky Bill had a hankerin' for the wife of a good, hardworkin' store clerk named Ralph Pepper. Ralph and his pretty young bride, Juliet, set up housekeepin' in a small adobe at the edge of town. Lucky Bill got roarin' drunk one night and broke into the Peppers' home. He stabbed Ralph, and then, when he attempted to rape his wife, she fought back. In a rage, probably over her rejection, he beat her senseless with the butt of his six-shooter, then raped her while she was unconscious. When I arrived for a visit the next day, I found her barely alive on the bedroom floor. A trail of blood showed that Ralph had bled to death trying to get to her. She struggled to tell me what had happened before her words stopped making sense. I reckon the shock of such a vicious attack was too much for her mind. The doctor was unable to do much for her. She died three days later. The doctor said it wasn't the beating that killed her; it was a broken heart over the rape and the loss of her husband.

"I went looking for Lucky Bill. I found him in the saloon, confronted him, told him I knew what he had done, then blew him into the next county with a forty-five to the forehead. I left town before the sheriff could decide I was guilty of something."

"So you figure you had every right to kill the kid?"

"Damned right I did. The girl he raped was my little sister."

"I didn't know. Sorry." The stranger looked away for a moment, rubbing his chin whiskers. His expression grew intensely serious. He stared at the ground, watching a beetle make its halting way across the sand, until Cotton broke the temporary silence.

"Who would swear out a warrant for me after all this time, especially over that animal?"

"Lucky Bill's father, a slimy crook by the name of Judge Arthur Sanborn. He was appointed to the bench three months ago by several of his cronies that recently took control of city government."

"Sounds as if you don't hold this judge in high regard," Cotton said, emptying the last dregs of coffee from the cup.

"I don't. The man is the lowest form of life. He's akin to all the other cockroaches scurryin' under things to feast on garbage."

"But he's the reason you're doggin' me?"

"Seems like."

"What led you to the Wagner ranch?"

"Reckon I do owe you an explanation of sorts. Interested?"

"Got nothin' better to do."

"Judge Sanborn isn't the only kind of trash blowin' across these lands. You've got yourself a handful with the likes of Bart Havens."

"I'm more than aware of him and his underhanded dealings. He's tried to bite me before."

"And on that particular occasion, so I'm told, you came out on top."

"Seems so."

"It may not be so easy this time. He's trying to boost his odds of winning this hand with a stacked deck. He's hedged his bet with some of the meanest gunhands in the Territory."

"How did you come by this information?" Cotton cocked his head questioningly.

"I've been paid a thousand dollars to be one of them."

Chapter 21

"You? You took money to kill me?"

"Yeah, I did. I took Havens's money to kill you the same as four others had. Of course, the man who was making the deal for Havens didn't know I wasn't who he thought I was."

Cotton's hand slipped ever so slowly to rest on the butt of his Colt revolver. While the man had just admitted to being in on a nefarious plan to kill him and likely Jack, as well, he was baffled by the man's admission that he was playing both sides of the fence. *Who openly admits to being part of a murder plot?*

"And just who are you?"

"You ever hear of a gunslinger by the name of Comanche Dan Sobro?"

"Of course. Never met the man, though. Just as soon not from what I've heard of his reputation for makin' trouble."

"Good."

"Good, what?"

"It's good you never met him. Nasty hombre that Sobro,

mean and ugly—well maybe not so ugly," the man said with a wry grin.

Cotton frowned at whatever the man was trying to say, which wasn't any clearer than mud at that moment.

"What's this fellow have to do with me?"

"He's one of several men who have been paid a thousand dollars each to gun you down."

"So that's Havens's new approach. I reckon I shouldn't be surprised. What's your part in all this?"

"Havens and his other gunslingers think *I'm* Comanche Dan Sobro."

Cotton's Colt was out of his cross-draw holster in a flash. The man calling himself Comanche Dan was looking down the barrel of the .45 before he could blink. But the man made no move for his own gun, nor did he even flinch at the sight of Cotton's gun pointed at his head.

"It'd be a good idea for both of us if you'd let me finish my story before you pull that trigger, Sheriff."

"I'm listenin'."

"About a month back, I came across Comanche Dan after tracking him for a stage holdup in Big Bend country. During my attempt to take him into custody, he made it clear he didn't want to be taken in. I had to eliminate him. Comanche Dan Sobro is deader than a rock. Havens and his hired killers, however, don't know the man they hired as Comanche Dan isn't who they think he is."

"Then who the hell are you?"

"Name's Thorn McCann. I'm a deputy U.S. marshal from Texas."

Cotton lowered his Colt, eased the hammer down, and slipped it back into its holster.

"So, how'd you come to take on this fellow's identity? And what brought you here?"

"Like I said, Bart Havens put up a lot of money to see you shot down. I happened to hear of it and figured since the word was going around that one of the men being sought after to join the effort was Sobro, I couldn't help but look into what the deal was. When I heard it was a plan to kill a sheriff—and a man I had a warrant for—I naturally had to figure a way to put a stop to it. Can't have thugs and miscreants shootin' down our duly elected lawmen, now, can we?"

"Reckon not, Marshal. You got a plan?"

"Since I'd accepted Mr. Havens's generous offer, I figured to see what the setup was, that is until I found out who the sheriff was they hoped to gun down."

"That make a difference?"

"Some. You got a reputation for bein' fast and deadly. It'd be a loss to your community if some of these lowlifes took it into their whiskey-soaked brains to back-shoot you, so that's why I figured to seek you out *before* I arrived at Apache Springs."

"How'd you know I might be at the Wagner ranch?"

"I heard a story a while back that you put a stop to some devilment instigated by one very nasty hombre: Virgil Cruz. I also heard you were wounded and had lain up at a nearby ranch to heal up. I asked at a couple of the ranches around here and they led me to the Wagner place. Some fella named Cappy Brennan put me on your trail."

"I don't mind tellin' you I'm happy as a pig in slop that I can look forward to one less gun pointin' my way," Cotton said. "Of course, there is that warrant you mentioned before."

"Let's worry about that later. First, what do you figure would be the best way to get word to you if I hear Havens has his plan complete and bullets could fly at any time?"

"I have a deputy goes by the name of Memphis Jack Stump. I'll have to tell him about you so he can rest easy that at least one of the gunslingers recently seen wanderin' our quiet streets isn't what he seems. Until the town gets downwind of Havens and his crooked dealin's, I reckon you best stop by the Wagner ranch whenever you need to contact me. Emily can get word to me."

"Emily? That the good-lookin' lady at the Wagner ranch?"

"Uh-huh, and don't go getting' any ideas. She's spoken for."

McCann held up both hands and said, "Worry not, Sheriff, I'm not a man to cut in on another fella's dance card."

Cotton stood up, leaned over to shake the marshal's hand, and said, "Since we both seem to be singin' out of the same hymnal, I reckon I can get back to town and relieve Jack of some worry about you joinin' the Havens bunch. He'll be a lot easier to live with knowin' there's at least one less back-shooter lurking in the shadows."

Chapter 22

"I hear you been real chummy with that deputy, Memphis Jack Stump. That *is* his name, isn't it?"

"We've, uh, known each other for a long time, Bart, long before I ever met you. It—it's nothing but an old friendship, nuthin' else. I swear."

Without warning, Bart reached out and backhanded Delilah across the face, hard enough to knock her sprawling to the floor. She struggled to get to her feet from a tangle of skirts as she rubbed her cheek. He'd hit her hard; his fancy gold ring cut the corner of her mouth. A trickle of blood dropped on her high-neck silk blouse. The shock of Bart's sudden reaction to finding out about Jack had taken its toll on her normally cool demeanor. She began to sob. Bart pulled his handkerchief from his breast pocket and threw it at her.

"Here, get yourself cleaned up and presentable to go down for dinner. And never let me hear that you've even *spoken* his name again, let alone met with him. Not that he'll be around much longer, anyway. As goes the sheriff, so goes the deputy," he said, with a contemptuous sneer.

Delilah was still shaking as she poured water from a hand-painted ewer into a ceramic bowl. On the wall above hung a small, round Chatham mirror. She dipped a corner of the handkerchief in the water and began dabbing at the cut to stem the flow of blood. She was still sniffling as she changed out of the bloodstained blouse and into another. Bart leaned on the window frame and stared at the comings and goings of the townsfolk and ranch hands as they conducted their business, oblivious to Bart Havens and his temperamental outburst. A light breeze wafted the curtains.

"Hurry it up. I've grown quite hungry all of a sudden. A rush of excitement does that to me."

Delilah sat across from Bart with her hands folded in her lap, reminiscent of a scolded child. Her face was still red, and her lip was beginning to turn blue. After ordering lunch for both of them, Bart pulled a folded paper from his vest pocket, opened it, and began issuing orders like a general planning a campaign.

"The Havens Bank will open its doors for the first time at precisely nine o'clock tomorrow morning. You will be there in front of the counter to greet each and every prospective customer. I'm certain there will be lots of townsfolk curious about who we are and what benefit we might offer to their businesses. You are to send each one directly to me, keeping all others engaged in friendly conversation until I am free after each interview. You can then send the next person in line to me. Is that clear?"

"Y-yes, Bart, er, Mr. Havens."

"Good. Many will try to get as much information as possible from you, but you are to defer to me on every occasion. You may simply explain that we intend to make the best loan arrangements possible, easily beating the competing bank's exorbitant rates. You may let them know, too, that we'll be offering excellent interest on deposits. That is as far as you may venture into the business end. Do you follow me?"

"I do."

"The first day will, I suspect, be fairly busy. After that, the curiosity will taper off and serious deals will start coming our way. We'll just have to be patient, letting the town get used to having two banks instead of one. Once we've secured sufficient loans and bank deposits to squeeze Darnell Givins to the breaking point, he'll want to make a deal. That's when we take him down and begin foreclosing on outstanding loans, the ones where nobody thought to read the fine print at the bottom of their contracts." He leaned over to whisper so that no one could overhear him as he spelled out his treacherous plan to destroy the community of Apache Springs. His disingenuous smile as he spoke belied his hatred for anything and anyone who had any contact at all with his most hated enemy: Sheriff Burke.

He sat back with a satisfied smile and looked around at the other patrons, giving each a nod and a cheery "Good day." When their lunches came, he quite properly helped Delilah with the plate of potatoes—too heavy by far for such a dainty lady—and passed the bread, butter, and beans. He dabbed at his mouth after each bite, replacing his napkin across his thigh and putting his fork down as he chewed. His manners were perfect, right out of the *Modern European Book of Etiquette*. Other patrons did not fail to notice that he stood head and shoulders above the ruffians and low-society types they were so used to sharing restaurant tables with. He instinctively picked up on the buzz of appreciation that floated about the room. His confidence grew as his successful performance played out. He knew these suckers were ripe for the picking.

He glanced over at Delilah, took her hand, and gave it a squeeze.

"We're on our way to winning a very high-stakes game of poker, my dear. Can you feel it as much as I do?"

She could only return a small smile in acknowledgment without wincing.

* * *

Comanche Dan strode into the hotel and up to the counter. The man behind it gave him a greeting and Dan asked if he had a room. The man turned the sign-in book around, handed him a pen, and said he had a nice room near the back. Dan agreed and signed in. The man handed him a key and turned away to continue his dusting of the shelves and mailboxes behind him.

Dan had no sooner leaned over to pick up his valise than Bart Havens and the most beautiful woman Dan had ever seen came through the front door. His mouth must have been agape as Bart smiled and approached him.

"Good day to you, Mr. Sobro. May I introduce Delilah Jones? She's my . . . uh . . ."

"I'm his secretary, Mr., er, Sobro was it?"

"Yes, ma'am. Mighty glad to make your acquaintance." He removed his hat and held it at his side.

"Mr. Sobro, perhaps we'll have some time to talk later," Bart said as he took Delilah's arm and escorted her up the stairs. She glanced back at the gunslinger and gave him a smile that turned his cheeks red.

"She *is* a looker, ain't she?"

"Huh?" Dan turned to see the man behind the counter following Delilah's every step up the stairs, almost drooling at the sight.

"Oh, yeah, she is at that," Dan agreed.

"Although, I must say she didn't look any too happy when the two of them came down to dinner an hour ago. I don't know the man personally, but he don't strike me as a gentleman. Oh, he puts on airs, but down deep, I can't say as how I'd trust him too far." Clucking his tongue, the man turned back to his labors as Comanche Dan took the stairs two at a time up to his room.

Dan tried the key to his room and let himself in. He stood momentarily scanning the meager furnishings, then tossed his valise on the chair by the bed. He thought back on what the hotel clerk had said about Havens. From what little he knew of the man, he had to agree. Havens was certainly no gentleman. It hadn't eluded him that the lovely lady bore a deepening bruise on her cheek. He doubted it had grown there on its own.

He walked to the room's only window, one that gave him a commanding view of the roof of the building next door, a butcher shop if memory served. At the end of the long hall was a rear door, likely leading to an outside stairway for use in case of a fire. It would serve him well in sneaking out unnoticed when the need arose. He was certain such a need was not far off.

As he stared out the window at shadows falling across the roof from the false front on the shop across the street, he recalled that his impression of Sheriff Cotton Burke at their brief meeting had been unlike what he'd expected. He couldn't exactly put his finger on it, but Burke exuded a calm confidence most men in his situation would not have. That and one of the fastest hands with a gun he'd ever seen.

He took off his hat and boots and lay back on the bed. It took very few minutes for him to fall fast asleep.

Chapter 23

When Bart entered the bank the next morning, promptly at eight-fifty, Delilah was standing near the door ready to greet anyone that came in. She nodded as her employer strode in with a pompous air, saying nothing to her, and watched him move to the back where his office sat behind a heavy door. Leaving the door open, he walked around the desk, scanning the room with a slight frown, then sat down. Delilah thought perhaps she should ask him if he wanted coffee or a cigar, anything to occupy his hands as he awaited his first curious customer. After a moment, she decided against it, remembering his treatment of her last evening, and the resulting bruise she had tried to cover with cornstarch powder.

The bank had been open for almost three hours and no one had ventured inside, not even a well-wisher or a disgruntled customer from the competing bank down the street. Bart was becoming noticeably anxious and frustrated by the lack of attention, easily seen by his pacing back and forth, first in his office, then in the lobby, and finally on the boardwalk out front. Delilah found Bart's discomfort strangely satisfying. No man had ever hit her, and she quietly vowed no one would ever do it again. She walked over to the teller's cage, where a clean-shaven young man stood patiently behind a barred window. He had counted the dollars Bart had given him for his drawer nearly fifty times. She found herself silently counting with him.

"Mr. Havens failed to introduce us. I'm Delilah Jones. What's your name?"

"B-Ben Saller. My pa is the blacksmith here in town. I'd always wanted to follow in his footsteps, 'cause every town needs a good blacksmith, but my pa said I had failed to beef up enough to wield the heavy hammer. Reckon he was right. I know I'm on the skinny side, mostly 'cause I was sickly as a kid, but . . ."

"I understand, Ben. No need to explain. It's nice to be working with you."

"Yes, ma'am, me too. Boy, I never did figure I'd be workin' with a lady as beautiful as you. Gosh durn . . ."

"Ben, thank you. You're sweet to say that, but I don't think it would be a good thing to say in front of Mr. Havens, if you know what I mean."

"Uh, yes, ma'am. I'm quiet as a mouse about such things, sure 'nough."

Delilah turned and walked back to her post near the front door. Bart was still outside pacing. After another half hour, he came back inside and summoned Delilah to his office, shutting the door behind them. They'd no more than gotten inside than he began to rave about the ungrateful miscreants who ran this miserable collection of mud and sticks. How dare they ignore the opportunities he'd laid out his good money to offer them as customers of his bank.

Delilah kept silent as he screamed obscenities at all the ingrates that roamed the miserable streets of Apache Springs. He figured it all had to do with that rotten son of a bitch, Cotton Burke. He'd probably spread the word that Havens wasn't to be trusted and they should stay away.

They must have believed him and were following his advice, he allowed.

"Do you have any knowledge of what Burke has said about me?"

"No, sir. I've never even spoken to the man."

"Yes, but you've spoken to that deputy, and I'll bet he's blabbed plenty. What'd he tell you?"

"N-Nothing, Mr. Havens, I swear. He never mentioned the sheriff's name. Not once."

"If I find out you're lying to me, Delilah, I swear I'll cut you up so bad no man could look at you without turning away in disgust. Do you understand me?"

"Yes, I do, sir."

"Get out of here and get me something to eat."

Delilah fairly ran out the door and across the street to the hotel dining room to fetch lunch for her boss, all the while chastising herself for succumbing to his promise to shower her with more money than she'd ever seen before. She'd watched what greed could do to a man, never considering that the principle might one day apply to herself, as well. Now she'd come face-to-face with the downside of dreaming of riches and actively chasing that dream.

Cotton had stayed in town for the past two nights. Since Jack had moved to Melody's newly redecorated saloon and house of prostitution, he had no reason to continue to impose on Emily's hospitality. Not that he really wanted anything other than to spend his nights with her. All of his nights. That morning, when Cotton stepped into the jail, he found a note lying on his desk. Jack had left it; it was a note from Emily saying she wished to talk to him. It said: *Cotton, I hope you will be coming to the ranch for dinner. I need to discuss a matter with you. Please come.*

Cotton had noticed Marshal Thorn McCann riding into town the day before, still assuming the guise of gunslinger Comanche Dan Sobro. He'd noticed no activity surrounding Havens's other gunmen, so he didn't think Emily's note had anything to do with them. On the other hand, what else could it be? She wasn't one to offer up an apology for some misunderstanding that had been born of his reluctance to be forthright with her. She had no reason to do that. He owed *her* the apology, but he was, as yet, not prepared to come clean and risk her seeing him as nothing more than another lawman riding both sides of the fence. In fact, he hadn't mentioned his killing of Lucky Bill Sanborn to anyone before his unexpected meeting with Thorn McCann. Not once in the five years since it happened.

Nevertheless, if Emily needed to see him, he had little choice but to comply. First, he'd need to locate Jack and tell him where he was going, and he had little doubt as to where he'd find the reluctant deputy.

When he stepped into Melody's Golden Palace of Pleasure—as she had so aptly named her revamped saloon—he couldn't help but notice how activity had picked up, even that early in the day. Melody drifted down the stairs wearing something long, flowing, and revealing. She made it clear she had no intention of acknowledging his presence. She walked to the bar, asked for a bottle of brandy, then tuned and went upstairs, never glancing back.

Cotton just shook his head as he asked, "You seen Jack today, Arlo?"

"Sure, Sheriff. He's up there," Arlo motioned with a shoulder while wiping down the bar top. "Lucky bastard."

Cotton chuckled at Arlo's assumption that living with Melody was akin to lying in a bed of roses. As the bartender got to know her better, he'd soon learn the error of his ways. Wondering if he should face Melody's wrath by walking in on their little love nest brought a frown to the sheriff. Rather than ruin an otherwise peaceful day, he leaned over to the bartender and whispered to him.

"Tell Jack, when he comes down, that I'll be out at the

Wagner ranch for a few hours. Don't forget, Arlo, it's important. No one else needs to know."

"Okay, Sheriff."

As the business day neared its end, not one person had stepped inside the new Havens Bank and Loan. Bart was furious by five o'clock, and he let Ben and Delilah know exactly how he felt. Ranting and raving, he roared through to his office, summoned Delilah, and again slammed the door.

"How dare they treat me like this. I'll teach them not to ignore Bart Havens. First, I want you to put an ad in that weekly piece of trash they call a newspaper. Make it bold. Tell 'em we're offering loans at no interest to the first ten people who come in. And say that the interest rate on all deposits will start at fifteen percent annually. You got that?"

"I don't believe it will be printed for three days, uh—"

"I want the damned thing out no later than tomorrow evening! Pay that ignorant editor enough to change his mind. The greedy bastard will do it for enough money."

"Yes, sir. I'll get right on it." She started to leave, but he grabbed her by the arm. She tried to pull away, but his grip was too strong.

"I'm not through. Find Sleeve Jackson and tell him and his boys to meet me here at ten o'clock tonight. Tell him to come in through the back door. They *must not* be seen. Is that clear?"

"Yes, sir."

He released his grip on her and waved her out of the room. He plopped sullenly into his chair, tapping his fingers on the desktop as he swore a stream of obscenities under his breath.

Chapter 24

"Jack, I'm concerned about some of those gun toters that have been hanging around downstairs. Where'd they come from? I haven't seen that many hard cases in one place since right after the war," Melody said as she slipped out of her lacy gown and sat on the edge of the bed. Jack was propped up on several pillows with his fingers interlocked behind his head.

"If what Cotton suspects is true, they are here at the request of Bart Havens. And that's not good news for any of us." He reached over to the table next to the bed and took up a glass of brandy, sipping it. "Including you."

"I don't give a damn about Cotton Burke, but I do care what happens to you, Jack."

"Then you better care about him, too, because whatever trouble is coming, I'm up to my ass in it. Remember, Whitey Granville tried to shoot me first."

"Yeah, but I suspect he meant it for the sheriff."

"Maybe, maybe not. We'll never know . . . now. One thing's for sure, his little brother Plink is in town, and my guess is he wants revenge."

"Is that your guess or Cotton's?"

"Does it really make a difference, Melody? A man out to kill someone can just as easily get the wrong man as the right one. Cotton's the best thing this town ever had, at least that's what I'm told by damn near everybody I come across. You'd be well advised to soften your hard heart a bit."

"And just why should I do that?"

"Well, if one of these cayuses starts a ruckus in your fancy new bordello, and I'm off elsewhere, Cotton could be the only one standing between saving the placing and letting it go to hell."

"He wouldn't let—"

"He might if you don't change your attitude about him."

"Are you tellin' me how to conduct my business?"

"Nope. Make up your own mind. I'm just tryin' to give you a little good advice, that's all."

Melody was steamed at being dressed down by her lover. She stuck out her chin, crossed her arms, and turned away from him. He knew he'd gotten as far with her as he was going to get. He stood up, pulled on his pants and boots, slipped into his shirt, retrieved his gun belt, and headed for the door.

"Just where do you think you're goin'?" Melody said with ice in her voice.

"Downstairs to watch the comin's and goin's of the riff-raff. A deputy's duty, in case you didn't know."

He pulled the door closed behind him as he heard Melody stomp her foot and utter a very unladylike comment.

Jack was looking over the shoulders of a couple of card-players when Delilah peeked in over the batwing doors and looked around. If she saw him, she made no attempt to acknowledge it. When she spied Sleeve Jackson sitting with two others along one wall, she slipped inside and walked up to their table. She bent over, whispered something in Sleeve's ear, then left quietly and quickly.

A few seconds later, Sleeve said something to the man sitting next to him, got up, scraped his meager winnings into his hat, and strolled out the door. Jack watched the discourse, then followed Sleeve out front, where he could see the man hurriedly making his way down the boardwalk in the direction of the hotel.

Seeing Jack come out of the saloon with a puzzled look on his face, Cotton crossed the street and came over to him.

"You got a bug up your nose, Jack?"

"No. But I saw Delilah whisper something to that gent strollin' down towards the hotel. Since we know Delilah works for Havens, I was considerin' followin' that hombre, maybe find out who he is. And what he's up to."

"Now you're startin' to think like a lawman. Let me know what you find." Cotton turned and walked away as Jack set off after the mystery man.

Jack stopped three doors down from the hotel in position to be able to watch the Havens Bank. Staying back in the shadows, he waited. He didn't have to wait long.

Ten minutes later, Sleeve came out the hotel's front door followed by four of the town's newly acquired gunslingers, Plink Granville bringing up the rear. Plink wobbled from post to pillar in an attempt to keep from falling down. It was late enough in the day that his drunkenness had now fully overtaken his senses. All five of them slipped around back of the Havens Bank and Loan. There were no sounds of horses leaving, so it could be reasonably assumed they had all entered through the bank's rear door. Jack moved close to the building and stood in the darkened space between the bank and the gunsmith's shop.

"We're all here, Mr. Havens, all except J.J. Bleeker. Didn't have time to ride out and bring him in. But first light, I'll go tell him whatever you're about to say," Sleeve said.

Havens was clearly distressed about something. He couldn't stop pacing around the room. After several minutes, he pounded his hand on his desk, making a sound as sharp as a pistol shot.

"Boys, there wasn't one citizen of this wretched town that had the gumption to come in and inquire about opening an account or checking on loan rates. Not one! I figure Cotton Burke's got something to do with that. If he's out spreading lies about me, well, the time has come to eliminate that which is standing in the way of our success."

"Does that mean you want us to take him down, Mr. Havens?"

"It does. And the sooner the better. But we need to conjure up a plan first."

"You got something in mind, sir?" Buck Kentner asked.

"Now that you mention it, Buck, I do indeed."

"We're all here and ready to hear what you got to say," Sleeve said.

"If you were to all go up against him at once, right out there in the middle of the street, it would scare the hell out of the townsfolk. That wouldn't help our cause. We need the folks hereabouts to keep whatever might happen to our unfortunate lawman separate from this bank. The overall plan is to fleece the town and light out with every damned cent we can get our hands on. That clear?"

"It is. But I thought you said that you wanted to get even with the sheriff. If we kill him, how's he goin' to know why we're here? A dead man can't see the error of his ways, can he?" Plink's words were somewhat garbled, coming as they were through an alcoholic fog. But in a twisted sort of way, he made sense, enough so that the others muttered their agreement.

Bart squinted and pinched his lips. While the others were probably assuming he would put Plink in his place, that wasn't what the wily thief did. Instead, he waited for several moments before replying.

"Plink, you've given me an idea. What you said has the ring of truth to it. To make the plan the success I'm seeking, we need to find a way to make that damned sheriff our scapegoat."

"How we gonna do that?" Comanche Dan said.

"I don't know just yet, but I'm thinking Delilah just might be the answer." Havens smiled and sat down in his swivel chair. He pulled a piece of paper in front of him and began scrawling words on it with a scratchy pen that he dipped repeatedly in an inkwell.

"If I may ask, what'cha writin' there, sir?" Black Duck Slater asked.

"The beginnin' of the end for Sheriff Burke, my boy." He wrote several more sentences, then blew on the paper to make sure the ink was dry. He then folded the paper in half and held it out to Sleeve, who took it with trepidation.

"What is this, Mr. Havens?" Sleeve asked.

"Never you mind. Just take it to Delilah at the hotel. You needn't wait for her to reply. She'll know what to do. Make sure she gets it without delay."

Sleeve took the paper and left the room, again by the back door. The moonless night made finding his way through the many obstacles in the alley treacherous. There were boxes, barrels, broken glass, and empty cans with lids jagged from being pried open. He stumbled several times before making it to the street, nearly bumping into Jack, who was retreating from his recent hiding place out front.

"My apologies, sir. I wasn't watching where I was goin'," Jack said.

Sleeve said something unintelligible and kept on going straightaway toward the hotel. On the porch, before going inside to find Delilah, Sleeve's curiosity got the best of him. He unfolded the note and leaned under a lantern to read it. "Son of a bitch," he muttered.

"She expecting you?" answered the clerk when asked Delilah's room number.

Sleeve's burning glare told the clerk an answer would not be forthcoming.

Chapter 25

"I got a message that you wanted to see me, Emily. Something happen out here?"

"No. But I do need to discuss a matter of importance. Come inside, Cotton, and let's have a brandy." Without waiting for an answer, she led the way into the large main room. She went to a side table, picked up a cut-glass decanter, and poured two small glasses half-full. She handed him one and then proceeded to sit on the long leather couch. When he started to take a seat in the chair across from her, she patted the empty place beside her. He took it.

"What's this all about?"

"You, me, us," she said, taking a small sip, then half turning to look him straight in the eyes.

Whatever she was about to say was making him nervous. He began to fidget in his seat. If she was about to tell him that their relationship was all over, she had sure picked a bad time to do it. Keeping a clear head was of utmost importance right now, particularly since the town seemed to be filling up with rattlesnakes. The two-legged kind.

And losing her would certainly add to the stress of the situation.

"Uh, what about us?"

"When I was growing up, my mother told me something that has stuck with me ever since. She said, 'Never keep secrets. Secrets tear down trust, and no relationship can survive that.' She was right, you know."

Cotton felt a chill. The very thing she was saying was what he'd been guilty of just two days before. He hadn't come clean about his past, and now it was coming back to haunt him.

"I reckon she was right. The thing is, sometimes the truth can hurt a relationship more than help it."

"Not if two people love and trust each other. If I had something in my past that I was ashamed of, or fearful that if it got out folks would think less of me, I'd have to get it out in the open before it smothered me. Or worse."

Cotton sat staring at the fireplace, empty of wood but ready for the coming fall temperatures to beckon a roaring blaze and fill the room with warmth. It was a beautiful fireplace, large and well built. Built by hand from rocks found around the clearing where the house now stood. Otis Wagner had put his talents to the task and built it solidly. Cotton wondered if Emily thought about her deceased husband every time she lit a match to it.

"Do you understand what I'm sayin', Cotton?"

"I'm afraid I do, and I'm not certain what to say. Some things should be locked away, I'm convinced. Sneaking a cookie when you are a child is one thing, but deliberately killing someone is quite another. I don't think all truths can be counted as equal."

"You are right, of course. But building a complete trust between two people requires truth that knows no such limitations."

"I'm not sure I'm ready to confess some of the things I've managed to put away. There are things better hidden than brought to light, at least to my mind."

"If there were some terrible secrets *I* had hidden away,

and *you* found out years down the road, wouldn't that change how you look at me?"

"Nope."

"Even if I'd broken the law?"

"Nope."

Emily stared at him for several minutes as if she were attempting to delve deeply into his thoughts. Finally, she shook her head and sighed.

"I suppose I'll never really understand you, Cotton Burke, but I intend to love you anyway. I'm sorry for pushing you away for not giving me an answer the other evening."

"Emily, there's nothing in my past that I'm ashamed of. Sure a couple of indiscretions with a lady of the evening here and there, but that's all in the past. As for other things, there have been times I've strayed from the *strict* letter of the law, but I'm still not backing down from the righteousness of my part in them. And I care not one whit about your past, only that our future is one of togetherness."

She put her arms around his neck and kissed him.

Sleeve rapped on Delilah's door. He could hear her shuffling about, probably putting on some slippers or whatever it is a woman wears when greeting guests.

"Who is it?" she called out.

"Sleeve Jackson, ma'am," he answered.

"One moment, Mr. Jackson." The moment turned into nearly five minutes. Sleeve was getting nervous standing in the hallway, for fear of being seen by someone who might report him as trying to spy on hotel guests. He really didn't have any idea what the sight of a gunslinger loitering in a hotel hallway might evoke, but he knew it probably wasn't good. The door opened a crack, just enough for him to see a pair of beautiful eyes peering out at him.

"Now, Mr. Jackson, what is it you've come for? I'm really not dressed to receive guests."

"I was sent here to give you this note from Mr. Havens, ma'am. That's all."

She opened the door sufficiently to reach out and allow him to put the paper in her hand. In doing so, her robe fell open just enough that Sleeve was instantly aroused. His breathing quickened and his palms began to sweat. He could smell her perfume, a fragrance that drove him crazy each time he saw her. He hadn't been with a woman for months, and never even close to one this beautiful.

"I, uh, would be happy, uh, to come inside and wait for an answer, if you—"

Delilah quickly recognized the position she was in and acted to avoid what could fast become a dangerous turn of events. Gathering her robe together, she slammed the door shut and turned the key in the lock. She spoke to him through the door.

"That won't be necessary, Mr. Jackson. If the note requires an answer, I shall get dressed and deliver it myself. Thank you."

Sleeve was embarrassed by the rejection. She'd been shrewd enough to see through his offer to await an answer inside her room. *Damn*, he thought. *She sure as hell was lookin' purty.* He left the hotel, but stopped in the middle of the street, paused as if in deep thought, then proceeded to Melody's Palace of Pleasure. *She's got some women there that can take care of a man's problem.*

He'd just walked through the door when a skinny girl of no more than twenty greeted him with a come-hither smile. Her hair was a mousey brown, straight, and still damp from her last encounter with an anxious cowboy. She took Sleeve's hand and walked him to the bar.

"You look like you could use a drink and some female company," she said.

"You're right on both them things, ma'am." Sleeve was nervous and overly eager to get down to business. "But, offhand, I'd have to say the female company is uppermost in my mind."

"Well, then if you have a dollar, we could go upstairs and visit for a spell. How's that sound?"

Sleeve hastily began fishing around in his pocket. He

withdrew a dollar and thrust it into the girl's outstretched palm. "Sounds fine, now can we get to it?"

He couldn't get the sight of Delilah out of his mind. But he was damn sure going to try, at least temporarily. He took the girl by the hand and almost yanked her out of her shoes in his haste to climb those stairs.

Safely inside her room, Delilah sat on the edge of her bed and unfolded the note from Havens. She read it over carefully, three times. She was boiling hot at what she'd just read. It was one thing for Bart to use her to help promote his crooked banking operation, but it was quite another to be considered nothing but a cheap slut to be used in any way he saw fit. This time, he'd turned about-face and was ordering her to send a message to Memphis Jack suggesting she hungered for his company and begging him to meet her. It went unsaid why Bart had concocted such a plan, but it was clear it had something to do with the overall plot to destroy the sheriff who he felt had stood in the way of his success long enough.

She was at a crossroads. If she refused his orders, she was certain to suffer an even more severe punishment than a bruised cheek and cut lip. On the other hand, what would happen to Jack, a man she'd loved once, and likely could again, given the opportunity?

She paced back and forth for nearly an hour before finally coming to a conclusion. Bart had made it clear she was to do exactly as he bid. And she didn't like it one bit.

Chapter 26

The next morning, as Delilah entered the bank, Havens came rushing out of his office to meet her.

"I assume you got my message," he said.

"Yes, I did."

"You will carry out my instructions as specified in the accompanying note. And do it to the letter exactly. Is that clear?"

"It is. But I don't understand why you had to send that sleazy man to my hotel room at night."

"Call it a test, my dear. I was interested in keeping the message quite secret, and I also wondered whether you would let him in."

"Did I pass your little test, *Mister* Havens?"

"You did, my dear, you did." With that, he spun around and headed back to his office, whereupon he closed his door.

Delilah was steamed by Havens's rationale as to why he sent Sleeve to her room so late, as a test of her loyalty to him. She returned to her post as greeter to any customers that might venture in. Her usually cheerful smile was now turned upside down. The reasons to hate that man were mounting up faster than tumbleweeds against a fence. She crossed her arms and made a feeble attempt to look pleasant in case someone might come through the doors.

But, after two days of standing all day, her legs were throbbing and her back had begun to ache. Havens had made it clear he wanted her at the ready the instant a customer arrived. So far, none had. And hers was not a position that allowed sitting. Finally, as if in answer to her prayers, a man and his wife wandered in. Delilah had nearly forgotten what to say, but the man spoke up first.

"I see in the paper that you're giving loans for no interest for the first ten customers to apply. That right?"

"It is, sir. Let me introduce you to our president, Mr. Havens. If you'll follow me." She led the couple to Havens's door and rapped softly.

"Come in," Havens said, standing quickly as Delilah pushed open the door and he saw that she wasn't alone.

"Bart Havens is my name. And you are . . . ?"

"This here's my wife, Agnes, and I'm Donald Blanchard. We own a little spread in the hills out towards the Brennan ranch. Not much, but we got a few head of pretty fine stock. Like to build that bunch of Herefords up a mite."

"And how much of a buildup you got in mind, Mr. Blanchard?"

"Like to start with an additional hundred head. I figure, if the winter ain't too bad, I can make that hundred grow to at least one-fifty, maybe more. I should easily pay off my loan by spring."

Havens pulled some papers from his desk drawer and spread them out in front of Blanchard. "Sounds like a sound investment. I think you'll find we're a good place to do business with. Now, if you'll just sign these papers, I'll get you the money. Now, exactly how much do you figure you'll need?"

"Two thousand ought to do it, Mr. Havens."

"Two thousand it is, Mr. Blanchard. And since you're

one of the first ten people to come looking for a loan, there won't be any interest for a full six months."

"Six months? I thought the ad said 'no interest' at all."

"Well, now, Mr. Blanchard, I'm sure you understand, being a businessman yourself, that it would not be feasible to not require any interest at all, forever."

Blanchard scrunched up his face into a scowl that was magnified by his rough, weathered skin. It was the face of a man who had spent many winters and summers under some very harsh conditions. He sighed, then bent over to sign. His wife said not a word.

"Just curious, Mr. Blanchard, was it the lack of interest that brought you in?"

"Yup. That fellow Darnell Givins tried his damnedest to keep me from bringin' my business to you. When I asked if he'd match your offer, he said he couldn't. That's why I'm here. I been doin' business with him for five years and now he don't think I'm worth keepin'."

When the Blanchards left, Bart said, "Delilah, run that ad again next week. And the week after that."

Melody shook Jack from a sound sleep. He mumbled something foul as he tried to escape her persistent jabs. "Jack, damn your hide. Get your lazy ass up. I want to talk to you."

"Melody, just come back to bed, will you. Whatever it is will keep till mornin'."

"It won't if that gambler downstairs gets caught cheatin' by one of them gunslingers."

"How do you know he's cheatin'?"

"Honey, I can spot a card slick a mile off. And I'm bettin' they can, too. Now, get dressed and hustle yourself downstairs. You got to keep an eye on things."

"And if I catch him cheatin', what am I supposed to do?"

"You *are* the deputy sheriff, aren't you? And ain't card sharks illegal?"

Jack had buried his head in his pillow. It stayed there until she got to the deputy part. He grumbled, but he finally, out of desperation, swung his legs off the bed, gathered up his shirt and pants, and slipped into them. He strapped on his gun belt and started for the door.

"Uh, Jack, maybe you'd look a little more imposin' if you'd put on your boots. A barefoot deputy ain't likely to strike fear in those snakes."

Finally, properly shod, and slightly embarrassed, he started down the stairway. Below he could see Buck Kentner and Sleeve Jackson engaged in a card game with a man who had a long coat and a bowler hat he had taken off and placed conveniently near the edge of the table. From where Jack was standing, any fool could see the gambler was a beginner. He was fumbling the cards as he shuffled the deck and showed no finesse dealing. *This man will be dead before morning if this keeps up.*

Jack sauntered up to the table, where he howdy'd each of the two gunmen. He stuck out his hand to the gambler.

"Name's Memphis Jack Stump. *Deputy Sheriff* Jack Stump. Don't think I've ever seen you around here before."

The gambler was suddenly more nervous than before. He'd started to cut the cards, but the deck slipped from his hand and scattered on the floor.

"Oh, dear. Gentlemen, I'm so sorry. I'll get a fresh deck right away."

Just then, Sleeve scooted his chair back and eased his revolver from his holster. "Aww, that ain't necessary. You been cheatin' so long a new deck ain't gonna change nothin'. I figure your dealin' days are about to come to an end anyway."

The gambler's eyes grew wide and his face turned pasty as Sleeve brought the gun up to eye level with the hapless card shark. Jack stepped in, placed his hand on Sleeve's gun, and shook his head.

"This gentleman is correct, Mr. Gambler. You been cheatin', and that's against the law in Apache Springs. I'm obliged to take you to jail, where you'll find accommodations until the judge comes to town and sets your fine. Now, get up."

"No need to get involved, Deputy, we can handle this ourselves," Buck said.

"Oh, no problem, gentlemen. Besides, since you fellows will be dividin' all the money on the table amongst yourselves, I figure this fella has a few extra dollars tucked away in his hat or vest. And the town *does* need funds to pay for its law keepers. That'd be me and the sheriff."

Sleeve slipped his gun back in his holster and sat back with a grin.

"Fair 'nough this time, Deputy. But the next pasteboard hustler to drop by may not be so lucky."

Jack hastened the gambler's departure from the saloon so fast the man nearly forgot his genuine felt bowler. *Maybe a night in jail will at least keep this fumbling jackass alive awhile longer,* Jack mused as he escorted the gambler to the jail.

Chapter 27

Jack was in the middle of doing something he'd probably never done before. He was sweeping out the office. The door was open as he took one final dusty swipe at the little pile of dirt, nearly choking the sheriff, who had dismounted in front of the jail.

"What the . . ." Cotton muttered when Jack stepped outside.

"Uh, sorry, Cotton. Just figured the place needed a little tidying up."

"Hmm. I reckon you're right." The sheriff stepped inside and removed his hat. As he was about to hang it on the nearest peg, he spotted a new tenant in the first cell. "Who's that?"

"Oh, him, well he's just about the worst crooked gambler west of the Mississippi. Caught him trying to bamboozle a couple of Havens's owlhoots. Figured a night in jail might keep him alive a bit longer."

"Good thinkin', Jack. We can put him on the Thursday stage out of here."

"That's what I figured. The town's close enough to explodin' as it is. Don't need a senseless killin' for all hell to bust loose."

Cotton seated himself behind his desk and leaned back in the swivel chair.

"I figure that's just what's about to happen. The hell of it is, I don't know when or how or by whom. I swear I should have shot Havens the moment he stepped off that stagecoach."

"I got the same feelin'. Everybody is actin' like they was sittin' too close to the fire."

"Melody let anything slip that's been said to her girls by their customers?"

"Nope. And to top it off, I'm not real sure she'd let on if she had heard something."

"Why's that?"

"Well, if you was to fail, she likely figures the mayor would appoint me sheriff and she'd be sittin' pretty."

"That figures. She's one power-hungry bitch."

"But a damn sexy one, you got to admit that, Cotton."

"I reckon."

"You come up with a plan to get ahead of this bunch without tippin' them off to our knowin' about it?"

"Not yet. But unless I've been hornswoggled, that information should be showin' up any day now."

"You obviously know somethin' I don't. You care to share with your ol' pard?"

"Soon, very soon. Too early and I could jeopardize our chances of success."

"Ahh. You're thinkin' I might blab to Melody, and everyone knows she can't keep her mouth shut unless she sees some profit in it. That about it?"

"Not exactly. I don't think you'd *intentionally* blab anything, Jack. You know I trust you, but you *do* have one shortcoming that could prove deadly."

"What the hell does that mean? What shortcoming?"

"You talk in your sleep."

* * *

Sleeve's late afternoon ride out of town took him to a campsite along a creek, well hidden from the road, among a copse of cottonwood and oaks. He reined up short of the burbling water and turned his horse loose. He felt a presence and spun around to find J.J. Bleeker seated on a boulder with a shotgun across his legs.

"Where the hell you been, Jackson? You said the wait wouldn't be long. I'd call four days one damn long time for a fellow to wait for the money he was promised."

"Yeah. Mr. Havens had me doin' errands and such. But don't worry, I brought the money with me. I also got you a room at a little boardinghouse on the edge of town. The hotel is full up. Got any coffee?"

J.J. slid off the boulder and sauntered over to the remains of a small fire. A coffeepot sat on the fire ring, a collection of rocks placed around the fire to keep it from spreading. He picked up a cup, poured some coffee in it, and handed it to Sleeve.

"Thanks," Sleeve said as he took a sip while fumbling in his pants pocket. He came up with a wad of bills and held it out to Bleeker. J.J.'s eyes lit up at the sight of all that cash. "Sorry it took so long."

"The sight of all them bills has done took away the pain."

"Good. We can ride back towards town together, but we gotta split up before we get there. Havens don't want us lookin' too friendly with each other. I'm hopin' Havens don't find out I was in a card game with Buck Kentner last evenin'. Damn near come to blastin' some sidewinder we caught cheatin'."

"What kept you from it?"

"The deputy sheriff stepped in. Saved that ornery gambler's butt."

"You said we was to kill the sheriff. You didn't say nothin' about a deputy, too. There more in it if we gotta take him down?"

"Havens ain't said a word about the man. As far as I know, he ain't part of the deal. I'll let you know if that changes."

"What's this deputy's name? He any good?"

"Name's Memphis Jack Stump."

"Reckon I just answered my own question."

"How's that?"

"I've never actually met him, but I heard about him in El Paso. 'Bout four years ago."

"He's alive, so I reckon he won," Sleeve said.

"Uh-huh. Against three of 'em."

Sleeve began stroking his chin. *Damn*, he thought, *I didn't figure on Memphis Jack gettin' in the middle of this. I got to think Havens knew about him all along. I wonder if he's figurin' that we ain't all gonna come out of this alive. Maybe cut down on his investment. Wouldn't put it past the bastard. I may need to move things along a little faster than I figured. I don't intend to be left out of that two-thousand-dollar bonus, after which Mr. Havens will quickly get to see the real Sleeve Jackson.*

"You sayin' he's fast?"

"Didn't say that, but he's damned accurate."

"How accurate?"

"You ever see Wild Bill Hickok shoot?

"No."

"It was a sight. You didn't never want to be the one he was aimin' at. Gone now."

"What happened to him?"

"Got back-shot. That's what."

Chapter 28

The town had been quiet—too quiet—for several weeks. Cotton didn't like how unnatural it felt. All the while unsavory characters seemed to be gathering in Apache Springs like it was a convention site. Normally, he'd be taking in drunks for sleeping one off in doorways or trying to bust up the saloon after losing a month's pay in a card game. Nothing of the sort had happened. It was as if someone had lit a very long fuse and was just waiting for it to reach the dynamite and blow everything to hell and back. Havens's crew had as yet caused no problems, and they seemed to be keeping everyone else in check just by their presence. None of the cowhands from nearby ranches dared come up against men that, judging by their very looks, would be formidable adversaries—drunk or sober. Man's natural instincts for survival kept those less adept at gunplay alive to return to their families and out of the town's Boot Hill.

And the longer the lack of normalcy lingered, the more Cotton was fraught with turmoil, although he'd been trying hard to keep it inside. He didn't want Emily to worry about him, and he sure as hell didn't need Jack getting ahead of himself by trying to push one of Havens's men into making a move. He'd seen that response in Jack before. Memphis Jack Stump was an easygoing, soft-spoken man whose needs seemed to be met with a bottle of whiskey and a willing woman. He didn't need a fortune, nor was he driven by the need to take a chance on one more hand of cards or roll of the dice. Not that the occasional game didn't have its appeal, but never a man driven to succeed, for the most part Jack was content to sit back and let others do the heavy lifting. Being a deputy was a perfect position for such a man. Of course, as with many men with the same lack of ambition, he *did* have a couple of quirks that could be downright dangerous.

Pushed to pull his Remington or die, Jack Stump had always chosen to risk a responsive hail of bullets by thumbing back his own hammer and letting fly. Never one to try talking his way out of a fight, Jack would shoot. And he was damned good at it. Sometimes, maybe, too good. That was just his way. Jack Stump had never precipitated a gunfight, but he'd ended his share of them, and almost always with a fatal outcome. That was one of the reasons Cotton had yanked Jack out of Melody's house of prostitution in Gonzales and brought him here to help with that good-for-nothing bunch that had kidnapped Emily. Jack had proven perfect for the job.

"Cotton, did you take note of that big fella that rode in about an hour ago?"

"Yeah, what about him?"

"Couldn't place him at first, but I got to thinkin' maybe I've seen him before."

"And . . ."

"And I have. I went back through some of the wanted dodgers we got piled up. I found him. Name's J.J. Bleeker. He's apparently not a man to trifle with."

"Where's he wanted?"

"Now that's the question. Says he was wanted for robbery and murder about three years ago in Colorado. That's long enough that things might be different today."

"Send a telegram off to the sheriff of wherever he was wanted and see if he served some time or if he's still got folks lookin' for him."

Jack left and went to the telegraph office. When he walked in, he found the telegrapher tapping away at the key with one hand while writing something down with the other.

"Be with you in a minute, Deputy," said the man, without missing a beat.

Jack nodded and turned toward the door. He stood in the doorway watching two riders pass by as they left town, while a wagon loaded with crates was arriving. A lady across the street stepped out of the millinery shop, trying to close the door with one hand and keep her new hat on with the other. She managed the door just in time to catch her skirt as it began to billow from a brisk wind whipping down the street. Dust whirled along the boardwalk causing a black-and-white dog to scuttle around the corner for refuge.

"Now, Deputy, what can I do for you?"

Jack turned. "I need to send a telegram off to Colorado, place called Lake City. I need information from the sheriff there about a man named J.J. Bleeker. Can you get that out for me?"

"Sure. You want to know if he's wanted or what?"

"That's exactly what I want. And if he knows, whether he's got anything newer than three years as to the man's more recent crimes."

"I'll let you know soon as I get a reply. Do I bill it to the sheriff's office?"

"Yup."

And with that, Jack braved the wind and, since he would have to go by Melody's saloon on his way back to the jail, decided to stop in for one quick beer.

When he pushed through the batwing doors, Arlo was

staring off into the distance, gritting his teeth, clearly annoyed about something.

"Say, Arlo, you look like you're having a bad day. Why don't you tell me about it over a beer?"

The bartender stepped away, returning in seconds with a foamy glass. He set it down in front of Jack without a word. Jack sipped, gave Arlo a questioning look awaiting an answer, then sipped some more. The bartender wasn't talking.

"Melody step on your toes, Arlo?"

"It ain't her. It's them damned pistoleros comin' and goin', causin' trouble, demandin' service, never askin' politely. They chase the decent folks away. Half the time they leave without payin', and between you and me, I'm sick of it. I get a cut of what gets taken in by the bar, you know that?"

"Nope. Did you complain to Melody?"

"Yeah. Didn't do no good. She said one of these days they'd up and leave, and things would get back to normal. She must know something I don't."

"You might not be alone."

Jack downed his beer, dropped a dime on the bar, and headed back to the jail. Cotton had gone by the time he got there, so he took off his gun belt, rolled it up, and laid it on the corner of the desk. He sat down and put his feet up. That's when he noticed the piece of paper with his name on it. It was from Cotton.

I'll be gone for a while. Just continue handling things as if I was still there. Also, keep an eye out for anything unusual concerning the town's newest scruffy inhabitants. If we get an answer to your telegram back from Colorado, hang on to it until I return.

The note intimated he'd be back in the morning.

"J.J. Bleeker is in town, Mr. Havens. I gave him his money, and I think he's down at the boardinghouse as we speak."

"Good. You told him the rules, didn't you? No trouble before I give the word?"

"I, uh, reckon them's not exactly the words I used, him bein' who he is and all. But I can't see him creatin' a stir over nothin', 'specially since he don't know no one hereabouts."

"He'd better not. Things are starting to pick up at the bank. I don't want anything to get in the way of our success. I'll depend on you to keep a lid on those gunmen you signed on. You do understand, don't you?"

"Yessir."

"And you told him everything that's expected of him?"

"I did just that, sir."

"Sounds like you've done a good job, Sleeve. Keep it up."

"Thank you, Mr. Havens. You can count on me."

"Good. Now go out the back way and leave me to my bookwork. But keep me informed if you hear anything I should know."

Chapter 29

"Cotton, it's him. He's come back."

"Who's come back, Emily?"

"That man with the vest and the sliver conchos. He scares me, Cotton, truly he does."

Cotton got up from the table and walked to the window. He pulled back the curtain to see Thorn McCann quietly sitting astride a dun mare. He had just pulled out a cigarillo; he lit it, blew a cloud of white smoke, then placed his gun hand on the pommel.

"Stay in here, Emily. I'll go out and talk to him."

"I'll go around back and fetch Henry Coyote. He'll back your play."

"No! Please don't do anything. It will be okay. I promise."

He stepped out the door and onto the porch. The man tipped his hat and blew a ring of smoke into the still air. "Nice mornin'."

"Yup. You come for a reason?"

"I did indeed. We should talk about it. Maybe we could wander down by the little bridge at the end of the lane."

"Sounds reasonable."

Cotton stepped off the porch as McCann dismounted. They strolled slowly toward the nearly dried up creek at the bottom of the hill.

"Been a fearsome dry summer," McCann said. "Could use some rain."

"We could, at that."

"We far enough away that we can't be overheard?"

"I reckon. You got some news?"

"That's *just* what I got. I told you I'd let you know Havens's plans as soon as he told us."

"And . . . ?"

"Thought you ought to know, all of Havens's gunslingers have finally arrived in Apache Springs. Plus one additional varmint."

"J.J. Bleeker?"

"Uh, yeah, how'd you know that?"

"Bad news travels faster than good news. You should know that."

"Yeah, reckon I do. Here, this should help you know who you're up against," Thorn said, handing Cotton a folded paper.

"What's this?"

"Names and descriptions of all Havens's crew of gunmen."

"Thanks." Cotton slipped the paper into his pocket.

"Yeah, well anyway, Havens has made sure they all understand they got *one* mission and one mission only: to take you *and* your deputy down."

"That's no surprise, but what's he waitin' for? I haven't been hidin'."

"He wants to get as many customers as possible into his bank before the shooting starts."

"Why? What does he hope to gain by that?"

"Havens thinks differently than most folks. I figure his head is all screwed up inside, because a lot of what he says doesn't make sense."

"Like what?"

"Well, the customer thing, for one. The more customers he has, the more people are beholden to him. He can stand in the doorway, cluck his tongue, and blame all the town's sudden violence on you and your deputy. Then, I figure, assuming you are killed, he'll suggest the best way to tame the town is for him to act as sheriff until the dusts settles."

"And just how does he figure to keep the peace without a gun?"

"Oh, he has a gun all right. Its name is Sleeve Jackson."

"So, Sleeve figures to chase the others out of town all by himself?"

"Nope. They'll leave of their own accord once Havens pays them off."

"Makes sense. It's not a bad plan, as plans go. When does he figure on the shootin' to start?"

"He's runnin' an ad in the weekly newspaper. He's giving loans at no interest for six months, plus very high interest on deposits. The Apache Springs Bank and Loan won't match his terms, so customers are naturally giving Havens their business, most figurin' they'll pay it all back before the six months. But Havens isn't stupid, either. He's got *somethin'* up his sleeve. He hasn't confided in any of us yet as to what that is, but I'd bet anything the customer is going to lose, sure as hell."

"Devious bastard, ain't he?"

"Yup. But that's where it don't make sense. If he ends up makin' enemies of all those folks that come to him for loans, who's going to come back for more?"

"Damn," Cotton muttered as he kicked at a clod of dirt. "That's just it: he doesn't need more customers if his plan to destroy the town succeeds. He'll skedaddle for some other place and do it all over again. His *real* purpose is revenge against me."

"You're probably right. However, there is one piece of good news before I go: you can count on my gun to back you when the shootin' starts. That's when I stop bein' Comanche Dan and get back to bein' myself."

"That's goin' to come as quite a surprise to the man who recruited you."

"Yeah. Ol' Sleeve ain't goin' to like it one bit, either. It cuts his odds down."

"Maybe we can figure a way to even the odds a little more before it all comes to a head."

McCann walked back to his mare. He held the reins in his hand as he said, "Your lady seems a bit skittish around me. Hope I haven't thrown a scare into the pretty filly."

"Don't worry about it. I'll tell her everything's okay. It *is* okay, isn't it?"

"For the time bein', Sheriff," Thorn said with a noncommittal grin.

McCann rode off in a cloud of dust as Cotton went back inside, only to be greeted by an anxious Emily Wagner.

"Who is that man, Cotton? And what did he want? Please. I need to know that everything's all right."

"He's a bit of a mystery to me, too," he said. "But not one I'm goin' to dwell on. All I can say for sure is, he's not on Havens's side. You got no cause to worry. We'll talk on it later. Right now, I've got to get back to town."

Sleeve Jackson was beginning to worry about J.J. Bleeker. He didn't really know the man, and their happenchance meeting seemed too well timed. What did he really know about this man other than the reputation that followed him around like the stench of a skunk—and a rough reputation it was. He'd handed J.J. a thousand dollars of Havens's money mostly because of his doubts about Plink Granville. He was starting to wonder if he'd tried to cover his butt for one mistake by making another. The whole thing turned his stomach sour.

He decided he'd better go down to the boardinghouse and have a talk with his new shootist. But what could he say at *this* point? Bleeker had been pretty easy to get along with during their brief meeting and ride back to town. But a man who had killed as many men as Bleeker had could hardly be considered reliable. Temperamental was more like it. And what if Bleeker took offense at his questions?

Would he lose all sense of reason and begin blasting away with that shotgun?

Sleeve began pacing back and forth outside the boardinghouse. *Do I go in or do I risk letting things play out as they will? Damn! I don't like being in this position. Havens can go to hell for all I care, but he damn well isn't goin' to take me with him.* He finally came to the conclusion that he'd better at least go inside and fill Bleeker in on the details that he hadn't mentioned earlier.

Sleeve stomped up on the porch and knocked on the door. He waited a couple minutes and then knocked again. From inside he heard the gravelly voice of the old woman who owned the establishment.

"Hold yer damn horses, will ya? I don't get around so well anymore."

The door opened to reveal a lady who could have passed for ninety if she was a day. Sleeve took off his hat. He wasn't certain why, although at that moment he envisioned his own mother standing there.

"Ma'am, I would like to see—"

"He ain't here. Went out. Hopefully he's goin' to get a bath. Foulest smellin' beast I ever did come upon."

"Uh, do you know where he went?"

"Don't know, don't care neither. Wouldn't have taken him in if he hadn't give me this hundred-dollar bill. I never for the life of me laid eyes on such a thing. Glory be. I'm thinkin' of framin' it." Just as abruptly as the door had opened, it was shut in Sleeve's face.

"Grumpy ol' biddy," he mumbled as he walked off the porch and into the street. He stood for several minutes trying to figure where the big man would have gone. He scratched his head, put his hat back on, and shuffled off toward the center of town.

Maybe he went for a drink at the saloon, Sleeve thought. That's when he heard the shot.

Chapter 30

Whether it was the sheer size of the man or the intense smell accompanying him that made all eyes turn as J.J. Bleeker lumbered through the doors to Melody's Golden Palace of Pleasure is a matter of conjecture. But he wasted no time making himself known to everyone in the place. He carried his shotgun in his right hand, while pounding on the bar with his left. Arlo had dealt with rough, impatient men before, so he was no stranger to the belligerence that could follow if the customer was ignored too long.

"Get me a damn beer," Bleeker exhorted him. "And I ain't of a mind to wait, neither."

"Yessir. Right away," Arlo said, and he scurried down the bar to a barrel with a spigot. In seconds he returned with a foamy-topped glass of golden liquid. Bleeker gulped it down in two swallows.

"Another," he ordered with a growl. Bleeker then looked around at several customers who were staring at him with mouths agape. "What the hell y'all lookin' at?"

Everyone returned to whatever activity in which he had theretofore been engaged. Everyone, that is, except Melody, who had apparently overheard his uncouth bellowing from her room and came storming down the stairway with the obvious intention of confronting him.

"What is all the hollerin' going on down here? Mind your manners or get out!"

"Well, well, lookee here," Bleeker said. "I got my beer and now I got me someone for pleasure." The leer in his eyes made his intentions obvious. Melody's reception of his suggestion was equally clear.

"If a woman is what you want, mister, I got some upstairs. You'll have to wait a spell; they're all busy right now. One of 'em will be down soon. While you're waitin', you might consider takin' a bath." She turned to walk away, but Bleeker grabbed her roughly by the arm and yanked her back. He held her so tightly she winced in pain.

"Take your hands off me, you big ox. I'm not available to you or anyone else not of my choosing. Now, I'd suggest you drink up and get out unless you're just achin' for trouble."

"Listen, darlin', *I* make the rules about what women I share my pleasure with, and for tonight, *you're* my choice. Now, show me the way to your crib."

Melody tried wriggling free of his grip, but he overpowered her easily. He shoved her toward the stairway, causing her to lose her balance and nearly fall to the floor. She caught herself on the first step. He shot a beefy hand out and grabbed at her, yanking her up and ripping the front of her dress almost to the waist. Furious at his rough treatment of her, she fumbled to try to cover her now exposed breasts as she yelled for Jack.

"Who the hell is this 'Jack,' little lady? And what do you expect him to do?"

"That would be me: Deputy Sheriff Memphis Jack Stump. And just who the hell would you be?" Jack's quiet arrival through the batwings caused several patrons to hurriedly depart their tables and scoot for the safety of the street, leaving cards, chips, money, and whatever else was already in the pot still laying there.

"J.J. Bleeker's the name. Now, I reckon you best step away before I loose this cannon your way and blow you into the street for the horses to stomp into the dirt." He chuckled.

"'Fraid I can't do that. You got ahold of *my* lady, and she's already told you she has no intention of goin' anywhere with you. Now, turn her loose. Or else."

"Or else what? I must tell you, I *have* heard of you, but now that I see you standin' right here in front of me, I can truthfully say, I ain't impressed."

"Sorry to hear that, Mr. Bleeker, but that don't change anything. I'll say it just once more. Let go of the lady!"

Bleeker suddenly turned, cocking the shotgun as he swung it around in Jack's direction. Melody had yanked loose of his grip and jumped aside. The saloon's silence was broken by the roar of Jack's Remington. The look on Bleeker's face, as he found himself instantly hoisted off his feet and slammed against the bar, could barely be seen through the smoky blast of Jack's .44. Bleeker's grip on the shotgun was involuntarily released as his huge body slid down the apron of the bar to the floor, leaving a bloody trail behind. The twelve-gauge fell with a thud. J.J.'s puffy face seemed to still be questioning what had just happened as his head drooped to his chest. Bleeker took one last gurgling gasp and died.

Melody looked on in horror. She gripped the railing and slowly pulled herself up, holding the front of her dress closed where it had been ripped. She didn't take her eyes off the deceased giant as she edged over to where Jack stood. She fell into his arms in a dead faint. He picked her up and carried her up the stairs.

After placing her on the bed, Jack returned just in time to see Cotton come rushing into the saloon. Jack headed for the bar. Cotton stood staring at Bleeker's body.

"Arlo, get me a whiskey. Make it a double," Jack said with a note of nervousness in his voice.

"Is that J.J. Bleeker?" Cotton asked.

"Was." Jack gulped the first drink, slid the glass toward the bartender, and asked for another.

Cotton nodded as he handed Jack the telegram he'd just received.

"Better read it to me, Cotton. Got my hands full right now."

"It just confirms what we thought. This man is wanted from here to hell and gone, and for every vicious crime in the book. There was a rope waitin' for him in any of a dozen towns."

"No big loss, huh?"

"Only to Havens. Looks like you timed it right."

"Cut down the odds against us, you mean?"

"That's exactly what I mean."

Jack swallowed his second glass of whiskey and shook his head as if it burned all the way to his boots. "I wasn't lookin' for trouble, you know. It just seemed to come grab me by the throat."

"Melody play any part in it?"

"A small one, I reckon."

"How small?"

Jack turned away from him and tapped the bar for another drink.

Cotton left by the same way he'd come in, muttering, "I told you so, Jack; I told you so."

"Arlo, go get the undertaker to remove this carcass. And do it quick. The stench is makin' me sick," Jack said before starting upstairs.

"Son of a bitch," Sleeve said as he watched three good-size men half carry, half drag the body of J.J. Bleeker through the saloon doors. Out front, he could hear people hurrying toward the saloon, hoping to get a glimpse of whatever terrible thing had just occurred. He looked over the batwings and saw Deputy Stump starting up the stairs with a bottle in his hand. He also saw Sheriff Burke on his way back across the street. *Too bad I didn't go to Melody's place first*, he thought. *Maybe I could have put a stop to whatever J.J. did to precipitate his getting shot down.* But he hadn't, and it was too late now. That's when the reality of the whole thing hit him.

Havens is going to explode when he hears of this. He'll blame me for bringing the oaf to town in the first place, giving him all that money, and now possibly jeopardizing his plans.

This incident would certainly emphasize to everyone that dangerous men were in town, and Havens had made it clear he didn't want to draw attention to that fact. Not that he figured the sheriff couldn't see for himself, but if everyone was behaving themselves, even the sheriff would be hard-pressed to raise a hand against any of them. *A man is free to go where he wants, isn't he?*

But all Sleeve's inner unrest wasn't going to make Havens's reaction any less explosive. How was he going to tell him? He went inside and eased up to the bar, sidestepping the stain of blood that still covered a two-foot area like a crimson puddle right below the brass railing. Arlo came up to Sleeve and asked what he'd like.

"Uh, I'll have a beer. But I'd like to know what happened here, too."

"Well, sir, that big smelly gent tried to manhandle the lady owner of this establishment and Deputy Stump took offense to her mistreatment. The big man decided he'd settle it with that shotgun, not realizing, at least the way I figure it, that Memphis Jack ain't someone to trifle with when it comes to his woman. Only took one shot. That's about it. I'll get your beer."

When Arlo returned with his glass of beer, Sleeve took it and walked to a table and sat. He needed some time to work out a story to tell Havens that would take the pressure off himself. He'd learned the hard way that just because a man seems friendly enough on first meeting, it don't mean he can't be set off by some trifle. In this case, it appeared that Melody was that trifle.

It looked like he'd made two blunders: hiring first Plink Granville and then J.J. Bleeker. And now Sleeve had to face Havens's wrath. He drank his beer and asked for another.

Chapter 31

Jack came into the sheriff's office looking like he'd been on a two-day drunk. His eyes were bloodshot and droopy. His clothes appeared to have been slept in. He dropped into a straight-back chair facing Cotton. The sheriff looked up, leaned back, and crossed his arms.

"Are we feeling shooter's remorse this morning, Jack?"

"Naw. Drinker's remorse—brandy, actually. Shoulda stuck to beer."

"Uh-huh."

"Any response from any of those other jackals over losin' one of their own?"

"Nothin' yet. I expect there will be as soon as Havens has finished chewin' on everyone's ass."

"I expect you're right. I wish we had another gun to back us up. We could use someone to watch our backs," Jack said.

"Fortunately, I think we have one. I been meanin' to tell you some good news, or at least good news for the time bein'."

"I could use some good news about now."

"That gunslinger that calls himself Comanche Dan Sobro? Well, he isn't."

Jack blinked at Cotton's words. "Huh?"

"Comanche Dan is actually U.S. Deputy Marshal Thorn McCann. McCann took down the real Comanche Dan a month or so back, and when he found out someone was lookin' for him to help kill a sheriff, well he decided to assume Dan's identity until he could find out what was goin' on. Once he found out none of the other gunslingers had ever seen Comanche Dan, the whole thing fell into place."

"Where did you hear about this?"

"From McCann himself. He's given me his word that he'll back our play when the time comes."

"And you *believe* him?" Jack scratched his head. His eyes showed he doubted such a tall tale.

"I do until I hear somethin' different. I reckon I'll have to."

"I'm not sure I can muster that kind of faith in a man I don't know. One who looks as much like a gunslinger as he does. Besides that, he don't have the eyes of a marshal."

"What the hell does that mean?"

"You know, a man can see another's trustworthiness by lookin' into their eyes."

"Uh-huh. Well, don't worry, we'll *both* be keepin' a close eye on him. Besides, he thinks he's got somethin' on me."

"What's that?"

"I'm not up to sharin' it right now. I will when the time comes for reckonin'."

"You can be a real puzzle at times, Cotton, and now is one of those times."

"Go get some sleep, Jack. Come back when you're rested. We both need to be ready for when the fireworks start, and if I'm any judge, they should be about ready to give us a show anytime now."

The next morning, Jack sauntered into the sheriff's office, whistling. Cotton was reading the weekly newspaper and frowning at something he'd just read. He glanced up as Jack plopped into the chair across from him.

"Sounds like you had a good night's sleep. Melody treatin' you nice?"

"Uh-huh."

"You look like you got somethin' on your mind besides Melody."

"Yeah, Cotton, there is somethin'. I just came by Darnell Givins's bank. He was standin' in the window starin' across the street at Havens's new enterprise and lookin' like someone shot his dog," Jack said.

"That shouldn't come as a surprise. With all that advertising Havens is doin', I'll be surprised if Darnell can survive the year." Cotton frowned at the thought. "There has to be some way to best that smoky scorpion Havens."

"*If* we survive his army. Another second and *I'd* have been chopped meat from Bleeker's scattergun."

"You're good, but you were also damn lucky. Bleeker had other things on his mind when you showed up. Not certain we can hope to come out on top every time. A couple of these gunnies have particularly nasty reputations."

"Don't need to be told. I'm aware of what we're up against."

"Wish *I* was," Cotton said. He shoved out of his chair and ambled toward the door.

"Where you goin' now?"

"Down to see Givins. He needs to know someone is on his side."

Cotton felt several eyes on him as he reached Givins's bank. He went in and was greeted by a large, mostly empty room, with only one of the two tellers' cages manned and Darnell sitting blankly behind a wide desk at the back. His expression was difficult to read. He was either thinking of shooting himself or considering jumping in front of a freight wagon. Havens's three-week advertising campaign obviously wasn't sitting well.

"Ah, Sheriff, to what do I owe this pleasurable visit?"

"Need to talk. And I figure you know what about."

"Yeah, the man who is already digging my grave. Havens. That bastard."

"How is he able to offer loans without interest?"

"He isn't. The whole thing is a scheme to defraud and destroy a lot of good people, and me in the process."

"Tell me whatever details you have. How does it work? Or do you know?"

"Oh, I know, all right. One of my old customers, Blanchard, came in waving his no-interest contract in front of my face. Said he just had to rub it in that he'd landed a deal when I refused the same terms."

"I take it you couldn't because . . ."

"Because I couldn't operate very long if I gave such terms. It's crazy. Although, after reading the contract that rattler put in front of folks—folks he knew damned well wouldn't read it—I thought seriously about going over there and putting a bullet in his head. He's bamboozled a lot of good folks hereabouts, and I don't like it one damned bit."

"The details?"

"Okay, here's how it plays out. Havens makes you sign a loan, interest-free for six months, using your property as collateral. Sounds like a great deal, but it isn't. Not considering the fine print at the bottom of the contract. He knows nobody reads that small stuff. The terms are if you pay the loan off early, there's a huge penalty. And if you don't pay until *after* the term of the loan is up, you forfeit your property. Devious, dishonest, and downright despicable, if you was to ask me."

"So anyone who signs up for a loan with Havens is tossed into a nest of vipers with no chance for survival?"

"That's right. Not a chance."

"You're sure these contracts are ironclad?"

"I'm not a lawyer, mind you, but I haven't found a way to bust 'em."

"What did Blanchard do when you explained what he'd signed?"

"He was furious. Said something about making Havens pay for his deception."

"You think he'd actually go after Havens?"

"Don't know. Don't much care, neither."

"So, what are *you* going to do? You can't wait until Havens starts foreclosing on everyone. If he ends up owning half the land around here, you won't have enough customers to warrant a second bank."

"That's what he's counting on. His whole plan revolves around my demise."

"Why? What's he got against you?"

Givins seemed to sink in on himself. His face changed. Grew dark. Despair was written all over him. He leaned forward, stacking his hands on the desktop.

"Oh, hell, what have I got to lose? I'm finished here anyway. Might as well spill the beans. Havens and me, we go back a ways. Back to Kansas right after the war. Border raiding was rampant. The Red Legs, William Quantrill, Bloody Bill Anderson—murder, robbery, plundering—there was so much bloodshed everywhere, a man had to look both ways before making a run to the outhouse."

"You don't appear to be the type of man who'd do anything like that."

"I wasn't, but someone had to help folks get back on their feet, and that meant they needed money. Havens and I went into business together and started loaning money to businesses to rebuild."

"Sounds like an honorable venture. What happened?"

"I caught Havens embezzling from folks' accounts. I called him on it, and he told me to keep my mouth shut or he'd make sure I got what was coming to me, whatever that meant. I never did find out."

"Why?"

"Because I turned him in to the U.S. marshal. He skedaddled out of town just ahead of some vigilantes with a roll of hemp. Went to Texas with some new scheme to defraud people. He's been doing it ever since. I suspect when he found out that both you and I were here in Apache

Springs—two folks he has no love for—well, he just naturally saw a way to kill two birds with one . . ."

"Yeah, I get what you're sayin'."

"Of course that isn't all he's doing here. He's also telling folks if they put their money in his bank, he'll pay three times the interest rate I can offer. If this keeps up, I'll be out of business within a month."

Cotton sat back, stroking his chin. He knew Givins was right: no one reads the little print at the bottom of anything. Half the time, people can't even get their eyes to focus on anything that small unless they've got a pair of store-bought spectacles. And people are naturally greedy when it comes to making money. If their deposits can give them a substantial rate of interest, well, who wouldn't jump on a deal like that? *Surefire, Havens is a snake, but is he really so clever that there's no way for a man to get out of his crooked contract without losing his shirt?* Cotton narrowed his eyes and turned to look out the window at the same place Givins had been staring when he came in. He eased out of the chair, leaned over to shake Givins's hand, and said, "Darnell, I'll think on this for a spell. Maybe between us, we can come up with a way to get one over on this jasper."

Cotton left the bank wondering what made a man like Havens tick. He pulled out his pocket watch and, seeing it was almost time for lunch, went back to get Jack. There was something niggling at the back of his mind. A little food in his belly might help spark the idea that was lying there, just out of recognition.

"Miss Delilah said you wanted to see me, Mr. Havens?" Sleeve Jackson stood in front of Havens's desk, hat in hand and very nervous.

"Sounds like you can't figure out why I'd be interested in having a little chat with you, or can you?"

"Why, er, no, I can't rightly say as how I have any idea."

"Then let me refresh your memory about a certain

shotgun-toting polecat with a powerful odor wafting off him to whom you handed a thousand dollars of *my* money for the purpose of killing a certain sheriff, and who then proceeded to get *himself* killed over some damned whore."

"I, uh, can explain. You see . . ."

Havens slammed his hand on his desktop. "Shut up!"

Sleeve's hand slipped to the butt of his revolver and rested there. He was shaking with anger as Havens chewed him out. Bleeker's getting himself killed had been his own fault. Sleeve had been assigned the task of hiring gunmen to take care of a job that Havens wanted done. That job would take men with a will of their own and nerves of steel. He paid to get men he figured could succeed. And he sure as hell wasn't some nursemaid. And no one was going to treat him like a wayward child. He pondered his next move as Havens blathered on. Sleeve didn't hear a word.

Chapter 32

Cotton was too restless to stay in town that evening. So he rode out to the Wagner ranch to spend time with Emily. She could see how distracted he was, so she tried to stay out of his way. She knew he was struggling with something but figured to keep silent unless he asked for her opinion on whatever it was that had him so upset. She scurried around tidying things up, straightening pictures, dusting, sweeping dirt off the front porch. As the evening wore on, she became lost in whatever business she could find to attend to and paid no attention to the morose sheriff sitting in her living room like a buzzard waiting for something to die. She looked up in surprise when Cotton suddenly leapt out of his chair and announced, "That's it! That might work!"

"What might work, Cotton?" she asked, a broom loosely held in one hand.

"I've been trying to figure a way to break Havens's hold on all the people that have taken loans with him. They were all bamboozled by his offer of no interest, and they failed to look his contract over carefully. Darnell Givins says the terms are ironclad, but I figured there *had* to be a way to break them."

"And now you have found it?"

"Well, at least I think I have. It will take the cooperation of more than one person, but if I'm right, we *could* break Havens's hold over the people he's fixin' to cheat."

"That's wonderful. How about some supper, and you can tell me all about it?"

He followed her into the dining room. The other hands had already eaten hours before, so they were alone as she fussed around gathering together leftovers and putting a skillet on the stove to fry a piece of beef. Cotton seated himself at the long table and watched her appreciatively. She brought freshly sliced bread, a pot of reheated beans, and some coffee to tide him over as he waited for the meat. She placed a plate in front of him, along with silverware, and sat down.

"Your steak will be ready in a few minutes. Go ahead and start eating. You must be starved."

"Uh-huh. You're right about that," he said, sipping the coffee.

"So, your idea, what is it?"

"Okay, here it is. First, I have to get Givins to go along with it. If it doesn't work, he could get burned."

Emily jumped up suddenly. "Oh, my goodness. Thanks for reminding me. Your steak."

Cotton snickered at her rush to take the skillet off the fire and fork up the steak. She placed the sizzling meat in front of him. His eyes showed how appreciative he was. "Thanks."

"Now, go on with your plan."

"I'll have to convince Givins to loan every customer that Havens doled out money to the same amount they borrowed from him. Then they pay Havens on the exact day their loan is due. That's the key to making this thing work."

"I don't understand."

"You see, Havens made sure that each loan was locked

up by the fine print. If a loan was paid early, there was a huge penalty in interest, likely several percent. But if it was late in being paid back, even by a day, the borrower forfeited whatever he'd put up as collateral for the loan."

"So, if he pays the money back on the exact day it is due, the contract doesn't address that eventuality, is that right?"

"That's exactly right. Havens will have no choice but to mark the loan paid, without getting his dirty hands on one red cent of interest or penalty, and he's gained nothing by his little charade. Not only that, but he won't be able to pay the high interest rate on deposits he's been offerin' to get people to put their money in his bank instead of Givins's."

"Will it work?"

"I hope so. If it does, instead of Havens putting Givins out of business, the tables will be turned."

"When are you going to suggest your idea to Givins?"

"First thing tomorrow." Without further conversation, Cotton began carving up a juicy hunk of steak that all but melted in his mouth.

Sleeve Jackson left Havens's office in an ugly mood. He'd had about all he could take of his pompous, ill-tempered employer. Every tirade, every angry outburst over the past few weeks seemed to have been aimed squarely at him. And his patience was nearing its end. He'd only hung around and taken the abuse this long because of the two-thousand-dollar bounty on Cotton Burke, a bounty he fully intended to walk away with, along with what he figured he owed Havens in payback.

Havens had told his gunslingers they could go ahead and take the sheriff down anytime they wanted, then he changed his mind and decided to hold off until his bank-loan scheme was fully operational. He'd been making interest-free loans hand-over-fist for several days now. Most folks didn't really need the money, but if it was going to cost them nothing for its use, well, what the hell. Sleeve didn't understand the details of those loans, only the certainty that Havens would come away richer than ever. The man knew how to bilk folks out of their hard-earned money, and he somehow had eluded any consequences for his actions for years. He'd guaranteed Sleeve that everything he did was legal. But who could believe a man who'd been run out of town after town? If Havens had been a man to carry a gun, he'd probably have been shot by now.

Before making his own move, Sleeve decided it would be a good idea to talk to some of the other gunslingers he'd convinced to join in on the devious banker's plan to turn Apache Springs into another Lawrence, Kansas. He liked the idea of all those guns hanging around, ready to leap into action and cut down anyone that stood in their way, even if that probably meant a sheriff and his deputy with reputations of their own. If he worked it right, he'd have the backup he needed, while he walked away with the prize, and he fully expected to shoot Havens for good measure just as soon as he had the reward in his hands. He figured he'd find most of the others at Melody's saloon and that's right where he directed his steps.

Plink Granville was asleep at a table by himself, facedown in a puddle of spilled whiskey. Buck and Comanche Dan were playing cards with two cowboys Sleeve didn't know, and Black Duck Slater was leaning on the bar in conversation with Arlo, the bartender. A lumpy girl was leaning on the gunslinger's shoulder trying her best to get him to go upstairs with her. Sleeve had no sooner entered the noisy room than the skinny girl he'd accompanied to her crib several days back approached him with a gleam in her eye.

"Where you been, stranger? I've been pining away waitin' for you to return. What say we go upstairs and stare at the wallpaper?"

"Uh, you actually remember me?"

"Well, of course, sweetie. A girl don't never forget a *real* man. So, what do you say? Want to invest a dollar on a sure thing?"

Sleeve's resolve to engage the other fast guns in a conversation about Havens and when they might expect to begin dropping a cap on ol' Cotton Burke began to wane. Women had always been the one weakness he just couldn't seem to put away in favor of more important things. But then, no one had ever convinced him that there *was* anything more important than lying beside a filly on a soft mattress after taking care of business. He sighed and took her hand, slipped a dollar into her palm, and followed her up the winding staircase Melody had had built special for her new Golden Palace of Pleasure.

The lumpy girl didn't seem to be having much luck with *her* attempts to drag Black Duck away from tossing down shot after shot of whiskey and exchanging jokes with the bartender. She looked bored and frustrated as she turned and wandered away to find a more willing customer.

Chapter 33

The next morning, Cotton sat cross-legged in the captain's chair across from Darnell Givins. He'd explained his plan to the banker, who had, as yet, not commented on what he thought of it. The expression on Darnell's face plainly expressed his misgivings. Cotton fully understood the position it put the banker in. If the bank president was unwilling or unable to take a chance on an admittedly risky scheme to best his chief rival, Burke could do nothing. He'd have to come up with some other avenue to make certain Bart Havens didn't do to this town what he'd done to so many before. Cotton hoped he could do it legally. If not, it wouldn't be the first time he'd had to step outside the law to accomplish a just and proper outcome. Givins cleared his throat and leaned his elbows on his desk.

"You have to understand, Sheriff, if this doesn't work, Havens could end up with *complete* control of Apache Springs. I'm sure you see my reluctance."

"Indeed I do. And if you can come up with a better,

safer plan to help these folks out, I'll be right there to cheer you on. But, for now at least, I've given it my best shot."

Givins sat back with a sigh. His sack suit was rumpled, giving the impression he'd slept in it for days on end. Cotton figured the truth was that Darnell Givins hadn't slept *at all* for some time. His eyes were bloodshot and dark circles gave the impression of a raccoon.

"I have to admit I like the sound of it. The timing, of course, would be crucial. One slip-up, though, and we'd be done for."

"And, for the whole thing to work properly, we'd need everyone who borrowed from Havens to jump on the idea. And, the payments would have to be paid back exactly six months from the day they took the loan out. To the hour."

"I'm not sure how we find out who all has fallen for this deception."

"I've been ponderin' that, too."

"Although, I reckon most of the ranchers hereabouts know each other's business to some degree, don't you, Sheriff?"

"I do."

"I suppose we don't have to make a decision on this for a few days, even weeks, do we?"

"Nope."

"Maybe with a little more time, we can come up with something even better."

"Yup."

"Well, Sheriff, until something better *does* come along, you may assume *your* plan is *my* plan."

"Good. We'll make it work, Darnell. Don't worry. Now, I suggest you get some sleep so you can handle all the business that'll be walkin' back in here once folks find out how they've been hoodwinked."

Cotton blinked in the bright sunshine as he stepped outside the bank. He hadn't wanted to mention it, but he *did* have an idea how he might get his hands on the list of loans Havens had made in the last several weeks. And he hoped Jack might be the key to finding it. As he walked down the boardwalk back toward his office, he noticed Buck Kentner keeping an eye on him while leaning on a post outside Melody's place. And across the street, Comanche Dan Sobro was keeping an eye on them both. He had to stifle a chuckle.

Cotton went inside his office to await an answer to any one of several telegrams he'd sent out to various towns both in New Mexico and in Texas. Never a man to take another's word for anything that could carry with it a life or death penalty, his inquiries all focused on two particular subjects: Comanche Dan Sobro and Judge Arthur Sanborn. So engrossed was he in his deliberations, he failed to take notice of a lone rider coming into town, carrying a shotgun, and heading straight for the Havens Bank.

Blanchard opened the door to the bank, looked around, then stepped toward Delilah, who was posted at the ready, a willing greeter to all who entered.

"Where's your boss, pretty lady?" Blanchard asked. His face was dark and lined with anger.

"H-he's in back, uh, with a customer, Mr. Blanchard. May I, uh, tell him you're here?"

"Nope, I'll tell that polecat myself."

Delilah took a step to divert Blanchard, but he just pushed her aside. She ran after him in an effort to warn Havens. But before she could reach the door, Blanchard had kicked it open and was already cocking the shotgun. Havens looked up at the intrusion, at first surprised; then seeing who it was, he broke into an amused smile.

"Why hello, Mr. Blanchard. To what do I owe this distinct pleasure?" His statement dripped with insincerity.

"Ain't gonna be no pleasure when I blow your lyin' head clean off'n your shoulders."

As Blanchard raised the shotgun, Havens stood up with one hand in the air.

"Now, hold on, my friend. Whatever it is that's bothering you, I'm certain we can work it out."

"Highway robbery, that's what it is. And out here we deal with your kind in a most decisive manner. That'd be what I'm totin' this here iron for."

"Did you say robbery? I say, you can't believe I would stoop to such behavior. I'm an honest businessman, and as such cannot condone anything other than absolute righteousness in my bank. Now, sit down and tell me what it is that makes you think you've been mistreated."

"You know damned well what it is, you rattlesnake. You got me to sign a contract that lets you either squeeze a tidy sum from me if I pay off early or turn over my deed to you if I pay up late. Either way, I lose."

"Now, who's been filling your head with such nonsense?"

Delilah had retreated toward the front door of the bank. Sleeve Jackson was coming her way. Seeing she was in some distress, Sleeve asked what was wrong.

"Mr. Blanchard is really upset at being cheated in his loan contract."

"So what? There's nothing he can do about it. He's already signed it."

"He seems to think there *is* something he can do about it. He's got a shotgun."

"And where was you headed, gal?"

"I was going to get the sheriff."

"Never mind. I'll handle this."

"But, wh-what are you going to do?"

"Reckon I better save Mr. Havens from being murdered by a bloodthirsty rancher."

"No, wait, I don't think Mr. Blanchard would really . . ."

Sleeve paid her no mind and pushed past her. He drew one of his Schofields as he entered the bank, stalking straight for the back. He heard arguing coming from Havens's office. Since the door was already open, he stood just out of sight for a moment.

"Here's what I propose, Havens. You tear up my contract and I'll walk out of here, and you'll live to cheat someone else, just not me."

"Mr. Blanchard, I assure you that the contract was made in good faith."

"Then, I have no choice but to—"

The roar of Sleeve's Schofield threw the skinny rancher to the floor in front of Havens's desk. Blanchard gasped for air as blood burbled from his back.

Havens sat back with a rush of air, pulling his handkerchief. He mopped his brow. "I do believe you came just in time, Mr. Jackson. That crazy old coot was fixin' to kill me."

"I do believe he was, at that, Mr. Havens. Now, I wonder why." Sleeve's sarcasm wasn't lost on Havens, who gave him a scowl.

Cotton burst through the front door, followed closely by Delilah Jones. His Colt was drawn.

"What the hell happened here, Havens?"

"Old man Blanchard was about to blow my brains out. Fortunately, Mr. Jackson was nearby to witness the whole affair. And of course, the fair Ms. Delilah also saw my imminent danger. She's likely the reason you got here so fast."

"No, it was the blast of this man's revolver that brought me. I don't allow gunfire in my town, except on the rare occasion that someone *needs* killin'."

"You don't intend to arrest Mr. Jackson, do you?"

"No, not as long as it was self-defense, as you claim. I'd better not find out to the contrary. Too bad the wrong man got shot, though." Cotton leaned down to the dead man. He frowned, visibly angered by this turn of events. When he stood, he shot Havens a look of disgust, then turned and strode out.

Chapter 34

"What happened?" Jack shouted, as he came at a dead run down the middle of the street toward where the gunfire had come from.

"One of Havens's killers shot down Donald Blanchard. Your lady friend said the old man confronted our crooked banker about the rotten deal he got on his loan and wanted to have the contract torn up. Havens didn't see it that way. Blanchard had a shotgun and Sleeve Jackson pulled down on him. The wrong man went down, shot in the back. And now I got to go talk to a widow."

"You *do* have to tell her what happened, I suppose, but . . ."

"More than that. I'm sure she knew what he was comin' to town for when he hauled out his shotgun. My fear is that we've just seen the first volley in what could quickly erupt into a general uprising against Havens."

For the next three days, both Cotton and Jack overheard grumblings from various citizens, all lamenting the lack of an arrest over Blanchard's killing. The town was growing increasingly uneasy about the gunslingers and about the rumors of Havens's mistreatment of some who'd taken out loans from his bank.

"Cotton, you can't just sit there and do nothin'. What do you aim to do about Blanchard's murder? You know it can't rightly be called nothin' else," Jack said. He had grown weary of Cotton's disagreeable silence and of keeping his thoughts on the subject to himself.

Cotton slapped the desk with both hands and stood up. "First, I'm goin' to have a whiskey. Join me?"

"Try to stop me. I can't remember the last time you bought. This I do with pleasure," Jack said, keeping stride with the long-legged sheriff, a broad grin across his face.

Cotton strode to a table at the rear of Melody's saloon and sat. Jack followed suit. When Arlo asked what they would like, Jack jumped in with, "Couple of whiskeys, the good stuff this time. And put it on the town's tab." Cotton gave Jack a frown, but sidestepped making a comment. He put his elbows on the table, folded his hands, and leaned forward as if a secret was about to be shared. Jack waited until Arlo served them before he spoke.

"Now, since you aren't overly generous with sharin' whiskey, which by the way, I've almost never known you to drink, what's on your mind?" Jack said.

"As soon as other ranchers who've signed up for one of Bart's interest-free loans find out about Blanchard, they're goin' to start askin' questions. Why did he go after Havens? They'll ask his widow what happened. She'll tell 'em they were all cheated, and that Havens had her husband murdered. Then all hell's goin' to break loose. Most of the farmers and ranchers either don't read at all or have so little book learnin' they for sure never read what they were signin'. I'll bet some of those loan contracts have only an 'X' for a signature."

"And you figure as soon as they find out they've been hornswaggled, they'll do the same thing Blanchard did."

"Worse. I wouldn't put it past a couple of those early settlers to set things right with a rope or a torch. Either way, the town comes out the loser. I have to stop that. But I'm goin' to need your help."

"What do you want me to do?" Jack's eyes showed wariness Cotton hadn't seen since he tricked Jack into coming to Apache Springs in the first place.

"Since I'm the main target of Havens's gunslingers and you're a better talker than I am, I'd like you to go out to Blanchard's ranch, talk to his wife, and try to keep the lid on things."

"Who's goin' to watch your back while I'm gone?"

"Reckon that's a chance I'll have to take on my own. Just watch yourself. We don't know yet how those ranchers are going to take the news of Blanchard's bein' killed by one of Havens's men."

"You'll be here with that Plink Granville and Sleeve Jackson and Black Duck Slater. Even if what you say is true about Comanche Dan, which I'm damned well gonna need proof of, those aren't good odds. How about gettin' Henry Coyote to hang around with that Spencer of his while I'm gone?"

"Now you're thinkin' like a true lawman. I'll ride out and fetch him and you can leave as soon as I return."

Jack's ride out to the Blanchard place took him the better part of three hours. The small ranch lay between two hilly ranges in a high, green valley. Good grass, sufficient water, and easy to defend if the need arose. Why Blanchard needed money was anyone's guess. Maybe he wanted to increase his herd before winter sets in. Jack reckoned it wouldn't be a bad investment. But why didn't he read the fine print before signing such a contract? Didn't Darnell Givins warn him about Havens beforehand?

Jack's silent questions weren't going to supply any answers until he had a chance to talk to Blanchard's widow. It was a task he didn't relish. When he rounded the bend in the road that led directly down to the ranch house, he was met with a sight he hadn't counted on. There, gathered in the yard front of the house were about twenty men, and they didn't appear to be in a celebratory mood. One was even carrying a coiled rope. The shouts and grumblings didn't bode well for him having much success talking them out of a hasty reaction to the tragedy. He rode up slowly and dismounted. He hadn't been spotted through the commotion until he reached the outer ring of men.

"Well, well, if it ain't the deputy. Come callin' for a reason, *Deputy* Stump?" Mrs. Blanchard said bitterly.

Jack understood her anger, but it was misdirected. Neither he nor Cotton had had any way of knowing that Blanchard would do something so foolish as to threaten Havens in front of his own gunman. But now it looked to be *his* job to defuse the situation before it got out of hand. Way out of hand by the looks of the crowd.

Jack removed his hat as he addressed the lady. "Yes, ma'am, I have come for a reason."

"And what might that be? You come to say it was all a mistake and that my poor Henry wasn't shot down in cold blood by that snake Sleeve Jackson?"

"Wish I could, ma'am, but the truth of it is, Henry didn't give Jackson no choice. Henry was fixin' to pull the trigger on that scattergun and blow Havens into the next world. By the time we heard the shot, it was too late to do anything. Henry was already dead."

"So, why *are* you here, Deputy?" asked the man holding the rope.

"I'm here at the behest of the sheriff to keep a whole lot more of you folks from bein' killed. If you all go stormin' into town with revenge on your minds, sure as blazes there'll be a lot of bloodshed. Havens has some stone cold killers that would love to earn their keep by brute force. In fact, that's just what Havens hired them for."

"You got a better idea? We can't just let that son of a bitch Havens steal our land over some piddlin' little printin' at the bottom of a piece of paper. Ain't none of us could understand it, anyways," said Mrs. Blanchard.

"I understand. And so does the sheriff. That's why he sent *me* out here instead of comin' himself. He's cookin' up a plan to get rid of Havens *and* his schemin' ways. But you gotta give us a little time. That's all I'm askin' for. A little time. Believe me, we want rid of Havens as bad as you do, along with those snakes he bought and paid to cover his ass—uh, beggin' your pardon, ma'am." Jack chewed on his lip as he awaited an answer.

Considerable grumbling rumbled through the crowd as Jack waited to see which way the wind would blow the rope. He noticed that most of the men were armed with either rifles or shotguns. There wasn't a man among them that had a chance in a close-in fight with revolvers, which is exactly what would ensue if they tried to take Havens on his terms.

"Besides, just look at you. You're plannin' on goin' up against hired killers with rifles and shotguns. It'd be a turkey shoot, with you bein' the turkeys."

After several minutes, one man nodded to Jack and said, "All right, Mister Deputy, you got until the end of the week to come up with a way to get rid of that thievin' owlhoot, or toss him in jail to wait for a judge. If there ain't nothin' changed by Friday, you can count on us and about a dozen more to come ridin' in with one thing on our minds: a necktie party."

A chill came over Jack as he rode away. He knew there were many eyes on his back, and that brought with it an uncomfortable realization. The end of the week was but four days away. Four days until one sheriff and one deputy might have to fend off a mob of men with blood on their minds.

Chapter 35

When Jack reined his horse in at the front of the jail and dismounted, the door was open. He could see Cotton sitting at his desk, apparently jawing with someone across the room. Jack looked around to see if any of Havens's men were hanging around. Seeing none of them, he eased inside, to find Henry Coyote grinning over a cup of coffee.

"Ah, Jack," Cotton said. "Good to see you made it without any holes in that nice shirt. I told you I wasn't the talker, you are. Did you get anywhere with Mrs. Blanchard?"

"Uh-huh. Well, I *can* say there's a passel of folks hoppin' mad at Blanchard's death. I came upon a mess of 'em. They were well on their way to comin' to town for a party."

Henry got a quizzical frown on his face. "What is *party*?"

"Well, Henry, in this particular case, it was goin' to be a necktie party in honor of Bart Havens. Jack seems to have talked them out of the festivities. Right?"

"Uh, yes and no. They gave us four days to solve the

Havens problem or they're on their way to town in force. I'd say about twenty or so were gathered at the Blanchard place. The leader, whoever the hell he was, made it sound like they could gather up an army if necessary. I'd say it wasn't a bluff."

"Four days, huh? Well, I reckon that's some better than four hours. Thanks for doin' your best, Jack."

"Cotton, you mind if I go meet Melody at the hotel? Told her if I got back in time we could eat together."

"Go ahead. I got plenty of ponderin' to attend to right now, anyway."

When Jack left, Cotton tented his fingers and began chewing his lip. He looked over at Henry and said, "My friend, it is beginning to look like I'll be needin' your help with that Spencer in about four days. If you're willin', of course."

"I be here," Henry said, and he turned and left as quietly as he'd come.

Jack started down the boardwalk toward the hotel. He'd gotten about halfway when he saw Delilah coming from Bart's bank. He waved at her. As they got closer, he asked how she was.

"I've seen better days, Jack. I'm not sure how I came to be in this place with that bastard Havens. First chance I get, I'll be on the stage for Santa Fe."

"What's in Santa Fe?"

"I don't know. Just as long as I'm not getting slapped around by a jealous jackass, I don't really care. I'll take in laundry if I have to."

"Ha, now that I'd like to see. Delilah Jones sweating over a tub of water washing out some fella's long johns."

"It'd be better than black eyes and bloody noses."

"Say the word, Delilah, and I'll have a talk with Mr. Havens. I'll bet we could come to an understanding, me and him." Jack rubbed his hand over the butt of his Remington, raising both eyebrows and smiling at the lovely brunette. He held out his arm. She slid hers inside his, hiked up her skirts with the other, and they walked up the steps to the hotel together. Once inside, she thanked him for his offer, saying it wasn't necessary, though, and she went upstairs.

Jack sauntered into the dining room, where Melody sat sipping a glass of wine.

"Glad you could free yourself from the rigors of kissing Cotton Burke's boots, Jack."

Jack glared at her for a moment, then took a seat across from her, saying nothing.

Across the street from the hotel, Bart Havens had been watching from his front window. His face was flushed with anger. He slammed his fist down on a table, knocking over a vase Delilah had filled with flowers to add some class to the bank. The vase crashed to the floor, breaking into a million pieces and scattering cut flowers and water everywhere.

"Damn you, Delilah, I give you everything a woman could want, treat you like a queen, and the first man you come up to, you take him to your hotel room and bed him. Bitch!"

He spun around and stormed back to his office, slamming the door behind him. He fell into his chair, put his head in his hands, and cursed everything he could think of, even though there was no one within earshot. He pulled out a desk drawer and fumbled for a bottle of whiskey. He yanked out the cork, put the bottle to his lips, and began guzzling the amber liquid like it was spring water.

Well, my dear, enjoy your time with that worthless deputy while you can, because I have a plan for him that will even the score for J.J. Bleeker. It's about time you realize just how much power I wield around this godforsaken collection of run-down buildings, whores, and drunken cowboys. Tomorrow I start my final push to destroy Cotton Burke's little kingdom. Mark my words!

* * *

The next morning, Bart Havens was waiting at the door of his bank.

"Delilah, it's time for you to deliver my note to Deputy Jack Stump," Bart said. He'd asked her to be in his office a half hour early so she could set things in motion now that he was well on his way to success. His particularly stern look and the tone of his voice gave her a start. She took the folded paper from her cloth purse and turned to do his bidding.

"Yes, Mr. Havens. I'll do it right away."

"That's my girl. You hurry back as soon as you hand it to him. I need you here greeting all the sheep right when we open," he said with an insincere grin. He ran a finger across his thin mustache.

Delilah rushed out of the bank and headed straight for the sheriff's office. This early in the morning she wasn't certain Jack would be there, but at least Cotton Burke should be. They had never met, but she liked what she'd seen from a distance.

She rapped on the door and, hearing no answer, tried the knob. It was open, so she went inside. "Hello, is anyone here?"

"It's about damned time you brought my breakfast. I'm starving in here."

Delilah peered around the corner and came almost face-to-face with a disheveled man wearing a rumpled vest, holding on to the bars of his cell. A frock coat was folded on the cot to make a pillow.

"I, uh, who are you?" she asked.

"Just one unlucky gambler, or maybe lucky, I haven't decided which."

"Why are you in here? Gambling isn't illegal in Apache Springs, is it?"

"I reckon it is the way I was doing it. I, er, sorta got caught dealin' off the bottom. I suppose I'm only alive to tell about it because of that deputy. He saved me from some rattler named Jackson who was fixing to put a hole in me.

But never mind me, why is a beautiful lady standing in the doorway to the jail?"

"I, uh, I am here to see that deputy you spoke of. I'm sorry, but I didn't know you were expecting someone to bring food."

"Yeah, well, service is piss poor around here. Better than being in Boot Hill, though."

"Has Jack, er, the deputy been in this morning?"

"Nope. Hope he comes soon. I got some things that need tending to, if you know what I mean."

"I'll tell him if I see him."

Delilah rushed outside to complete her mission and get back before Bart beat her black and blue for being late. He had been quite specific about her being in the bank when it opened promptly at nine o'clock. She looked up and down the street, half-expecting to see Jack coming with a tray of food for his prisoner. All she saw was a couple of storekeepers sweeping the dirt away from their doors and the stagecoach loading up passengers for its run to Albuquerque.

She knew Jack was living with the woman that owned the saloon she'd turned into a bordello. She assumed he was thusly engaged, so she went across the street, stepped up on the boardwalk, and peered over the batwings. She saw no sign of Jack, and her time was running out. She went inside and immediately spotted a man behind the bar stacking glassware.

"Excuse me, but have you seen Jack Stump this morning?"

"It's a tad too early for Jack to crawl out from under the covers. Do you need him for something?" Arlo said.

"I need to get this note to him. It's very important," she said.

"I'll be happy to deliver it soon's I see him stumbling down those stairs for his first drink of the day." Arlo grunted, grinning at the picture he'd painted.

Delilah handed him the folded paper, thanked him, and hurried out and down the street. She walked in just as Bart was unlocking the door to the bank.

"Did you give it to him, girl?"

"Y-yes, Mr. Havens." She pushed past him to take her position before he could detect the lie on her face.

"Good, very good. Now, let's get ready for the fleecing."

Melody had been at the top of the stairway as Delilah was leaving the saloon. She drifted downstairs, holding her skirts up so she wouldn't trip and end up in a heap at the bottom. She walked over to Arlo, leaning one arm on the bar.

"What'd that woman want?"

"She gave me something to give to Jack."

"What did she give you, Arlo?"

"A note, Miss Melody. Said to give it to him personally."

"Hand it over, along with a bottle of brandy. I'll take both of them upstairs to Prince Charming."

"I, er, don't know. She said I was to—"

"Hand it over, Arlo, unless you want to be unemployed in about ten seconds.

"Yes, ma'am."

He handed Melody the paper and a bottle, both of which she yanked out of his hands. She slowly ascended the stairway, opening and reading the note. By the time she reached the top, her face was beet red. She wadded up the paper and threw it on the floor. She glanced back to see Arlo watching her as she entered her bedroom with a cheery "Good morning, sweetie. Here's your breakfast."

Chapter 36

At exactly eight-thirty that evening, Melody was standing on the wooden bridge over Spring Creek. That was the time the note had stated for Jack to be there. She looked around, assuming something had held Delilah up. *That's all right, I can wait*, she thought. *In fact, I can wait till hell freezes over to tear your eyes out for trying to steal my Jack, you witch.*

She heard a rustle behind her. Furious at having another woman even think of enticing Jack away from her, she spun around expecting to see Delilah. Instead, there stood Buck Kentner, gun in hand.

"Where is he? Where's Memphis Jack?" Buck said through gritted teeth.

"Wh-who are you and what do you want with Jack?" she hissed, hands on hips, feet apart like she was preparing for a real knock-down, drag-out.

"None of your business, lady. Now, where the hell is he?" Buck's impatience was reaching its peak. "He was supposed to be here. Is he such a coward that he sent a woman to fight his battles?"

"What battle are you talking about? He was supposed to meet . . . damn! It was a *setup*, wasn't it? A trap to kill Jack," Melody sputtered, as she slowly caught on to the subterfuge. "You bastard!"

"Shut the hell up, lady! Where is he?" Buck raised his gun, pointing it directly at her chest. "Be a shame to ruin that pretty dress, but I will if you don't tell me where Jack Stump is."

"I'll tell you nothing, you pig." Melody's eyes were aflame with anger. She showed no intention of acquiescing to this gunslinger, even if it meant risk to her own life. Melody had always been a selfish, self-absorbed woman, but she didn't react well to threats.

Buck cocked his Colt. Melody, out of a natural instinct for warding off pain, took a step back, catching her heel on a rotten piece of the old bridge. She lost her balance and fell just as Buck pulled the trigger. She hit her head on the railing, blacking out instantly. Buck stared at her lying there. A shiver of thrill ran up his spine. She didn't move. He stayed for a moment, and then, finally assuming he had killed her, he turned to walk away before someone came after hearing the shot. That's when he found he wasn't alone.

"Comanche Dan! Wh-what're you doin' out here?" Buck said as he slipped his Colt back into the holster.

"You kill her?" Dan asked.

"Yeah. Noisy bitch. No big loss. I figured if I left her alive, she'd tell Jack Stump I was plannin' on back-shootin' him, and he'd want to face me down. I wasn't eager to lose the advantage this little surprise meetin' was meant to be."

"Part of Havens's plan, eh?"

"Yup. Didn't he tell you? He sent a note by way of Delilah that Jack was to meet her. I don't know why he didn't show up. I planned to gun down the maverick."

"Maybe he didn't get the message," Dan said. "Anyway, killing an unarmed woman was a mistake. Havens isn't goin' to like that. I'm afraid I'm goin' to have to help you make amends."

"Make amends? What the hell you talkin' about?"

"I'm not Comanche Dan Sobro. I got rid of him some time ago. My name is Thorn McCann, and I can't abide any man who'd shoot a woman."

Buck didn't take McCann's confession well. He had always been a man of action, not one for contemplation, thinking a situation through. He went for his Colt. McCann drew and pulled the trigger before Buck could clear leather. The outlaw fell, a red bloom staining his shirt and vest. McCann went to where Melody lay in a heap of satin and lace. He knelt down and put his arm under her back. He was at once puzzled by so little blood. A trickle of red ran down her forehead and onto her cheek. He pulled out his handkerchief and dabbed her face but was unable to see where the bullet had struck her. Just as he moved her, she groaned. He gently lifted her up to a sitting position.

"Wha-what happened?" Melody mumbled, still not completely in her right mind. She was trying to blink away her confusion when Thorn's face came into focus. Her hand went straight for her head. She winced as her fingers touched the wound. She quickly drew her hand away, staring at the blood on her fingers. "A-am I dead? Did that skunk kill me?"

"No, you're very much alive, miss. It appears you must have knocked yourself out when you fell. Good thing you did, too, because that must have been when he fired. He didn't realize he'd missed you. You're one lucky lady."

"Where'd he go?"

"I had to kill him, I'm afraid."

"Who are you?"

McCann suddenly found himself in a bad situation. He could tell her the truth and risk her blabbing his real identity all over town, at which time he would be marked for death by Havens's other gunslingers. Or he could continue with the Comanche Dan cover and tell her he killed Kentner because he couldn't stand by and watch a woman shot. He studied her face for only a moment.

"Name's Comanche Dan Sobro. I, uh, am new to Apache Springs."

"What brought you out here to the bridge?"

"Luck of the draw, I reckon. Decided to take a walk after dinner, and, well, here I am."

"Fortunate for me, I allow."

Dan helped her to her feet. She was a little unsteady at first but soon got her footing sufficiently for Dan to let go of her arm.

"Thanks," she said. "Come by my saloon anytime. I owe you a couple of free drinks, maybe even a little something more." She gave him a come-hither wink.

"I'll gladly take you up on your offer, ma'am." He walked alongside her until she was in sight of the saloon, and then he started across the street toward the hotel.

I need to get word to Cotton that Havens tried to have Deputy Stump back-shot. He'll also need to send someone out to pick up the body of Buck Kentner. Then, maybe after supper I'll stop by and look in on Havens. He'll want to know his scheme failed.

As he headed up the steps in front of the hotel, he saw Delilah coming across the street toward him. He stopped, tipped his hat, and said, "Evenin', Miss Delilah."

"Oh, Mr. Sobro, isn't it?"

"Why, uh, yes, it is. Have you had supper yet?"

"As a matter of fact, no. I was just going up to my room. It's been a long day, and I'm feelin' poorly."

"I'd sure appreciate the company, if you'd reconsider. Nothing makes a juicy steak taste so good as looking across the table at a lovely face."

Delilah blushed and averted her eyes from him. She hesitated for a moment.

"Well, since you work for Mr. Havens and all, I suppose it would be all right if I joined you for a bit of repast. Thank you."

She took his arm, hiked up her skirt to keep from tripping on it going up the stairs, and the two of them went straight into the hotel dining room. McCann's mind had just been diverted from any duty he might have felt to tell the sheriff about a dead body cluttering up the path to the bridge. In fact, his mind was on something entirely different.

"Jack, Jack! Get the hell up. I've something to tell you. Something important," Melody said, leaning over his still body and punching him with her fist.

"Wha-what the hell? Melody? Have you lost your . . . ?"

"My what? Never mind, whatever you're tryin' to say isn't as important as what I have to tell you."

"Uh, okay, spill it," he said, struggling to sit up while getting his leg caught in her billowing silk skirts.

"Someone tried to kill you tonight. He almost succeeded in getting me instead."

"What the devil are you blathering about? Kill me? I've been right here."

"One of those gunslingers that's been hanging around town for some weeks. Buck somebody."

"Buck Kentner?"

"Yes. That's him."

"What happened?"

"A note was delivered to Arlo to give to you, by that Delilah witch."

"A note from Delilah to me?"

"Yes."

"And how did you get it?"

"I took it from Arlo and brought it upstairs to give to you, but I didn't because I read it first and it said for you to meet her down by the bridge over the creek and . . ."

"Whoa! Slow down. You're sayin' you read a note meant for me?"

"Uh, well, uh, yes. I—" Melody sat on the edge of the bed, and her eyes seemed to be searching for some elusive answer to Jack's question.

"You sure do have a lot of nerve reading someone else's messages, Melody."

"I-I know, Jack, I shouldn't have, but after what happened, I don't feel all that bad about it because if I hadn't, it'd be you lyin' out there dead instead of Buck."

"Buck's dead?"

"Uh-huh."

"And you killed him?"

"No . . . no. He shot at me, but I tripped on a piece of rotten wood and fell. Musta gone down right at the same time as he pulled the trigger. Hit my head and sorta went all black and woozy for a while. Don't know how long, but when I came out of it, there was this fella tryin' to help me up."

"What fella? And who shot Buck?"

"That's what I'm tryin' to tell you. It was that fella who was helpin' me to my feet."

"Do you know him?"

"Not before then."

"Well, did he give you his name?"

"Yeah, it was Comanche somethin' or other. I was still pretty woozy."

"Comanche Dan Sobro?"

"Uh, yeah, I think that's it."

"Let me get this straight. One of Havens's killers, Buck, was shot and killed by another of Havens's killers, Comanche Dan, that about right?"

"Uh-huh. That's what happened."

Melody stood up, pale and disconcerted, straightening her wrinkled skirts. She looked like she couldn't decide whether to laugh or cry. She finally settled on the latter. Jack took her in his arms.

Chapter 37

"So, that's the story on Buck Kentner, Cotton, at least as Melody tells it."

"Looks like I need to talk to Comanche Dan. But before I do, I told you we might have more backup than we figured."

"You figure he'd go against Havens even after taking the thousand dollars?"

"He came out to the Wagner place to find me. Scared Emily to death. She doesn't take to gunslingers stoppin' by for a casual visit. Still a little gun-shy from her encounter with Cruz, I reckon. But he *did* tell me about him bein' a deputy U.S. marshal and all. Still, I don't plan to fold my hand until I see all the cards."

"And none of the others knew what Comanche Dan looked like?"

"That's what he said."

"I reckon that's possible, especially if these rats came out of their holes from all over." Jack scratched his head and frowned. "You think he's tellin' it straight?"

"I'd like to think so, but I also like to see a bill of sale before I accept a man's word that the horse he's ridin' is his."

"I like your thinkin'. Where do you figure to go from here?"

"Havens has lost three of his hired guns already, and he's no closer to getting rid of me than he was the day he arrived. I'd say he's about to get himself real worked up over this last turn of events. Could bust the whole plan loose."

"You thinkin' of givin' him a little extra push to kinda get things started?"

"Indeed."

"What do you want me to do?"

"I've been watchin' him, and I think I know the chink in his armor."

"And that is . . . ?"

"Your beautiful friend Delilah Jones."

"You're fixin' to get me killed, aren't you? Either by Bart or by Melody."

"One of the risks of being a deputy. You should know that by now."

"What am I supposed to do?"

"Pay extra attention to Delilah. Drop by the bank just to say hello, meet her after the bank closes, walk her to her room, ask her to dinner . . . Hell, I don't know, you're the lothario around here."

"I don't know what that means, but I'll assume it's an insult since it's comin' from you, Cotton." With a deep sigh, Jack pushed out of his chair, hiked up his sagging gun belt, and strode outside, muttering to himself. *Melody will use that derringer on me without giving it a second thought if she even suspects I'm fooling around. I know Havens doesn't sport a gun, but he's proven he'd not stop at payin' one of his back-shooters to even the score for him.*

Sleeve Jackson was once again standing in front of Bart Havens's large oak desk. He had been berated for the past half hour by the red-faced man shaking his fist and pointing his finger at him. He'd about had his fill of being treated like a galley slave. One thousand dollars didn't give any man the right to chew on him like an old piece of meat. As he stood silently, gritting his teeth and seething inside, Delilah arrived and was immediately invited, none too politely, to receive her share of the blame for Buck's death, which Bart perceived to be a failure on the part of them both.

"Can you explain why Jack sent that slut out to the bridge instead of going himself?"

"I . . . really . . . can't, uh—"

"I'd lay money that you didn't give that note directly to him as I instructed. Isn't that right?"

"The bartender said he was still asleep and that he would be certain that Jack got it as soon as he came downstairs."

"Do you suppose that's what happened?"

"Perhaps not. The woman who owns the saloon must have somehow gotten hold of it and figured I was asking Jack to meet me for, er, something romantic. She's very jealous, or so I've been told, and I suppose she showed up fully intending to tear my eyes out."

"Well, well, the lady has solved the riddle." Havens stood up suddenly, slamming his fist on his desktop. "But your incompetence got Buck killed! Get out, Delilah! I'll deal with you later."

Delilah turned and abruptly left. Feelings of anger mixed with fear for her own safety. Tears dribbled down her cheeks as she returned to her hotel room.

After Delilah left, Havens redirected his fury back to Sleeve. Although the gunslinger had yet to figure out what part he'd played in Buck's demise, he could but quietly withstand the tongue-lashing he was getting. Had there not been another two thousand dollars awaiting his successfully shooting down the sheriff, he would have killed Havens on the spot.

"Who got the drop on Buck?"

"I don't know. I went down to the undertaker to see the body. Had one bullet in him."

"In the back, I suppose?"

"No. He saw it comin'. Undertaker said it looked like he'd failed to get a shot off before he went down," Sleeve said, shaking his head.

"I'm betting that damned deputy was waiting for Buck. Probably dry-gulched him. Well, never mind, I'll take care of *him*."

"How do you figure on doin' that?"

"After the loss of Whitey Granville, J.J. Bleeker, and now Buck, we can't afford to wait any longer. We'll put the second part of a plan I been thinking about into motion. I want you to take this to the telegraph office and get it sent pronto. Do you understand? No screwups!"

Sleeve took the paper being handed him and left, grumbling to himself.

Having overheard Black Duck Slater and Sleeve Jackson discussing plans on how best to ambush the sheriff after the loss of Buck Kentner, and now Havens's plan to bring in more help, Plink put down his whiskey glass long enough to try concentrating on exactly what they were saying. Drunk as he was, enough of their conversation had broken through the haze and gotten his attention. And he didn't like what they were saying one bit. He saw their whispering as just a way to cut him out of his rightful money for being the one to do in the sheriff. He had no intention of giving up what he considered his right, the right of one brother to avenge another brother. He started to pour himself another drink, then stopped, thinking better of it. His blurry eyes and slow speech aside, he recognized that he must sober up long enough to do the deed. As tough as it was, he scooted the bottle aside, turned the glass upside down, and pushed his chair back from the table. He needed some fresh air to clear his addled brain. He knew the time had come to put together his own plan before any of Havens's other gunslingers could beat him to the punch. He couldn't allow any of them to take what was his and his alone. He, Plink Granville, would be the one to go down in history as the man who killed Sheriff Cotton Burke. And that was all there was to it.

He stumbled through the batwing doors, nearly falling on his face once before catching himself on a post out front. He hugged the heavy timber, the one that held up the porch, for several minutes as his head stopped spinning. It had been quite a while since he'd stood up. His body was still adjusting when Bart Havens came strolling toward him.

"G'day to you, sir," Plink muttered.

"And to you, my good man. Where are you headed?"

"Uh, thought I might get some fresh air, maybe take a short nap."

"Do I detect a man driven by a purpose? Or do I just see another slovenly drunk looking for a place to pee?"

Plink was at once infuriated by the man's callous words. The sting of Havens's comments was like a rattler's fangs sinking deep into his flesh. But what could he say? Havens was the source of the money he'd need if he hoped to make a clean getaway after the shoot-out. He could only blink away the blur of liquor and mumble his acceptance of the insult.

He stepped off the boardwalk in front of the saloon and stumbled down the street, nearly losing his footing every so often in the uneven road. If he could manage to stay away from any whiskey until morning, he'd surely be sober enough to accomplish his task. That is, if he could control the shaking hands he'd experienced with every previous attempt to sober up. He was well aware that alcohol had consumed him for several years now, and any attempt to break free of its control over him would likely be futile in the long run. But for now, he needed only to be alert for a short time, and fast, like he had once been. He could take this sheriff, of that he was certain. Why, it wasn't that long ago when he backed down one of the most notorious gunslingers in Texas. The man's name didn't immediately come to him, but he could still see clearly how the man had thrown up his hands at the realization that Plink Granville would easily best him if the confrontation came to that point. It hadn't, though.

Plink entered the hotel lobby still bleary-eyed and stumbling. He fell twice on the stairs up to his room. After fumbling for his key, he opened the door, went inside, and fell facedown on the creaking bed. Sleep came quickly but fitfully. His head was awash with unsettling images of guns going off and bodies being thrown to the ground to lie in pools of blood that seemed to grow and grow until the street was a river of red. At one point he awoke screaming and sitting up in bed. His revolver was in his hand and he was pointing it at his own head. Perspiration poured off him and he lay back shaking, filled with fear.

The nightmares were becoming more and more violent, and almost certain to again emerge each and every time he closed his eyes.

Chapter 38

"Jack, I want you to ride back out to Mrs. Blanchard's place and see if you can get a little more time from those folks. We've got to keep them from comin' into town with fire in their eyes and a rope in their hands. If they come rampaging in here like a mob of vigilantes, Sleeve and his boys will cut them to pieces. And we'll be caught in the middle. We can't take them both on at the same time." Cotton seemed uncharacteristically nervous.

"You're right about that, but I doubt I can do much if their minds are still set on only givin' us four days. Half of that is gone already. They didn't seem overly eager to listen to a tin star," Jack said.

"We have to try. Since you're the one who talked to them in the first place, it should be you that does the asking. Make it sound like you understand their cause."

"Trouble is, I do," Jack said as he frowned, grabbed a rifle off the gun rack for his saddle scabbard, and left.

* * *

As he approached the Blanchard ranch, he pulled up. What he saw was disturbing. There were about a dozen riders in the barnyard, ambling around aimlessly like they were waiting for the order to saddle up. They were well armed and gave the impression they were about to lay siege to a fort. Jack sat still for a few minutes pondering whether to ride down into the midst of a gaggle of angry men with guns. Finally, he could see no other option, and he spurred his horse to a gallop. When he reined up in front of the house, Mrs. Blanchard came onto the porch with her hands on her hips. She wore an apron as if she'd just finished feeding a passel of hungry soldiers. As Jack looked around, it appeared that's exactly what she'd done.

"What is it you want this time, Deputy?" Her mood was decidedly cold.

"What's goin' on? I thought we'd agreed you folks would give us at least four days to solve the Havens problem."

"Most of the ranchers that have been taken in by that scoundrel voted to go against our agreement. I figure they're all out of patience with waitin'," she said.

"If those men ride into Apache Springs figurin' to dislodge Havens and his hired gunslingers, there's goin' to be a lot of bloodshed. Many of those men out there in your barnyard won't be comin' home to their families. I know you don't want that to happen."

"Ain't nothin' I can do about it. They're grown men and they make up their own minds. Ain't a darned thing an old woman can say to change that."

"Mrs. Blanchard, I know those men will listen to you. Please consider what I'm sayin'. I need a little more time. The sheriff and I are both on *your* side, but we are also sworn to uphold the law, and what you're about to do is illegal. Arrests will be made, blood will be shed, and all over one crooked banker. He's the only one who'll come out of this thing untouched. Please, listen to me—"

"What's this fella fillin' your head with, Miz Blanchard?" said one of the men who'd gathered out back, as he walked his horse around to the front of the house.

"He's come to talk us into stayin' put for a spell, just so's the sheriff can get this Havens to move on of his own accord, I reckon."

"That it?" the man asked Jack. "You figure to convince Havens to pull up stakes and give up waitin' around to clean us all out? Why, son, you're as full of buffalo dung as he is. He ain't goin' to skedaddle; he's goin' nowhere until all those loans come due and then he'll own half the county."

"I never said it would be easy. But we have to try doin' it legal-like. Havens won't win this fight; you got my word on that. But what you're plannin' can't succeed, either. Havens has hired a bunch of killers and he'd like nothin' better than to see some of you brought down so's you won't be alive to pay his bank back. That way, he wins by default, your families will lose everything, and he don't have to wait for his money, nor anything else. Your women and children will be kicked off the land you worked hard to develop. That what you want?"

"You got a good argument, son, but our minds are made up. We're gettin' rid of that skunk for good. Now is as good a time as any. We'll still give you till Friday, but that's it," he said over his shoulder. Every one of the riders shouted their agreement without protest, even though many had heard Jack's words.

Jack could see the futility of wasting more time talking. He mounted up and spun his horse around. He spurred the gelding to a run, heading straight back for town. He could only hope Cotton would come up with a solution before the army of angry ranchers blew the lid off things, turning the streets of Apache Springs into a possible massacre.

He came to a dusty halt in front of the jail and dismounted in the cloud swirling around his horse. He stomped onto the boardwalk and pushed the door open.

"Cotton! Things a—"

He saw then that except for the one prisoner the jail was

empty. He went back outside, looking up and down the street for the sheriff, without any luck.

"Crap!" he grumbled aloud, mostly to himself. "If Cotton's gone back out to play parlor games with Emily Wagner at a time like this, I'll—"

"You'll what?" Cotton said as he came around the side of the jail.

"Uh, nothin'."

"So, what happened? Did you get them to hold off?"

"Hell, no! Fact is, they're still bent on comin' on Friday. I couldn't steer that herd away from the cliffs. And they're pretty lathered up, too. Couldn't talk *any* sense to 'em."

"Damn! Okay, here's what you do. Go down to the livery and tell whoever's there to drag out every bale of hay and straw he's got and pile 'em on either side of the street at the edge of town. That's the most logical way for 'em to come. I just saw Henry Coyote ride into town. I'll get him to stay in town a couple of days. I'll have him take up a position on the balcony of Melody's saloon."

"And when they see we've blocked their way, what do you figure they're goin' to do? Hope you ain't figurin' on them boys turnin' tail and runnin'. They won't, believe me."

"Didn't figure they would, but they'll not be wantin' to shoot it out with the law as well. I don't figure they're goin' to face down you, me, Henry Coyote, and Havens's men, too."

"Havens's men? What the hell are you talkin' about? They won't lift a hand to help us. They'll see it as a perfect opportunity to gun us down in the process."

"I'm bettin' they won't. After I tell Havens what's about to transpire, he'll tell his men to back our play to guarantee his safety. You see, he isn't just a scheming tyrant, he's also a coward, but his hirelings will do as he says."

"Hmm. Might work. Okay, I'll get someone to start readyin' a barricade." Jack wandered off in the direction of the livery while Cotton sought out a conversation with Bart Havens himself, something he was suddenly looking forward to.

* * *

Cotton stopped just inside the Havens Bank, where he came face-to-face with Delilah Jones. He took off his hat as he approached her.

"Good day, Sheriff. What can we do for you?" Her sweet voice was in stark contrast to everything he knew of Havens.

"I'd like to speak to your boss, Miss, er—"

"Jones. Delilah Jones. And I'll see if he's able to talk to you," she purred, turning to knock on Bart's door.

Havens opened the door and, seeing the sheriff standing there, stepped aside. Delilah ushered Cotton into Havens's office and closed the door as she left. The awkwardness of the two of them standing there, staring at each other, was palpable. Havens walked around his desk and sat. He waved the sheriff to do the same in the chair that faced him. Cotton obliged him.

"To what do I owe this visit from our esteemed sheriff?"

"Well, Havens, I'll get straight to it. The town is on the verge of being overrun by a gang of pissed-off customers—your customers—and I figure their plan is to storm this bank, drag you outside, and string you up by your worthless neck. And I'm almost of a mind to let 'em."

"Now, why would my customers ever feel the need to take such a rash and primitive action?"

"Because you've cheated them, every one of them. Those contracts you had them sign—the ones with the no-interest clause—will end with either huge penalties or forfeiture of property. And they damned well got it all figured out. You thought them too stupid to see through your scheme, but they did. And to make things worse, you stood by while one of your rattlers gunned down one of their own. Stupid, really stupid. So now, unless you listen to my plan and listen good, I'll have no choice but to turn them loose to do as they wish. They are *seriously* riled up!"

"You wouldn't. You're a straight-shooting minion of the law, and your reputation as such is far too valuable to you to contemplate abandoning your legal responsibilities."

"Here's where that kind of thinkin' could get you killed: there are too many of them for me and my deputy to handle. So you can put your gunslingers out there on that street to back us up, or I walk away. But make up your mind quickly because they'll be here day after tomorrow."

"I see no reason to interfere with the way the law handles such situations. You're the sheriff, and you have an obligation to protect the citizenry. I am a citizen. Now, if by some chance a couple of bullets happened to get you and your deputy, I'll simply ask my men to stand in the doorway to the bank and repel any with the stomach for risk. My men are the best around at what they do. Make no mistake about that."

"I see where you're comin' from, Bart, but there's a couple of serious flaws in your thinkin'. First, you seem to have forgotten about your hired killers J.J. Bleeker, Whitey Granville, and Buck Kentner. They're all dead. Second, I could easily step aside and let that mob come straight to your doorstep."

"My men can handle them," Bart said with a smug grin.

"All fifty of 'em?" Cotton turned and strolled out the door.

As Cotton left Bart's office, he heard the banker nervously ask Delilah to fetch his men.

Chapter 39

Friday morning dawned clear and cool. Shortly after dawn, Cotton arrived at the jail to see if preparations were under way to handle what he figured to be a dangerous situation. Jack, the liveryman, and two young men he'd recruited to help with the straw and hay bales, had the street at the end of town pretty well blocked off. They'd even found some empty crates and a couple of broken-down wagons to add to the blockade. Jack was shouting orders like a drunken general. When he saw Cotton, he thanked the others for their help and ran up the street to meet the sheriff.

"Mornin', Sheriff. Figured we'd best be ready for whenever they decide to come," Jack said.

"Good job, Jack. All that stuff in the street ought to at least slow them down."

"You know, if they come a-shootin', we're goin' to have to throw some lead their way. How do you feel about shootin' at our neighbors?"

"I don't plan to have to. I hope when they see the firepower we've mustered, and the blockade you've put together, they might just rethink their intentions."

"You hope?"

"I hope."

"Not sure hope is goin' to be enough. You should have looked those men in the eyes as I did. There ain't a lick of hope left in 'em."

"There better be a few cooler heads in the crowd."

"Did Havens say he'd send his polecats out to play in the dirt?"

"The stubborn jackass didn't say. But he will. I had to appeal to his logical side."

"Logical side? What side is that?"

"The one that's scared to death of bein' strung up like a smoked ham."

"You haven't said what we do if shootin' starts."

"Shoot over their heads or at the ground in front of 'em. Maybe we can spook their mounts and cause enough confusion they'll see it ain't worth the pain."

"That's fine for you, me, and Henry, but who's goin' to tell those gunslingers that they aren't supposed to kill no one? That's what they do for a livin', you know," Jack said with a scowl.

"I plan to place them between us and the ranchers. That way, if one of the cowboys goes down from bein' shot by a Havens man, whoever shot him pays with a bullet himself."

Jack stroked his chin.

"You know, Cotton, that idea just may be a stroke of genius, something I seldom am forced to portray you as bein'."

Cotton looked around to see Sleeve Jackson, Plink Granville, Black Duck Slater, and Thorn McCann coming toward them. McCann, still in the guise of Comanche Dan, spoke up.

"Sheriff, Mr. Havens said you might need some help with an army of disgruntled ranchers coming to take him to task for his contractual language. That right?"

"Interesting way to put it, but, yeah, that about covers it."

"What do you want us to do?"

"First off, I don't want the street littered with dead ranchers. They aren't gunfighters, just regular family men with an axe to grind with Havens."

"So what are you askin' us to do, throw rocks at 'em?" McCann said.

"Nope. Just want to scare them enough that they'll turn around and hightail it back to their ranches. I want you men to shoot over their heads. I figure if we show we've got enough guns to hold off a small army, maybe, just maybe, they'll rethink their plan. Any shots that get fired should be aimed *well* over their heads. Any of 'em that goes down, the shooter does, too."

McCann looked at his companions and shrugged. No objections from any of the others, so he turned back to Cotton and said, "Okay. How soon they comin'?"

Before Cotton could say anything, a thunderous pounding of the ground sounded and a cloud of dust appeared over the hill no more than a quarter mile away. There appeared to be thirty to forty of them and they were riding hard.

"Right about now, Mr. Sobro," Cotton replied to McCann. "Better get ready."

Everyone but Plink Granville drew his gun. All were cocked and pointing in the general direction of the oncoming riders. Cotton and Jack both had rifles in addition to their sidearms, and both stepped slightly back of the line of gunslingers. Henry Coyote was stationed on Melody's balcony with his Spencer repeater. As the ranchers reined in at the barrier, the man in the lead shouted to Cotton.

"Sheriff, better get that Havens fella out here or we're comin' in to get him."

"Sorry, Abe, but you know I can't do that. Now, why don't you use your heads and turn around and ride on out. As you can easily see, there are seven men here, all armed and all very good shots. We could, if pushed to do so, kill every one of you twice over. I don't aim for nothing of the kind to happen. But it's all up to you."

Plink Granville was weaving in an attempt to remain

standing. When he looked around and saw that all the others had their guns out, he started to pull his. His hand was shaking so badly, he couldn't manage to get a firm grip on it, and he dropped the gun in the street. Because he didn't keep his six-shooter loaded with just five shells rather than six, as most gunslingers do, in case it should be dropped, Plink's gun went off the second it hit the ground, sending a .45 slug into the pommel of the lead rider. The bullet missed the rider and the horse, but came close to both.

Cotton spun around ready to take out the shooter, but instead came to a realization of considerable importance: Plink Granville really wasn't a threat to anyone but himself. The look on Plink's face was that of a child expecting a scolding for spilling his milk. Cotton turned back to the crowd, as the kid stood embarrassed and shaky, unable to even pick up his own gun. His bleary eyes were unable to focus on what was happening around him, and he slowly turned to stumble back into the saloon.

But the shot had accomplished one thing. The ranchers must not have expected to see a bullet hit so close to the lead rider, and they were growing nervous. Cotton decided now was the best chance he'd ever get to push them to make their move.

"Last chance, Abe. The next one will be aimed right at *your* head and it'll come from that Indian on the balcony with the rifle. I promise he won't miss. Don't make me give the word."

Abe glanced up at the Indian, and then around nervously, all the while trying to keep his horse under control. The others were doing the same, looking from one to another for verification that riding out was an acceptable solution to their dilemma.

"I'm waitin'," Cotton shouted.

Abe looked at the ground sheepishly, then turned his horse about and signaled the rest of the riders to head back the way they came. There didn't appear to be any resistance to the decision.

Cotton said nothing as he headed back to the jail with Jack. Henry climbed down from his perch and joined them. Havens's gunslingers wandered into the saloon. Not a word was spoken between them. One of Havens's men picked up Plink's revolver and stuck it in his gun belt.

Chapter 40

The Coleman brothers, Farley and Cress, were taking their ease in their second-floor hotel room in Albuquerque when a knock came at the door. Cress was sitting at a table near the window smoking a cigar, reading a newspaper. Farley was sipping a glass of Kentucky Bourbon, as he gazed out on the street below.

"Door's open," Farley called out.

A young boy opened the door timidly, his face showing both trepidation and inquisitiveness. The room he entered was the temporary quarters of two of the most feared gunslinging gamblers for many miles around. He carried a piece of paper, which he gingerly handed to Farley.

"What's this, boy?"

"A telegram, sir."

Farley fished in his pocket, retrieved a quarter, and handed it to him. The lad left without hesitation, uttering a whispered thanks and nearly tumbling down the stairs in his haste to leave all in one piece.

"Who's it from?"

"Someone named Havens from Apache Springs."

"What's it say?"

"Says we're about to come into some money. A thousand dollars apiece," Farley said, handing the telegram to his brother. "Couldn't have come at a better time, too, seeing as how we've pretty much worn out our welcome here."

"Uh-huh. Say, do you know who the hell this Havens character is?"

"Heard he's one mean hombre. Never met him, but this here offer's clear. We get to shoot ourselves a lawman."

"I don't suppose it happens to say which lawman, though."

"That's true. But what difference does it make? There's two of us and only one of him. Simple. Ain't a man alive that can take both of us at the same time."

"Reckon you got a point. And last night seemed to prove it. When are we supposed to be in this Apache Springs? Never heard of that place, either."

"Southwest of here, somewhere. At least I think so," Farley said. "We'll ask at the desk."

"How long you figure it to take?"

"Couple days, maybe longer."

"Then I reckon we best get started. All that money is callin' to me like a long lost friend." Cress put down the newspaper and went to the wardrobe to begin pulling clothes out. He placed a valise on the bed, opened it, and began stuffing in shirts, pants, socks, and other items a gentleman gambler would be expected to wear. Farley watched for a moment, then gulped down the last of his bourbon and followed suit.

As they went downstairs to the hotel lobby to check out, Cress asked the clerk, "Do you have any idea where Apache Springs is located? And is there a stage that goes there?"

"Certainly, sir. The stage that leaves in about an hour goes through there on its way to Silver City. Stage office is two blocks over."

The two men thanked the man and headed for the stage office. "Let's cut down the alleyway to avoid any contact with the sheriff. I'm sure you'll recall him saying we were to stick around until he could talk to the others in the game."

"Yeah, I remember. Looks like this telegram came at just the right time to save our skins," Farley said. "Someone is bound to figure out that little trick of dropping an ace right at the feet of the man who had almost taken every cent we had and called you on it."

"It isn't like he didn't have it coming. Don't forget he'd near cleaned us out three nights in a row, too. I *knew* he was cheating; I just couldn't seem to catch him at it. So your choice was clear. Shoot the bastard."

"My sentiments, precisely," Farley said. "Lucky for us the sheriff couldn't decide whether it was self-defense or not. He didn't waste any time warning us to stick around until he figured it out, however."

He patted the bulge under his coat where rested a nickel-plated, .38-caliber Colt Lightning in a shoulder holster.

They hurried from alleyway to back street to alleyway, avoiding contact with anyone who might remember them from the card game that ended in the death of either a very good gambler or a very good cheater. They had no interest in hanging around to find out which.

Sleeve Jackson's patience had finally run out. His hatred for Bart Havens coupled with a deep desire to get his hands on the two-thousand-dollar bonus for killing Cotton Burke were uppermost in his mind on that misty morning. He never did like the idea of sharing the bounty with others, either. And Bart's distasteful treatment of a beautiful woman, Delilah Jones, had put the last nail in the coffin. He didn't know whether Delilah would actually acquiesce to the dream he'd harbored ever since their first casual meeting, but if he could get her free from the clutches of her benefactor, he felt certain she'd at least entertain the idea of leaving with him for the gold fields of California, where he'd heard tell folks were picking up nuggets the size of a man's fist. At least that was his dream, and Sleeve was a man known to dream incessantly. And now the time had come to put all things right. He'd first kill the sheriff, then brace Havens for the money—maybe even shoot the jackass for good measure after getting his hands on the cash—then ask Delilah to accompany him to even greater riches in that far-off land he'd seen only in his mind.

One at a time, he pulled his two revolvers from their holsters, half-cocked each of them, then rolled the cylinders through, slowly. Loaded, ready. He'd not fortified himself with whiskey, as the others seemed to like to do. He needed his mind clear, his reflexes at their peak. He pulled his hat from a peg and placed it on his head. He stood up and began a slow walk to the batwing doors of the saloon, moving casually so as not to attract attention to his purpose. He stood at the doors, momentarily looking over them to assess the town's activity, then pushed through. He walked to the corner of the saloon, then slipped down the alley—his mission set, his attitude one of confidence, his stride purposeful. His destiny lay a hundred feet away and he was ready. *Prepare to meet your maker, Cotton Burke.*

Cotton and Memphis Jack were in the sheriff's office making certain all the rifles and shotguns were cleaned and loaded. Three Winchester carbines were lined up on the desk, and a coach gun leaned against it. Several open boxes of ammunition were scattered about the desktop. There was a sense of impending danger within the community. Storekeepers felt it, as did those who came to town for supplies or entertainment. An unspoken awareness that one, or all, of Apache Springs' recently arrived gun toters were planning to embark on something violent.

"When do you figure those that are still standin' will make their move, Cotton?"

"Don't know. Just want to be ready when it comes."

"If Havens stays true to what I saw him do in Texas, he'll keep sendin' for more gunslingers every time we take one down. Seems like he'd be runnin' out of money before long."

"It does at that."

Just then a shot rang out. Cotton stepped to the door and eased it open. He peered out slowly, making sure no one was immediately outside waiting for him to emerge and then get filled full of lead. The street seemed empty, so he cautiously stepped out onto the boardwalk. His Colt .45 rested easily in his hand. Jack was behind him with a rifle, a cartridge levered in place.

Chapter 41

There had been a soft rain since just after dawn. Cotton felt a chill in the air as he stepped out onto the porch, and a slight breeze carried with it a hint of the coming rainy season. The morning had adopted the gray garb of a dowager queen. Only now and then did an occasional shaft of sun find its way through the cloudy overcast.

"Hey you, Sheriff Cotton Burke." The disembodied voice echoed off the wooden buildings.

In the waning light of the afternoon, vague shadows stretched across the false fronts of the businesses. Tiny puddles of sunlight splashed the rutted street. Cotton watched as a man moved out from between two buildings halfway down the street. It was Sleeve Jackson. A touch of sun glinted off the nickel-platted revolvers at his side.

"It's time we got to know each other a little better, Sheriff. Come on out into the street and let's us talk a spell," Sleeve yelled.

Cotton moved from under the porch overhang. He held his gun to his side.

"From all the mischief you've been into on Bart's part, I feel I already know you, Sleeve. No need to shake on it, though."

"Didn't figure on no handshake bein' necessary, Sheriff. And you can tell that deputy of yours this is just between you and me."

"What's on your mind, Sleeve?"

"Thought you might like to have a little shootin' contest. You up for that?"

"Well, Sleeve it *is* late, and I'm normally startin' to get ready for supper about this time. Maybe some other afternoon."

"I done had my supper, and I'm feelin' jus' fine. So what say we make it a quick contest?"

"I can't help noticin' the shine on those fancy revolvers of yours. Smith & Wesson Schofields, right?"

"Yep. They say Jesse James hisself favors these shooters."

"Yep. Nice, real nice. Nickel-plated ones are rare. What ammunition do you use?"

"The only proper one for such a fine instrument: Schofield .45s."

"Ah, that's what I figured. My Colt uses Long Colt .45s."

"Yeah, so?"

"Well, I hear tell that in a contest between the two guns, the fact that the S&W bullet is a shorter cartridge, so it takes longer to get out of the barrel, leaves that shooter at a distinct disadvantage."

"Huh?"

Cotton could feel Jack's questioning eyes burning into his back. *Ever the cynic*, Cotton thought. That didn't slow him down, though.

"Yep, a big disadvantage. I figured a top gunhand like you'd know that."

"You don't know what you're talkin' about, Sheriff. The length of the cartridge don't make no difference. That's crazy talk."

"I'm just sayin' what I've heard. More'n once. That's all. And from some pretty accomplished marksmen, too. Some of the best. So, it's up to you whether you want to pull them hoglegs or not," Cotton said with an air of nonchalance.

A slight hesitation before Sleeve got his two revolvers out of their holsters was all it took for Cotton to raise his Colt and put two quick bullets into the greasy-haired killer. Shock filled Sleeve's eyes as he dropped his guns and sank to his knees. He flopped over facedown in a puddle. Muddy water splashed the corner of the boardwalk as he fell. Cotton walked over to the man lying still in his street. He shook his head and clucked his tongue before turning around and marching back to his office, taking care to avoid the puddles that dotted the roadway.

Memphis Jack stood motionless outside the door, seemingly in disbelief at what had just happened.

"What the hell was all that *hogwash*, Cotton? There ain't a hill of beans' difference between the two cartridges and you know it."

"There ain't? Damn! Maybe I been misled."

"But, Cotton—"

"You're probably right, Jack. I reckon it *was* just hogwash." He placed his Colt on the desk, secured a cleaning rag from the drawer, and started rubbing. The undertaker, having heard the shots, came clomping down the street, attempting to miss the rivulets where rainwater had filled the wagon ruts, eager to gather up his latest customer.

The stagecoach rolled by on its way out of town. The driver slowed at the sight of a man lying in the mud. He guided the horses around the unfortunate loser of the latest gunfight in Apache Springs. The wheels splashed the mucky water over the shiny Smith & Wesson Schofields still lying near Sleeve's lifeless hands.

Bart Havens was understandably furious over Sleeve Jackson's death. Four men he'd paid a sizable amount of money to had now been killed either by the sheriff or his deputy. And he had nothing to show for his investment. His options were disappearing like wisps of smoke.

Delilah Jones, Plink Granville, Comanche Dan Sobro, and Black Duck Slater were all in his office waiting for some ranting and raving over Sleeve's demise. They weren't certain what he expected them to do about Sleeve. After all, he'd made the decision to call the sheriff out with no mention of it to the others, making his move with no backup. Delilah was nervously wringing a frilly handkerchief. Plink was trying to keep from exposing his still somewhat besotted state to the notice of others by leaning on a high back, leather chair, his six-shooter back in its holster thanks to Black Duck's retrieval of it from the street.

Dan and Black Duck both appeared bored by the whole thing and were clearly unwilling to accept any responsibility for the recent demise of either Sleeve or Buck. Expecting Havens to explode any minute now, they were surprised at what did happen. Bart broke into a sly smile when the door opened and in walked two well-dressed men wearing identical pearl-handled, .38-caliber Colt Lightnings—double-action with short barrels in shoulder holsters. It looked like they knew what to do with them. Havens stood up and extended a hand.

"Gentlemen, welcome to Apache Springs and what I hope will be a lucrative venture for you both."

Both men shook hands with Bart, then turned to do the same with the others. They both tipped their bowler hats to Delilah. One even took her hand and gave it a peck. She blushed.

"Let me introduce our new associates, Cress and Farley Coleman."

"They look more like city slickers than gunslingers, to me," Black Duck said with a sneer. He turned away with a look of scorn.

"I can assure you they are quite adept at the use of firearms. In fact, I have a special purpose in bringing them to town."

"I don't need any help beating Burke," Black Duck said.

"You are welcome to the sheriff, Mr. Slater; in fact

that's part of my new plan. They are here to eliminate *another* problem. They are gamblers of the first order. Their target will be to push Memphis Jack Stump—who I am informed considers himself a fair gambler—into a confrontation after they've taken every last cent he has. When two such proficient shootists go after a target, he'll not survive; I can assure you."

"Y-you want them to kill *Jack*?" Delilah was horrified at Bart's declaration. She knew he was jealous, but not to the point of a killing.

Bart gave her a cynical smile. "Why yes, my dear. That *does* meet with your approval does it not? After all, you *did* say he meant nothing to you."

"That was fast thinking, Cotton, playing on Sleeve's ignorance and all," Jack said. "What made you think he'd go for it?"

"I had no idea whether he would or not. I really just wanted to keep him talking as long as possible. I figured to get his mind off the purpose of him pulling a gun in the first place."

"That leaves Havens with only two more gun handlers, assuming that fella calling himself Comanche Dan is telling the truth."

"I think we'll know very soon."

Cotton walked to the door and stepped onto the boardwalk. He looked up and down the street. He didn't know who or what he expected to see, but the shooting still had him on edge.

Chapter 42

Cotton decided not to stay in town that night. He was restless and out of sorts. He told Jack he'd be out at the Wagner ranch and be back in the morning. Jack just shrugged and said maybe he'd go to Melody's and sit in on a poker game. Cotton went to the livery, saddled his mare, and headed out for Emily's soothing and understanding company.

By the time he'd ridden about an hour, crossed the creek that cut through the southern quarter of the ranch, and started up the well-traveled road to the house, his nerves had relaxed some. He was no longer thinking of pulling his Colt and plugging the first thing that moved. In sight of the house, he called out. Emily came out on the porch and waved. She stood with her hands on her hips, watching his approach with a warm smile. As he dismounted, she rushed to him and threw her arms around his neck.

"I was beginning to think you'd been shanghaied and taken out to sea. It's good to see you all in one piece."

"There *have* been some developments since I was last here."

"Sounds ominous. Better come inside and get comfortable before you tell me." She took his arm and they went inside in lockstep. "Let me get you some coffee, unless brandy sounds better."

"Coffee would be fine. Thanks." He took a seat on the leather couch.

She returned a couple minutes later. "Here you go, Mr. Sheriff," she said, handing him a cup and saucer. Steam rose from the cup, giving him ample warning to be careful of that first sip.

He sat for a moment before sampling the coffee, as if he were off somewhere else. Emily saw this and brought him back to reality.

"Okay, now, what is it that has you so preoccupied?"

"I'm, uh, sorry. Reckon I was kinda drifting off, wasn't I?"

"Yes, you were."

"I had to kill a man this afternoon. It never gets any easier. I suppose I'm still—"

"—still facing the fact that there is someone out there who wants to kill you and wishing things could be different?" she finished.

"Something like that."

"Reckon it's time you let us in on your plan, Mr. Havens, so none of us go off and do somethin' stupid like Sleeve did," Black Duck muttered. His voice carried a note of scorn that could not be missed.

"All right, Mr. Slater, I'll do just that. Cress and Farley are going to be letting everyone know there will be a big poker game starting up at Melody's saloon. From what I hear, Memphis Jack Stump is a sucker for a poker game. He won't be able to resist the temptation to make some extra money. Being a deputy isn't making him rich, and I happen to know he likes living well. The Coleman boys will be sitting in such a way that Memphis Jack will have to sit between them. They will let him win a hand or two, just to get him hooked on the possibilities, then his losing streak will begin in earnest."

"Lots of men lose at cards, that don't mean they're goin' to blow up and try to kill someone," Comanche Dan said nonchalantly.

"True enough, Mr. Sobro, however, in this case, *Farley* will be the one to explode. He'll jump up and claim he's caught the deputy cheating, draw his gun, and before Stump can even offer a defense, blow him to hell. Since Stump will be sitting across and at an angle to my boys, he'll probably not get off one shot. He'll be caught in their cross fire."

"And what are we supposed to be doin' while these Coleman boys do their circus act?"

"You, Mr. Slater, will be ready to take care of the man you've been waiting for. As soon as he hears the shots, he'll be stampeding through those saloon doors like a mad bull. That's your chance to complete your part of the bargain. You three can all fire at once, if you've a mind to. I'll up the ante to give each of you the bonus if it's unclear who actually kills him."

Black Duck and Plink looked at each other and shrugged. Comanche Dan gazed off with a questioning scowl.

"Questions, Mr. Sobro?"

"No, Mr. Havens, no questions. Sounds like a solid plan. When is all this going to come down?"

"Tomorrow night looks to be a perfect time. Gives the boys a chance to spread the word about the game."

All three of the gunslingers nodded and left Havens's office. Delilah started to follow, but Havens called her back.

"My dear, I strongly suggest you go directly to your hotel room and get some sleep. Be here early in the morning, as usual, but I don't want you talking to anyone without me present."

"Why is that, Bart? Don't you trust me?"

"I wish I could, but I can't. Therefore, please do as I say or the penalty could be severe. You may go now."

Red-faced and angry, Delilah stormed out of Havens's office and headed for the hotel. *I've had about all I can take of that insufferable man. His day of reckoning is coming. I can feel it. And it can't arrive too soon for me.*

When she started up the stairs of the hotel, a low voice from across the lobby startled her. She turned around to see Comanche Dan standing in the corner shadows. He took a couple steps toward her and removed his hat.

"Ma'am, would you join me for dinner? I hate eating alone."

"Did Bart send you to keep an eye on me so I don't violate his precious rules? Well, you can go back and tell him I haven't needed a nanny since I was two." She turned back to go up.

"No, ma'am, I surely wasn't sent by that pompous bag of wind. And my invitation is sincere. I would enjoy your company. So, could you see your way to reconsidering?"

She hesitated for a moment. Havens had told her not to talk to anyone. He was so adamant about that, his words had frightened her. But he surely hadn't been talking about one of his own handpicked killers. *Gunslingers.* The very word made her shiver. And yet, this particular gunslinger somehow made her feel different. She experienced no fear, no uneasiness whenever he was around. He didn't have the same empty, cold eyes as all the others had. Certainly he was a killer, but she had to admit, only to herself of course, that there was something quite appealing about this man. Her decision was made.

"Thank you, Mr. Sobro, that would be very nice." She came to him and took his arm. They went to the dining room looking very much like any normal, happy couple.

Chapter 43

Cotton had washed his face and was combing his hair when Emily came into his room. She was still wearing a housecoat over her gown, and her hair was a tangle of curls. She leaned on the door frame and crossed her arms. She let out a sigh.

"After our talk last night, I thought perhaps I could convince you to spend some time here, away from the constant threat of being ambushed."

He turned to her as he shrugged into his shirt. "There isn't anything I'd like better and you know it. But I have to break up Bart Havens's plan to destroy Apache Springs. I didn't ask for his devilment, but I seem to have inherited it just the same."

"Couldn't you ask the U.S. marshal to send some deputies to help corral these rattlers?"

"I could, sure enough. But if I allowed myself to beg the marshal for help every time some threat wanders into town, how could the town have faith that I can protect them? That is what they elected *me* to do, isn't it?"

"I understand what you're saying, but—"

"—but you don't want to come to another funeral, right?"

"That's right. Especially not yours. Cotton, you know how I feel and . . ."

"Yes I do, and I feel the same way. It's for that very reason, for *us*, that I must face this thing head-on. And see it through to the end. Which, I might add, isn't far off, I fear."

"What do you plan to do about Havens? Since he supposedly doesn't carry a gun, and has never personally threatened violence to anyone, how can you go after him? I know he's a devil, but that doesn't mean you can simply walk up and shoot him." Her look of despair suggested that she, too, had spent considerable time seeking an answer to his dilemma and had come up empty-handed.

"The idea of getting the folks who've taken loans out with Havens to pay up on the exact day their loans come due is a solid solution. The problem is, now that Sleeve Jackson, Bart's most trusted hired hand, is lying dead at the undertaker's, he's bound to feel pressure to eliminate me, and likely Jack, before he's forced to impose his scandalous loan contracts by himself. The one thing Bart has always understood is that without guns to back him, he's vulnerable."

"Do you think he has enough money to keep buying up hired guns until one of them gets lucky?"

"That I don't know. He's done all right so far. That's always been his ace in the hole. It appears the time has come to lay down the law to Mr. Havens. I think he needs to fully understand that in Apache Springs, he's dealing with *Cotton's law*."

Delilah and Comanche Dan spent nearly two hours over dinner at the hotel. His easy manner calmed her after Bart's proclamation as to what would happen if she didn't follow his rules implicitly. She had suffered enough at his hand but had been unable to come up with a way to divest herself of the restrictions he'd placed upon her as terms of her employment and his deranged perception of a relationship.

She had yet to understand this man she sat across from, either. Here was a well-known gunslinger, whose gun was available to the highest bidder, but he somehow seemed out of character. Inexplicably, he appeared to have the demeanor of a man of reason, a rarity in her experience. While not a woman of the world, she had certainly experienced enough of the underbelly of the frontier to know a decent man from a run-of-the-mill scalawag.

She'd found out early in life that being beautiful can be a double-edged sword, bringing both prize and condemnation in the same thrust. Her beauty had been something to wear as a badge of achievement for Bart Havens. For her, it had been like making one's way through a pitch-black forest without benefit of even the tiniest hint of light. Beauty had brought her nice things, clothes and jewelry, but neither peace of mind nor respect for who she was. Now the question seemed to be *What does this man Comanche Dan want of me, and what do I expect of him?* And what would be the result if he saw firsthand how Havens had treated her? Would he shy away or rush to her rescue?

"You seem distant, Delilah. Did I say something to distress you?"

"Huh? Why, er, no. I was merely guilty of giving myself over to the luxury of drifting off into a bit of fantasy, I suppose."

"And where did your imagination take you?"

"Away from where I've been for the past year, that's for sure."

"You aren't happy being the consort of Bart Havens?"

She was instantly impassioned with resentment. Her face was flushed and her eyes narrowed as she stuck a finger in his face. "Listen carefully to what I'm about to say. That word, *consort*, indicates something I am *not* where Bart is concerned. I would not willingly be either his *wife* or his *whore* under any circumstance. And I object strongly to the inference."

"I, uh, am sorry if I offended, but I, uh, was under the impression you were with him in, er, every way."

"Well, I'm not! So you can stuff that idea back in your hip pocket and not bring it out again, if you please." She turned her glance from him and pulled up her long skirts, preparing to get up.

Like an awkward teenage boy, he fumbled for the menu and looked it over as if it held some deep secret. After a few awkward moments, he mumbled, "Please accept my apology, Miss Delilah. It was my foolish mistake. I opened my mouth when I had no call to do so. Uh, h-how about dessert? I can recommend the apple pie."

Delilah's coldness turned soft at the suggestion, and she turned back to him, her sudden fury assuaged. *Perhaps this man has amended his first impression of me. Could he actually be more than just another ruffian?*

"Apology accepted. And dessert would be nice. And some coffee to go with it," she said with a sigh.

After dinner, he walked her to her room, bid her good night with a tip of his hat, and left the hotel by the alley entrance, checking all around to make certain he wasn't seen by Bart or his other minions.

The next morning, word was being spread that there was to be a poker game worth sitting in on that evening at Melody's Golden Palace of Pleasure. The stakes would be substantial. No penny-ante pikers need bother. The Coleman brothers had several flyers printed up by the print shop and distributed them around town, nailing a few extras to trees and fences. When they'd finished spreading the news, they wandered back to Havens's bank to firm up their plan of action.

"Anything in particular we should know about this Memphis Jack, Mr. Havens?" Farley said.

"He's no clod-buster, if that's what you mean. He's apt to drink too much, but he's smart. And fast on the trigger. Don't underestimate him, gentlemen. He gunned down J.J. Bleeker before the man could even take aim."

"He know much about poker?" Cress asked.

"He's spent many a day and night raking in some hefty pots. So play it close to the vest. He won't be an easy one to buffalo."

"Farley's pretty damned good at sleight of hand. Don't brush him off lightly, either," Cress said, proudly.

"All right. I'm counting on you both."

Chapter 44

When Cotton strode into the jail, Memphis Jack was removing the food tray from the cell where he'd put the gambler. He was whistling as he replaced the cell keys in the desk drawer. He looked surprised when Cotton came into the office.

"How's our prisoner doing?"

"Grumpy and foul-tempered. Like I'd be if I were in his situation. Maybe we should just let him out. I doubt he'll ever set foot in Apache Springs again."

Cotton chewed his lip for a second.

"Okay. Kick him loose. Town can't afford to keep feedin' him, anyway. Judge won't be here for, what, a month?"

Jack took the keys back into the cell block. He opened the door to the hapless gambler's cell and stood aside.

"Due to the generosity of our esteemed sheriff, you are hereby released. If—and I do stress *if*—you ever set foot in this town again, I'll shoot you on sight myself. Do you follow what I'm sayin'?"

"Y-yessir," the poor man sputtered, as he frantically

gathered his coat, hat, and brogans and rushed from the cell and out the door as if the building were on fire. All to Jack's great amusement.

Jack stood at the door watching the man try desperately to put on his shoes as he hopped around on one foot stirring up plenty of dust while at the same time trying to put as much distance between him and the jail as possible. Jack shook his head and chuckled at the sight.

"That boy had better learn more about poker or try some other endeavor."

Cotton clucked his tongue. "Reckon so. And speakin' of that very thing, I hear there's goin' to be a big game over at Melody's tonight. Couple of gamblers named Coleman. You know them?"

"Nope, Cotton, I never heard of 'em. But I wouldn't mind sittin' in."

"That's just what I was goin' to suggest."

"You *want* me to drink and gamble?"

"Why, Jack, you amaze me with your quick grasp of my intentions. Only the drinkin' part is out."

"But gamblin' isn't gamblin' unless accompanied by whiskey. Don't you know that?"

"Maybe some other night that might apply. But tonight, it doesn't."

"You got some reason?"

"Uh-huh."

"Well, spit it out. I'm waitin' for whatever pearl of wisdom is sure to come rollin' from your lips."

"Two things. The first is: I just got a telegram from another sheriff warnin' me to be on the lookout for two brothers who are wanted in Albuquerque for murder. They are thought to be headed this way."

"How's he know that?"

"The stage line, where they bought tickets, and their telegraph operator, who received a message from Apache Springs."

"Now, who here in town would send a telegram to a couple of gamblers in Albuquerque?"

"One of only two folks I can think of: Bart Havens or Melody. Which one would you put your money on?"

"Melody has never been all that keen on gamblers, at least not the professional ones. So I suppose it falls to Bart. But why?"

"I'm not sure. But I got a notion who might."

Jack narrowed his eyes. "Am I goin' to like this?"

"I don't know, but it isn't important. I want you to talk to Delilah Jones. She knows why Bart sent for those two. She'll tell you."

"I don't know, Cotton. The last time I tried to take her aside at the hotel, she seemed awful nervous and not too interested in bein' seen with me. I'm thinkin' Bart put the fear of God in her. He is one nasty bastard."

"I know, but you've got to try. And do it before that card game."

Jack was expected for dinner at Melody's. But if he was going to corral Delilah, he needed to do it quickly. He didn't dare show up late or Melody would skin him. She was very particular about promptness. So he went to the saloon early to tell her he was going to be late. He'd figure some excuse before he got there. He was sure of that. But when he pushed through the swinging doors, Melody was at the bar talking to Arlo. When she saw Jack, she waved him farther down the bar where they could talk without being overheard.

"I've been thinking of something I want to tell you about," she said.

"Yeah, I, uh, have something to tell you, too."

"You can tell me as soon as I'm through. Jack, sweetie, since your six months of servitude to Cotton Burke is about up, I want to move back to Gonzales, where things are a lot quieter. Too many shootings here in Apache Springs. It's safer back home. Anyway, I've decided to look for a buyer for the saloon."

"You want to sell the place after all the money you've

put into it?" Jack was clearly caught off guard, and not a little flustered.

"It's *just* business. The banker, Mr. Givins, told me he is often approached by someone, usually someone wishing to remain anonymous, seeking to own a saloon. He said they almost always have the cash to pay for it. If something like that came along, I think it'd be too good to pass up. Probably make a nice return on my investment, too."

"I, uh, didn't know you wanted to leave. Besides, I'd need to talk to Cotton before—"

"Talk to Cotton! Always 'Talk to Cotton.' Who the hell's more important to you, me or him?" She was now on her tiptoes no more than an inch from his face, fists balled tightly. She was so close he could feel the heat from her flushed cheeks.

Jack was taken aback by her sudden, unexpectedly belligerent response. He'd known all along that she didn't like Cotton, but he was unaware she'd let her dislike actually break them apart. He was instantly torn. Cotton had given him a chance to prove he could be a lawman again, and Jack was beholden to him for that. Melody was expecting him to agree with her idea, without argument, and her fury at not getting the response she expected burned in her like a sulfur match.

Getting into an argument with Melody wasn't something to be looked forward to. She was like a raging bull when she didn't get her way. It wasn't that he was afraid of her, exactly, more like he didn't want to lose her. She was, after all, the giver of nearly all things necessary to life, at least Jack's life. A place to sleep, a beautiful woman to sleep with, most of his meals, and all the whiskey he could consume was provided by Melody. And at no cost to him, other than having to grin and bear it whenever a tantrum was in the wind. Now was one of those times. He knew damned well he'd better come up with something to calm her down before the explosion became deafening. And his mission went south.

"Melody, you know how much I care for you, and I

would never do anything to change that. But Cotton knows this town, and likely anyone who might be a potential buyer for the saloon. So, what I'm sayin' is, let's let him in on our thinkin' and see if he'd consider lookin' over any deal that was tendered. Just so you don't get stung by some highbinder lookin' to take advantage of a beautiful woman. That's what I mean," Jack said. He was feeling pretty proud of himself for that little speech. He struggled mightily to hide it, though.

Melody unclenched her fists, but kept her frown. It was obvious she needed some time to consider Jack's rationale. That was obvious to him by the way she backed off, like a cat shies away from a skunk, thinking over whether it is friend or foe. He could see the thoughts swirling around in her head. She was actually rather transparent, especially to a man like Jack, who had always had a good grasp of what women were thinking. And if anyone knew Melody, it was Memphis Jack Stump.

Melody suddenly came out of her angry mood and said, "Oh, I'm sorry, Jack. What was it you wanted to tell me?"

"I, uh, just wanted you to know I'd be a few minutes late for dinner. Cotton has a little job for me. But don't worry, it won't take long. Besides, I want to be here for the big poker game everyone's talking about."

Melody frowned at the word "poker" because Jack was notorious for letting his involvement with a poker game keep him up all night, whether he was winning or losing. But his announcement didn't seem to have the negative effect he'd feared. She waved her hand as she started over to a table to talk to some cowboys who'd drifted in.

"As long as you're here, so I have someone civilized to eat with, a few minutes one way or another won't matter. See you later."

Jack left to see if he could track down Delilah before he had to get back to Melody.

Chapter 45

As he left the saloon, Jack noticed Bart Havens walking from his bank down a block to the livery. He was alone. Jack stood under the porch overhang for several minutes to see what Bart's intentions were. Not more than ten minutes passed before he saw Havens driving a buggy out of the livery, heading down the street to the alley that led to the back of his bank. Curious, Jack ran down to the livery. Inside he saw the old man who ran the place with a pitchfork in his hand getting ready toss more hay into a stall.

"What can I do for you, Deputy?"

"Just curious about Bart Havens. Did I see him rent a buggy from you?"

"Yes and no. He didn't rent it, he bought it. Made him a real good deal, too. Ten dollars cash and I threw in an extra cushion 'cause the one it had was threadbare and near wore out. Hope he don't plan on any real long sorties, though."

"Why's that?"

"Well, to be truthful, the wheel spokes looked to need

tendin' to. Darn thing's been sittin' out back for two years, ever since Mr. Cotter got gored by one of his bulls and died. Took it in as payment for his feed bill. His widow seemed happy to get shut of it."

"Thanks," Jack said as he headed out to find Delilah. *What the devil could Bart Havens need with a buggy?*

When he got to the hotel, he went to the desk clerk to ask if Delilah Jones was in.

"I do believe I saw her go up about a half hour ago, sir. She may still be there. Shall I go check for you?"

"No, thanks," Jack said, waving the desk clerk off, "I'll go up myself."

When he got to her room, he stopped outside her door. He thought he heard sniffling or crying, he couldn't tell which. He tapped lightly on the door. After a few seconds, the door opened a crack and one red, teary eye peered out.

"Yes. What is it?" Delilah said.

"It's me, Jack," he said in a near whisper, "I need to talk to you. Can I come in?"

She eased open the door, almost as if she couldn't decide whether to admit him or not. Finally, she stood aside to allow him to enter, then closed it immediately. The sight of her face brought him to an instant boil.

"What the hell happened to you, Delilah? Who did this?"

She turned away from him, crossed her arms, and walked to the open window. Curtains fluttered from the slight breeze coming through. She sniffled and then dabbed at her eyes. Her face was bruised and red. One eye looked as if it might turn black and blue given a day or so.

"Who do you think?"

"Bart Havens? That son of a rattlesnake. I ought to go over there and blow him away."

"What are you doing here, Jack?"

"I want to know what you know about the poker game at Melody's Palace of Pleasure tonight. Is it something Bart is behind?"

"Oh, yeah. And if you're smart, you'll stay far, far away. The whole thing is a setup. And you're the target. Or at least one of them." She started to cry again. Tears streamed down her face.

"What's the plan?"

"Those two gamblers are also gunslingers. They're going to say they've caught you cheating, and the taller one, Farley Coleman, is going to shoot you. Then, when Cotton comes through the door after hearing the shot—and Bart's certain he will—he'll be met by several blazing guns. Neither of you will stand a chance."

Jack walked up behind her, took her by the shoulders, and spun her around.

"You've put yourself in even more jeopardy by telling me this, but I want you to know I am grateful to have a friend like you. And don't fret; Bart's little ambush won't go off as planned. Cotton and I'll make sure of that. Now, dry those beautiful eyes, lie down, and rest. I'll see you after this is all over."

She laid her head on his shoulder for a moment, then looked him in the eye.

"Kill the bastard, will you? For me."

"So that's his plan, is it?" Cotton said, nodding at Jack's revelation at what Delilah had told him. "You think she's on the level?"

"You wouldn't ask if you'd seen what he did to her. Any man who'd hit a woman ought to be strung up on the spot."

"Okay. I reckon we're goin' to have to play the hand we've been dealt. Wish we had a few more guns, but . . ."

"Yeah, I know, but we don't. Too bad Henry Coyote has done rode back out to the Wagner spread. We don't have time to get him back here."

"Hmm. Maybe we do, at that." Cotton stroked his chin.

"How's that?"

"That Oliver kid still work at the livery?"

"Yeah."

"Give him this half dollar and tell him to ride hell-bent for the Wagner spread. Have him tell Emily we need Henry, and pronto."

Jack didn't say a word as he tore out of the jail and ran down the street to the livery.

"Don't know, ma'am, just that the sheriff said to get him to town lickety-split," Oliver said, not bothering to get down from the gray mare he'd ridden bareback all the way from town.

"Thanks, son. I'll take care of it. You can go on back and tell the sheriff he's on his way."

The boy had no more than reached the gate than Emily had gathered two other riders in addition to Henry Coyote and was herself also saddled and ready.

"Make sure you got ammunition for that Spencer of yours, Henry. I got a bad feeling about this. Bart Havens must be up to more of his dirty doin's. The four of us ought to change the odds in Cotton's favor. Let's ride."

Jack wanted to look the saloon over well before the appointed time for cowboys and amateur gamblers alike to gather for the much-ballyhooed game. He also wanted to talk to Arlo about the table arrangement. As he strolled in, Arlo was scooting chairs around one large table in the center of the room to allow for six players, and rearranging several smaller tables along the outer walls. He did this so that those not in the game would have a place to observe the goings-on as well as order drinks. Of course, in Arlo's and Melody's minds, the whole purpose of such a gathering was to up the revenue to the house.

Jack motioned Arlo over to the bar where he could talk without being overheard, even though there were only a handful of patrons scattered about, mostly sipping whiskey and engaging in idle conversation. Two tables held card games of little consequence.

"What's on your mind, Jack?" Arlo said, wiping the top of the bar and setting up a long row of glasses in anticipation of a busy evening.

"You still got that sawed-off twelve-gauge behind the bar?"

"Yep. Why?"

"I figure, if my information is correct, you'll be needin' it before the evenin's over."

"Who do you figure will be creatin' trouble?"

"Couple of gamblers named Farley and Cress Coleman. They're gunslingers Bart Havens brought in to take care of some business for him. Just be ready."

"What kinda business?"

"Killin' me and Cotton."

Chapter 46

A half hour before the game was supposed to begin, Cotton and Jack huddled at the jail to go over last minute plans to deal with Bart's intentions to have the evening end with their demise. Cotton checked his Colt and slid it back into his cross-draw holster. He had loaded a .45-caliber Winchester carbine, too. Jack was, as usual, carrying his Remington .44, but this time he planned a little extra armament. He'd slid Melody's two-shot, .41-caliber derringer into his belt. She wasn't aware he'd filched it from her dresser drawer, but he was confident she wouldn't mind, since it could end up saving a life, possibly his. And she liked the way he warmed her sheets.

"You figure that Oliver kid got to the Wagner spread in time? It's been nearly three hours since he left."

"He's a good kid. I can't see him dallyin' on the way, knowin' how important it is."

"Which side you figure that feller callin' himself Comanche Dan will fall on?"

"That's a damned good question. He's lookin' at collectin' a two-thousand-dollar reward whichever side he decides to take. However, I have to believe he wouldn't have stuck his neck out and told me who he was if he figured to turn on me. I have a hunch he has somethin' else in mind. I don't know yet what that is, but until I do, I aim to give him the benefit of the doubt. At least as much as I can."

"Okay, one more time: you're goin' to be outside the back door, so's you can come in behind Black Duck and that drunken Granville kid, right?"

"Right. I figure they'll be expectin' me to burst through the batwings and that just might give me an extra second of surprise. I'll need it."

"If Henry Coyote gets here in time, what's your plan for him?"

"You're goin' to need to warn Melody of the possibility of trouble, then let her know we want Henry situated on the balcony where he can see everyone in the room. You don't think she'll give you any argument on that, will she?"

"Who the hell knows where Melody stands on anything?"

"I see your point. Did you talk to Arlo?"

"Yep. He understands and promises to be ready with that blunderbuss he keeps hidden under the bar."

"Reckon we might as well get started. You have to get there and choose the seat you want. That'll force the Coleman boys to make their play on *your* terms."

They left the jail and split up halfway down the street, with Jack heading straight for the saloon, up the steps, and through the batwings. The tinkle of piano keys accompanied by a few sour notes from a fiddle drifted through the open windows. He went upstairs to inform Melody about Henry Coyote, then came back down, eyeing everyone who had entered the room.

He sauntered over to the large table Arlo had set up, walked halfway around it, scooted a chair out, and sat. The way he figured it, the Coleman boys would want to position themselves in such a way as to get him in a cross fire. His getting there first changed where the Coleman boys could sit. That meant that each of them would have his back to either the front or the rear door, putting them at a disadvantage.

Jack hadn't been seated more than a few minutes when Farley and Cress Coleman entered, looked around, and spotted the table for their rigged game—two well-dressed gentlemen, attired in pressed suits and boiled shirts with starched collars and string ties. They looked at each other and frowned. Jack figured it was because they had planned on getting there first and choosing the chairs they wanted before anyone else had any say-so. Jack just sat quietly shuffling a deck of cards, showing off his dexterity with the pasteboards. He knew Farley and Cress would want a new deck, since they'd immediately be suspicious of his handling the cards before anyone else could watch and make sure nothing funny was going on. Jack had absolutely no intention of marking or shaving any cards, but he wanted Farley to start a ruckus about getting a fresh deck. That was Jack's way of heightening the tension between him and the one Coleman brother with the deadliest reputation.

Jack was slouched in his chair with his Remington in his lap, out of sight. The Colemans approached the table, waved Arlo over to bring a bottle of whiskey, and Farley reached across to shake Jack's hand. Jack made him reach as far as he could, not accommodating him by leaning forward. Farley grimaced at the slight, and Cress didn't bother to introduce himself.

"You're Memphis Jack Stump, the town's *deputy*?" Farley said with a note of obvious disdain coloring his attitude.

"You win the first hand, Mr. Coleman," Jack said.

"Will others be joining us?" Farley asked.

"I reckon some will wander in after a couple hands. Folks around here are a cautious lot. They'll want to be sure everything is on the up-and-up."

"That's the only way we play, Mr. Stump, the only way we play."

"Call me Jack, and that's not the way I've heard it."

"What exactly do you mean?" Cress said.

"Well, it seems someone up in Albuquerque took offense to your pluggin' some fellow for havin' an extra ace. Sheriff over there says after investigatin' that didn't appear to be the case, and they're now callin' it murder. So, there's a reward out for you boys. I think I heard somethin' about five hundred dollars."

"You plannin' on collecting that reward, Deputy?"

"Nope. I'm just here for a friendly game of poker."

"Good. Good. That's the kind of talk we like to hear, isn't it, Cress?"

"Uh-huh." By his response, it was obvious Cress wasn't the talkative one. Jack also noted a touch of distress in his attitude after learning of the reward for murder.

Over the tinny music and the buzz of conversation from patrons who'd come to watch the action, Jack heard someone walking on the balcony above him. It wasn't Melody, as she wore silk and satin dresses that made a distinctive sound as they brushed the railing whenever she sashayed by. These steps were nearly silent. If it hadn't been for the creaking of a loose floorboard, he'd never have known there was someone standing right above him. And it could only have been Henry Coyote, whose stealth was unlike any other he knew. Jack grinned knowingly, but kept his eyes on the two gamblers.

"Mr. Bartender, could you please bring over a fresh deck of cards? One still in the box, if you wouldn't mind," Farley said. "No offense, Deputy, but I like cards that haven't been shuffled about. Too many possibilities of, um—"

"Tomfoolery?" Jack offered.

"Yes, I believe you've caught my meaning. So, shall we get started?" Farley opened the deck of cards Arlo had placed in front of him and cut them, after peeling off the joker and a couple of extras telling who'd printed the deck and where new ones could be ordered. Farley had obviously decided he'd be the dealer, at least for the first few hands. Jack made no objection.

Arlo was clearly nervous, so he brought the shotgun from beneath the bar and leaned it against the back bar. Since Farley and Cress were facing away from the bartender, they didn't see his attempt at subtlety. Slowly, cowboys and others intent on getting liquored up along with watching some out-of-town gamblers get cleaned out by their own deputy began to gather around. That's when Comanche Dan, Plink, and Black Duck wandered in, surveyed the crowd, then took up positions around the room, each with a clear shot at the batwings.

The stage was set for Bart's gunslingers to spring their trap, none of them knowing, however, that the sheriff and the deputy were aware of what was to come and were prepared. For the first half hour, Jack wasn't doing well. He was down by twenty-five dollars, nearly half the amount Cotton had given him to play with. Then, quite suddenly, he began to rake in some pots, three in a row, in fact. He could see how Farley was manipulating the cards to let him win after dealing off the bottom in the beginning. But Jack's insights weren't enough to keep the surprise from his usual poker face as the sound of leather shoes descending the stairs caught his attention. Then he heard that familiar voice, as the smoke and the smell of whiskey and beer were suddenly diluted with the sweet smell of gardenias.

"Jack, honey, you haven't introduced me to your new poker friends." Melody, making one of her famously flamboyant entrances, strolled to the table, leaned over sufficiently to reveal enough cleavage to make any man shiver clear down to his boots, and reached out to Farley to shake hands. Her long blond curls fell gently off her shoulders. She wore a cameo broach at her throat, attached to a black velvet choker. Her lips were moist and as red as the setting sun.

Farley swallowed hard, took her hand, and gave it a gentlemanly light kiss. Cress just followed her every move with his eyes, trying hard to hide his sudden desire. Jack was amused, at first. That disappeared at Melody's next move.

"Jack, have you seen my derringer?" she said, with an air of accusation. "I was certain I'd left it in my dresser, but now I can't find it. I seem to be getting forgetful. Did you borrow it?" She began to step away, giving the gamblers an enticing smile.

Chapter 47

Melody's interjecting herself into a dangerous situation had Jack unsettled. He'd always been a good gunhand, but he wasn't used to having to consider the safety of some innocent bystander, especially a woman, before making his play. And he was as certain as the sun would rise in the east that the Coleman boys were close to carrying out Bart's dastardly plan. He was right. Farley took advantage of Melody drawing attention to herself by suddenly leaping to his feet and shouting, "Cheat! Cheat! This damned card shark's been palming cards! Everybody in this godforsaken place saw it! *Damn* your thieving ways!"

Both Farley and Cress started for their guns. Farley's came up first, as Jack had assumed it would. He cocked his Remington that lay in his lap and fired right through the pinewood table, blowing a hole the size of a fist and catching Farley in the neck with a .44-caliber bullet, along with a fair amount of wood splinters for good measure. Farley grasped his throat and gasped in a useless attempt to call out to Cress. He toppled over backward like a felled oak and crashed to the floor. Blood gushed from his severed carotid artery.

Cress hesitated at seeing what had happened to his brother. But having started his move, he whirled toward Jack. That split second of indecision was enough to allow Jack to pull his revolver from beneath the table and level it at Cress, firing just as his adversary squeezed off a hasty shot. Jack's bullet hit Cress in the heart, knocking him backward into another table, scattering those who'd been seated there, before he slid to the floor from the overturned tabletop.

Jack grabbed his left shoulder as pain shot through him. Blood began forming a splotchy mess on his white shirt, the only good one he had. Cress's shot hadn't completely missed. Melody screamed and grabbed him, sobbing at the sight of him being wounded. She helped him back into his chair. But the action in Melody's Palace of Pleasure wasn't over by a long shot.

As Black Duck Slater, Comanche Dan, and Plink Granville all faced the front entrance, fully expecting the sheriff to come racing through at any second, a voice from the rear startled them all. Black Duck's hand went immediately to his Colt. Plink fumbled to retrieve his revolver. Comanche Dan made no move, remaining where he had been all along, leaning against the wall near a window, arms crossed over his chest, as he took notice of the Apache on the balcony with a Spencer rifle pointed his direction.

"Lookin' for me, gents?" Cotton shouted. All eyes turned in his direction.

Black Duck drew in the blink of an eye, but it proved to be too little, too late. Cotton's Winchester spit fire and smoke before the man could get a fix on the sheriff's position. Smoke still hung in the air from Jack's shots, making visibility difficult. Black Duck went down with his Colt drilling a hole in Melody's newly mopped and waxed floor, nothing more.

Plink Granville then made the biggest mistake he'd ever made. His sudden realization that his destiny lay right in front of him was an epiphany. Even in his ever-present drunken fog, his future as a recognized, feared, and respected gunslinger hung in the balance. His future was now.

Shouting that he would get even with the sheriff for killing his brother if it was the last thing he ever did, he kept fumbling to retrieve his revolver from his holster. Cotton yelled at him to stop and he'd live. But Arlo, now holding the shotgun leveled at the boy-turned-gunslinger, panicked and pulled the triggers on both barrels. Plink Granville was nearly cut in half by the blast of the twelve-gauge only five feet away, his six-shooter still hung up where the hammer had caught in his suspenders.

Cotton called up to Henry on the balcony. "You can hold off on your shot, Henry. Thanks for being here, though. I think the gentleman has chosen to remain neutral in this fight, at least on this occasion."

Thorn kept his hands away from his gun. He remained where he was with a big, dumb grin spread across his face.

Cotton quickly went to Jack and said, "Are you hit bad?"

Melody shot him an angry glance. "Of course he's hit bad, you jackass. He's bleeding, isn't he?"

"Somebody go get the doc," Cotton hollered over the din. He looked first to Arlo, who was frozen in place, shaking like a puppy in a thunderstorm. Cotton figured it was from the experience of shooting his first man. He didn't appear to be much in favor of doing it again. One of the men who'd seen it all said he'd go find the doctor, and he slammed through the doors of the saloon and raced down the street, leaving while a haze of smoke and the smell of cordite and death still hung in the air.

Melody refused to let go of Jack. She kept hugging him and patting his back. Jack grimaced with each pat but said nothing. She cradled his head on her ample chest.

"Why'd that gambler accuse Jack of cheating? Jack doesn't cheat. He never would," she said, gritting her teeth angrily and still trembling.

"It was just part of their plan from the beginning. You

comin' down the stairs lookin' the way you do and gettin' close to Jack gave them the opportunity they were lookin' for to catch him off guard."

"What the hell do you mean by 'lookin' the way I do'?"

"Sexy, Melody, just sexy. Don't get your feathers all ruffled." Cotton shook his head.

"Y-you mean, I almost got Jack killed by being sexy?"

"Maybe—no, not really. You just made it easier for Farley to make his move when he figured Jack was distracted. They would have found a way without your help."

"Jack?" Melody's wide open eyes stared into Jack's, imploring him to give her some word of forgiveness or a denial that what Cotton had said carried with it any truth.

"It's all right, Melody. What Cotton said makes sense. Those boys came in here plannin' to kill both me and Cotton. The big finale to Bart's plan."

"So, you forgive me?"

"Yes, Melody, I forgive you," Jack said. "Although it wouldn't hurt if you'd go easy on patting my shoulder."

"Oh, sorry." Melody blushed and pulled her hand away. The doctor came through the doors, saw Jack obviously wounded, and went straight to him. As he passed each of those less fortunate lying about in puddles of their own blood, the doctor clucked his tongue and muttered, "Will civility ever come to the frontier?"

Cotton looked over at Thorn McCann. "C'mon over here, Thorn, but keep your hands well away from that smoke wagon."

Thorn did make a concentrated effort to give no hint of a threat. He sat at one of the empty tables and called to Arlo to bring over a couple of beers. Cotton, remaining cautious, sat across from him. His hand remained well within reach of his Colt. Arlo was still nervous as he spilled half the contents of the two glasses while bringing them to the table, struggling to keep his distance from the carnage strewn about the room. Cotton thought Arlo might get sick.

"Go fetch the undertaker and tell him there's customers in the saloon. Make his day," Cotton said to a young fellow whose morbid curiosity had him leaning over to look carefully at Black Duck's corpse. Cotton's order shook him out of his state of inquisitiveness concerning death. When the young man left, Arlo was still standing near the sheriff. It was obvious he had something on his mind. Cotton knew exactly what it was.

"Am, uh, am I in, umm, trouble for shooting that boy?"

"No, Arlo, you aren't. You may have even saved my life."

Arlo returned to his station behind the bar and began wiping and wiping the same spot on the bar top, over and over. Cotton figured it would be a spell before the bartender got over the shock of what had happened that evening and his involvement in it. Blasting someone into oblivion isn't something a man forgets easily.

"You had some inside information about this little soiree, didn't you?" Thorn said, matter-of-factly.

"Might have."

"A pretty dark-haired lady, by any chance?"

"Could be. Why?"

"Bart doesn't have anyone left to take his anger out on. She's likely to receive the brunt of it. Wouldn't like that, not one bit."

"You got a personal interest in the lady, Thorn?"

"Might have. Hope that doesn't mess up anyone else's plans." Thorn glanced over at Jack. The doctor was still tending to Jack's wounded shoulder. Melody made it difficult with her insistent hovering.

"Go ahead, then, and keep an eye on her till this all gets settled one way or another. How about you drop by the jail tomorrow? We'll have a talk."

Chapter 48

"Jack, you don't look all that much worse for a little bullet wound," Cotton said, pouring two cups of coffee and handing one to his deputy.

"I reckon. Wasn't all that bad. Doc patched me up good and proper. Had more trouble gettin' Melody to stop fussin' over me so I could get some sleep." Jack took a sip from the steaming cup, made a face, and put it back on the desk. He groaned slightly as he tried to get comfortable in the aging wooden captain's chair at the jail.

"Why doesn't that surprise me?"

"What do you figure Bart will do now that he doesn't have any more pistoleros to keep him from the wrath of the citizenry?"

"Good question. I may just saunter down and ask him that very question. Right after I've had a little talk with Thorn."

"I thought he was comin' over for a chat with you this mornin'."

"He's supposed to have been here before now. May have to go to the hotel and roust him."

"Why don't you drop in on Bart and I'll sit here and wait for Thorn? I'm real curious to ask him what he'da done if you was to get unlucky last night." Jack tried another sip of coffee, this time with more success.

"Good idea," Cotton said, putting on his Stetson and walking outside. He stopped briefly before heading for Bart's bank. The town was already bustling with activity. Two ladies walked by and gave the sheriff a nod. He tipped his hat. Wagons passed in the wide street, each loaded with crates of goods bound for somewhere else. The stage was pulling away from in front of the hotel, and the clerk at the hardware store was sweeping dirt from the boardwalk in front of his store. Arlo was pounding nails in some boards to cover holes made in the front wall by errant bullets during last night's unpleasantness.

Cotton's stroll to Bart's place was leisurely. Since his archenemy was now toothless after he and Jack had put all of his gang of cutthroats out of business and in line to be planted underground, there was no reason to hurry. He noticed that the door to Bart's bank was closed and locked. *That's strange*, he thought. He went around back, peering in the only window on that side of the building as he went.

Reaching the back door, he found it open. He pulled his Colt and very cautiously stepped inside. He called out. "Bart! Bart Havens! You in here?"

Hearing no response, he eased over to the desk, looked behind it on the floor, and noticed that all the drawers were open. He left the office and went out to the bank lobby. He looked behind the teller's cage. Then it began to come clear to him. There, behind the counter, sat the safe. The door was wide open and the safe had been cleared out. There wasn't one penny to be found anywhere.

"*Son of a bitch*," Cotton growled, "the bastard has robbed his own bank."

He ran from the building to see if anyone had spotted Havens leaving town and, if so, which direction he'd gone. He stopped in the middle of the dusty street, partly to allow a horseman to pass, and partly to see if he could see Havens riding away. He didn't notice more than a handful of people in the whole town. None of them resembled Bart Havens. It all came suddenly quite clear to him. He ran back to the jail.

"That bastard pulled it off!" he said as he stormed into the jail. "Damn!" He threw his hat on the desk. Startled by the sheriff's sudden entrance, Jack had gone for his gun. He stopped short of pulling it when he saw it was nothing more menacing than Cotton in an uncharacteristic rage.

"What has set you afire?"

"Havens! He's stolen all the money from his own bank, the depositors' money, and taken off. That must have been his plan all along."

"Then, we best be goin' after him," Jack said, stating the obvious.

"I'll get the horses and be right back. You think you can ride with that shot-up wing?"

"I, uh—"

"Never mind. I'll go alone. You stay here and keep that chair warm till I get back," Cotton barked as he left for the stables.

He'd no more than gotten his mare saddled than he heard Jack yelling at him. He stuck his head outside the livery to see whatever Jack was making such a fuss about. It took only a second to identify a man slapping the reins of a horse pulling a buggy. It was Thorn McCann.

Thorn reined the horse opposite Cotton and jumped down from the recently patched seat cushion. "Mornin', Sheriff. Sorry I didn't get over to see you sooner. Got a surprise for you though." He directed Cotton's attention to several leather valises in the back of the buggy. "I think you're goin' to like it."

"Who owns this rig? And where'd you get those travelin' cases?"

"Hang on, Sheriff, I suggest we get in out of the sun where we can have a look-see without the whole town gettin' in on the action."

"We'll haul 'em down to the jail."

Thorn took the reins and led the horse alongside Cotton to the jail, where he tied the old horse to the hitching rail. The two of them each took two valises and carried them inside. Jack stepped aside with a curious glance at the valises. With the leather satchels placed side by side on the desk, Cotton opened one of them. He whistled when he saw the contents.

"This the money Havens stole from the bank?"

"Yep."

"How'd you get your hands on it, Thorn?"

"It's a long story."

"Then you best get to it."

Thorn let out a sigh and said, "Got any coffee, maybe with a chaser? It's mighty dusty out there."

Jack poured him a cup, spilling in a shot of brandy to liven it up. Thorn sipped, thanked Jack, then sat on a rickety chair by the wall next to the gun rack.

"Goes like this. I was figurin' on comin' down here to have our little talk early this mornin'. I saw Havens drive his buggy out from behind his bank like his britches was afire just after dawn, so I figured to take a look at why he was leavin' town when it was almost time to open the bank. I went around back and found the door open and no one inside. I also found the safe open and no money to be found. It seemed like a good idea to follow him. By the time I got my horse saddled, Havens was long gone. So I just naturally rode off in the direction I'd seen him head."

"Makes a heap of sense, don't it, Cotton?" Jack nodded, somewhat cynically.

"It does *indeed*, Deputy. Go on, Thorn. You have our attention."

Thorn cleared his throat, took another sip of Jack's coffee, and said, "About four miles out of town on the east road, I saw what appeared to be an unfortunate soul hangin' from a tree. There were a number of men, mostly cowboys, gathered around arguin' about somethin' or another."

"Arguin'?" Cotton questioned.

"Yep. So I rode down there to see what the fuss was all about."

"And they were discussin' what they'd just done?"

"Not exactly. They were arguin' about what to do with what was in these here valises."

"Let me get this straight. You're sayin' they likely saw Havens makin' a run for it and they grabbed him, strung him up, and *then* they start makin' a stink over what to do with the money? That it?"

"That's the story."

"So how'd you get your hands on it?"

"Once I told them I was a U.S. marshal, they began to listen to reason. Didn't have no trouble gettin' them to see there was no choice but to return it all to the bank, seein' as how it belonged to some of them, anyway. Makes no sense to steal your own money, does it?"

"And out of your dedicated sense of duty to the citizenry, you just naturally had to bring it all back," Jack said with more than a touch of suspicion in his voice.

"That's the way it was, Deputy."

"Havens still danglin' from that tree when you left?"

"He was. Reckon he still is," Thorn said.

"Jack, we best stop by the undertaker's and go out and fetch him," Cotton grumbled.

Chapter 49

"Don't you find it curious that Thorn suddenly remembered somethin' he had to do, that prevented him from joinin' us?" Jack said, slumping slightly from the pain of being jostled about in the saddle. The east road out of Apache Springs was rough and rutted from the many wagons traveling to and from the nearby mines.

The undertaker had brought his buckboard to haul the body of Havens back to town. It bounced over the dips where water flowing downhill from the nearby hills during rainstorms had eroded the roadway. At one particularly rough patch, the pine box that had been brought to carry the corpse nearly bounced out.

The sky was overcast, promising rain later in the day, which would do little to improve their trip back to town. Cotton had been silent the whole way, content to listen to Jack mumble about how convenient it was that Thorn McCann just *happened* to get to the scene of the lynching in time to save the money, but not Havens himself. The only response from Cotton was a grunt. Jack apparently couldn't tell if it was an agreement or not. Jack continued to mope.

When they arrived at the spot Thorn had described, Cotton sat and stared at the grisly sight dangling from a cottonwood. He urged his horse around, looking at Havens from different angles before he motioned for the undertaker to join him. He was beginning to have second thoughts about having told McCann to stay in town, rather than accompanying them in case other questions arose. Thorn had claimed to be bushed and needing some sleep. They'd mutually agreed that as soon as Cotton and Jack got back with Havens's body, Thorn would come down to the jail and they would settle the one score that had presumably brought him to town as Comanche Dan in the first place. For some reason that Jack couldn't fathom, Cotton had been amenable to Thorn's suggestion, and he made no attempt to hide his feelings.

"Cotton, I never have liked that man, and you know it."

"Thorn McCann?"

"Yeah. You know who I'm talkin' about. Don't act like you don't."

"What is it about him you find unsettlin'?"

"I just plain don't trust him. Don't give a tinker's damn that he seems a friendly sort and all that. I figure you're not of the same mind, but I say what I mean. Always have. No offense."

Cotton sighed. "None taken."

They sat beneath the tree from which the body of Bart Havens dangled, the rope creaking from the weight as a slight breeze blew through the limbs, giving the lifeless form an eerie presence. Cotton stared at the corpse. Seeing his enemy and tormentor in death should have made him happy, or at least given him considerable satisfaction. Instead, showing no emotion whatsoever, he dismounted and began examining the ground around the scene for twenty yards. Then, he walked around the body itself, before finally telling the undertaker to help him cut the body down.

Jack wasn't able to lift any weight, so he merely directed

the others. When they had the body loaded into the pine box, they started back to town. The buckboard rattled and shook, creaking under its added weight, slipping in and out of the ruts.

"What're we goin' to do with all that money?" Jack asked. "I gotta tell you I was a little squeamish about leavin' it all lyin' around the jail with nobody watchin' over it."

"Nobody knows it's there . . . except Thorn. And the door's locked," Cotton said with a wry grin.

"So, when we get back . . ."

"We take it down to Darnell Givins after we've gone through all four valises. He'll probably bring in someone from Albuquerque to audit the account books. They'll be able to determine how it all shakes out."

"That's a good idea."

"Glad you approve." Cotton looked over at Jack with a raised eyebrow.

"You makin' fun of me?"

"Never."

Cotton helped the undertaker unload the pine coffin bearing the remains of the late Mr. Bart Havens, then went to the stables to unsaddle his horse and put her up for the day. Jack had gone on to the jail, apparently anxious about those four valises of cash sitting in there, unguarded. When Cotton walked in, Jack was peering into one of the open cases.

"Have you determined that it's all there, yet?"

"Since I have no idea what 'all there' actually means, the answer is no."

"Hmm, well, you're right about one thing; we have no idea how much money Bart left town with. But that's only part of the story. We don't know how much he arrived with, either."

"I hadn't thought about that, Sheriff. We know he was receiving lots of cash from folks transferring their savings from Darnell's bank to his, all because the scoundrel promised a high interest rate," Jack said, frowning with curiosity. "Folks sure are fickle, 'specially when it comes to money."

"They are at that."

"So, you figure that Bart's own money is mixed up with others'?"

"I think it's highly likely."

"When do you want to take it to Givins?"

"No time like the present. I think I can handle three of these, if you can grab the last one. I'll feel better, and I damned well know you will, when this cash is safe and sound and locked up tight."

Jack grabbed the fourth valise and followed Cotton outside, down the boardwalk, and into Darnell Givins's Apache Springs Bank and Loan. Darnell's eyes grew wide as the four satchels, brimming with cash, were dropped on the desk in front of him.

"What the hell, Sheriff? Where'd all this money come from?" Givins began thumbing through the contents and shaking his head in disbelief.

"The long and short of it is: It came from Havens's bank. Whose it is, we don't know. And Havens is dead. So it appears it'll be up to you to answer all those questions. Oh, and as of this minute, the responsibility to keep it safe also falls squarely on your shoulders."

"I fully understand. It's going in the safe this very minute."

"Can you get an auditor down here from Albuquerque to unravel this mess? There ought to be a set of books somewhere, either in one of the bags or over at Havens's bank."

"I'll get right on it." Givins was beside himself. Cotton wasn't sure whether his joy came from having all that money drop from the sky into his lap, or because Bart Havens was dead and gone. And out of his life forever.

Cotton offered to buy Jack's dinner at the hotel, after which he planned to go the jail and await the arrival of Thorn McCann to wrap up a little personal business.

Jack never turned down free food.

Chapter 50

As Thorn McCann came strolling across the street, seemingly without a care in the world, Cotton stiffened in his chair. Still not completely comfortable with a man who constantly changed his story, Cotton pulled his Colt out and placed it in the top drawer of his desk. He leaned back in his chair. The first thing Thorn noticed was Cotton's empty holster. The second thing was Memphis Jack Stump leaning next to the gun rack, his thumbs in his gun belt, right hand very close to his Remington.

"Good afternoon, Sheriff, Deputy." Both nodded their response.

"So, are you ready to talk about settlin' that other piece of business we talked about a while back?" Cotton said.

"You're readin' my mind, Sheriff."

"Well, before we go further, I have in my desk a couple of telegrams I received in response to my query a few days back about my status as a wanted fugitive in Texas. Seems the Rangers, the county sheriff, and the U.S. marshal for the district all know nothin' about any warrant for my arrest. Furthermore, not one of them had one good thing to say about Judge Sanborn."

"Hmm. Sounds about right."

"And that ain't all. Not one of 'em ever heard of a U.S. Marshal Thorn McCann, neither. Although they all had a passel of words, mostly of a disagreeable nature, to say about a bounty hunter by that name."

Jack's hand slid down to the butt of his Remington, probably just in case this conversation didn't go where Cotton intended.

"And you are lookin' for some explanation, right?" McCann sighed.

"Uh-huh."

"Mind if I sit?"

"Go right ahead. And like I suggested last evenin', keepin' your hand well away from that smoke wagon on your hip would amount to some real good thinkin'."

McCann leaned forward with his hands on his knees. "All that stuff you just said is true, at least as far as it goes. I *am* a bounty hunter. Sorry about the deception. Sometimes I get a little carried away with schemes to get a fugitive to accompany me back for a trial."

"I also found that this Judge Sanborn is only a justice of the peace. He doesn't have the power do much more than levy a fine for spittin' in the street. What do you figure he had in mind by putting a price on my head?" Cotton stared Thorn straight in the eye with a hard look.

"Like I said, all that's true. Look, he's offering to pay two thousand dollars out of his own pocket to bring you back for killing his son, Lucky Bill. My job is fulfilling folks' wishes, that's all. That and, at the time, I was in dire need of the money."

"Uh-huh. But it's illegal for one man to put a price on another man's head for his own personal vengeance. You are aware of that, aren't you?"

"Of course."

"Then . . . ?"

Thorn looked away for a moment, as if he were seeking

an answer that would not make him seem like nothing more than a hired killer. His searching eyes told Cotton there wouldn't be an acceptable answer anytime soon.

"So, what *did* you intend? Since I'll not go with you willingly, and Jack'll gut-shoot you if you try pulling that hogleg on an unarmed man, I figure you better lay your cards out on the table so we can deal with 'em, proper."

Thorn took a deep breath and let it out.

"I've seen what you can do with that Colt. I don't know if I could beat you or not, but right now I don't have the stomach for finding out. I been thinkin' of finding myself a nice soft job somewhere that'll let me sit back with my feet up on the desk, kinda like what you got here."

Jack looked over at Cotton and raised his eyebrows.

"So you think dealin' with a bunch of yahoos that'd just as soon put a hole through your gizzard every time they see you is a soft job, huh? Maybe I ought to turn this one over to you and I'll just settle down to pushing cattle around and taking my leisure on the front porch with a beautiful woman. You interested?"

"No, thanks."

"Does that mean you'll be leavin' Apache Springs without me in tow?"

"That's what it means. I really don't consider trading lead with you a good investment."

"What about that fat reward?"

"There'll be other rewards with less risk involved."

"That what happened to the real Comanche Dan?"

"Truth is, he was too drunk to pull on me. I didn't have to shoot him, just hauled him to the next town with a sheriff that knew who he was and collected my reward. A bunch of vigilantes, mostly businessmen who'd been robbed or had friends shot by him, dragged him out of that flimsy jail and strung him up before anyone knew he had been captured. Easiest five hundred I ever made."

"You said it was *you* that killed him," Jack said.

"Yeah, well, in a manner of speakin', it was. If I hadn't brought him in, he'd still be alive and probably addin' his gun to Bart's army. Count your blessings," Thorn said, with a wily grin.

"I see your point," Cotton answered.

"Oh, before I leave, if somethin' comes up and you find yourself in need of another gun, you can reach me in Silver City," Thorn said, as he put on his hat, hiked up his gun belt, sauntered out into the sunlight, and unhitched his mount. He swung into the saddle.

"Silver City? What made you decide to go there?" Cotton said.

"I heard they're in need of a town marshal. Thought I'd go see if that's true. Sounds like a nice quiet place to me." Thorn gave a salute and turned his horse toward the road out of town, to the south, in the direction of Silver City.

"Good riddance," Jack said, leaning on the doorjamb.

"Uh-huh. You figure this whole thing is behind us, now?"

"I suppose. What else could there be? Bart's dead. All his gunslingers are, too. All wrapped up nice and tidy. And you and me are none the worse for wear—well, you anyway."

"Seems like that, doesn't it? Nothing left now but to wait on that fellow from Albuquerque to come peruse Bart's ledgers and give us the verdict."

"After he figures how much of the money belongs to the citizens and how much is Bart's, what happens to Bart's portion?" Jack asked.

"Reckon we'll have to cross that bridge when we come to it, won't we?"

Chapter 51

Two weeks had passed before Darnell Givins sauntered into the jail on a sunny morning, looking for the sheriff. Jack told him he was out at the Wagner ranch and that he'd be back by nightfall. Darnell deferred giving out information to Jack, preferring instead to await Cotton's return. He said something about assuming certain proprieties before elaborating on what he'd found out about the valises containing cash from Bart's bank. Jack didn't see that as an affront, but merely a careful banker playing his cards close to the vest, something Jack understood fully.

While Jack was, admittedly, intensely curious about the bank audit, he already had enough memories of Havens's attempt to destroy Apache Springs and him and Cotton with it. His wound was healing nicely, but there was still lingering pain. The doctor said it should be fine, given time. He had been admonished to take things easy and get plenty of rest. He figured drinking his share of brandy sufficed for taking it easy, but he wasn't certain whether Melody's energetic romps in the bedroom could be considered rest. He doubted it.

Cotton had taken to visiting Emily more often now that the danger posed by a town full of gunslingers had apparently passed. At least the atmosphere in town had lost the air of uncertainty that had put folks on edge, even if they didn't completely understand why. Cotton and Emily spent many a cool evening sitting on the porch swing chatting about this and that, but never delving into anything of real substance, much to her displeasure. She had been hoping for some time that Cotton would make the leap toward a firm commitment between them. He wasn't an easy man to read. If necessary, she would be happy with whatever time he could spare for her, rather than abandon all hope for any future together. She would much rather have him near her on his terms than tied to her apron strings and miserable. He was a wild stallion, needing his freedom and his space, and she knew and understood that. She was not cut out to be a mother hen, anyway.

"Have you any word on whose money it was that Havens took from his bank?"

"Not yet, but I think I'll ride into town early in the morning. The auditor has had four days to come to some conclusion. I want to be there when he releases his findings."

"You sound doubtful that the outcome will find favor with the folks in Apache Springs. Why is that?"

"This whole affair is more complicated than it seems. Bart Havens was a devious, deceitful man, never one to leave an obvious trail to his dealings. It's conceivable we'll not be any closer to finding all the answers to this sordid mess than when Thorn brought that money back."

"At least he *did* bring it back. That should be worthy of credit, shouldn't it?"

"At first glance, I agree. I don't think we know the complete story, that's all."

"Is there any chance Havens didn't keep accurate records, since it seems he planned all along to steal everyone's money and leave the town high and dry?"

"There's more than a chance. My guess is we'll find he deliberately manipulated the entries because, if someone should have called him to task before he could get out of town, he could have shown them his books. It would be their word against his. No one could prove anything against him, unless . . ."

"Unless, what?"

"Unless he gave each customer a copy of their deposit, figuring they'd probably lose it or destroy it, assuming they didn't need another piece of paper lying around. And . . ."

"And what?"

"And those crafty old ranchers and penny-pinching businessmen had a habit of keeping every scrap of paper that might affect their finances, yesterday, tomorrow, or ever."

"That sounds more like the ranchers I know. Well, while you're mulling over the workings of a dead man's mind, I'm getting ready for bed. There's coffee on the stove if you want some before you turn in," she said with a twinkle in her eye.

Cotton watched her leave the room with the grace of a swan drifting along on lazy waters. He got up and followed her, saying, "No, I think I've had enough coffee for tonight. Besides, you may need someone to watch over you, make sure you don't have any bad dreams."

Emily smiled seductively. "Good idea."

The next morning, Cotton kissed Emily before mounting his mare and riding down the gravel-strewn hill through the open gate. His thoughts had yet to leave the comfort of Emily's charms, but niggling questions left unanswered about Havens still haunted him. Where had Havens been headed, why was he killed, and what could even a qualified auditor ever hope to make out of the wads of cash in those bags?

He felt both relief from the demise of Havens and his henchmen, and a gnawing sense of his own vulnerability that a man with such devious intentions could so easily ride into town, set up shop, and begin fleecing the citizenry as if there were no laws or lawmen to prevent it.

The sun beat down relentlessly, promising another scorcher after a day of drizzly rain. The wetted ground held the moisture only for a few hours, for whatever time it took the roots of grasses and shrubs to have a drink before the heat of the day drew out the little remaining dampness and baked the ground once again, beginning the cycle of nature all over. He was surrounded by evidence of life struggling to hang on in a harsh land. How the hills managed to burst forth in spring and fall with the delirious colors of bountiful wildflowers was a mystery to him.

He wiped perspiration from his forehead with his shirt-sleeve.

Cotton let his horse pick the pace, and, for the time being, a slow, steady jaunt seemed to suit them both just fine. As he entered the town's limits, he was aware of the smell of the fresh-cut pine boards, newly hammered into place to serve as walls for yet another business, another hopeful entrepreneur seeking his fortune. The town had recently seen a boom in new businesses. And an eclectic mix of wooden, adobe, and temporary canvas-covered buildings greeted him as he headed down the main street. In front of the jail he saw a small crowd of people gathered. Some were shouting angrily, others merely standing by as observers, seemingly content to see what would happen if those more boisterous individuals got things stirred up sufficiently to warrant action by the law.

Jack was out front, armed with a coach gun, likely filled with nothing more than salt. After all, even in a confrontation with a crowd, the objective wasn't to blow folks into the next county, but to discourage them from becoming rowdy enough to do damage to property or bring harm to other people. As Cotton rode up, he purposely urged his horse through the crowd, bumping some people aside, or making bystanders make way. When he dismounted, he put his hand on the handle of his Colt, forging a path toward Jack.

"What's this all about?" Cotton shouted, turning to the noisiest of those gathered.

"That bastard stole our money and we want it back. Now!" shouted the man closest to him.

"Your money is safe. Now, go on about your business and I'll let you know when you can get your hands on it. Right now it's in the bank being accounted for by some bank fellow from Albuquerque."

"How do we know you aren't pullin' a fast one on us like Havens did?"

"Because most of you know me, and you know I don't operate that way."

"We figured we could trust a banker, too, and look where that got us."

"I understand your frustration. Bart Havens was nothing more than a con man. But he's dead, and the town has to unravel the mess he created. So if you'll just do us the courtesy of settlin' down and go on back to your businesses or families, you have my word things will work out."

The crowd slowly broke up, and with considerable grumbling and cursing under their breath, all departed. Some went to the saloon, probably to build up some more courage, while others went inside their own shops or walked their horses down the street to the stable. Cotton figured many planned to stay close-by until there was some resolution as to the disposition of their assets.

Jack wiped sweat from his face with a damp handkerchief. He stuffed it back in his pocket and blew out air. "Whew. Damned glad you decided to ride up when you did. Things weren't goin' real smooth." He led the way back inside and put the shotgun back in the rack.

"They did appear somewhat touchy, didn't they, but you seemed to be handlin' things fine. You hear from Givins yet?"

"Yeah. He said to tell you to come down to the bank the

minute you got back. I think he's got news—whether it's good or bad, I can't say."

"It better be good. Right about now, that's the only kind those folks are gonna accept. You comin'?"

"I think I better stick around and load up all the rifles, shotguns, and six-shooters just in case it don't turn out the way you want it to."

"Jack, you're too much of a skeptic." Cotton merely shook his head as he walked away.

Chapter 52

When Cotton walked into the Apache Springs Bank and Loan, Darnell Givins looked up from his desk and gave a wide smile, which from Darnell was startling to anyone who knew him. He had a reputation for being the most staid, expressionless individual anyone ever did see. Cotton had always felt he'd have been a better undertaker than a banker.

"G'morning, Sheriff. And I do mean *good*!" Darnell stuck out his hand in greeting.

"You suggestin' you can account for all those folks' money, Darnell?"

"It's more than a suggestion. We got proof. Whatever else that snake Havens was, he was damned good at keeping records. Every cent those folks deposited in his bank is in these ledgers. We found them at the bottom of each satchel. And they all added up."

"So, while he was tryin' to steal every red cent the citizens had, he still kept a good accountin' of it all?" Cotton was clearly puzzled by why a man who'd set out from the beginning to defraud a whole town was careful with his record keeping. He scratched his head, took off his hat, then settled it back on.

"I got no explanation, Sheriff, but I'm sure glad he did it," Darnell said, about ready to bust a button off his suspenders.

"The folks'll be damned glad to get the news."

"That's what I figured. So, how about me going to the newspaper and having the printer make up a batch of flyers to distribute around town? That way, everybody gets the good news at the same time."

"Now, just for the record, every last cent in those bags is accounted for, no shortages, no extras?"

"That's right. To the penny."

"Thanks, Darnell. I'll leave you to your work," Cotton said.

"That seems to be the long and short of it, Jack. Every penny, the man said."

"That'll be damn good news to a lot of folks. I think Melody even put her money with Havens, probably because of the promise of a big return. You know how Melody is. She never passes on a good deal, especially if she can add to her poke."

"Yeah, I know."

"Then how come you look so down in the mouth? Emily didn't make you wash dishes or somethin', did she?" Jack burst into a grin that was half devil and half little boy.

"It's just that the whole thing doesn't make a lot of sense. That's what."

"What sense? Folks are goin' to get their hard-earned money back. What's there to make sense of?"

Cotton shrugged and walked outside. He sighed and stepped into the street. Jack stood in the doorway and watched.

"Where you off to now?"

"I'm goin' to have some coffee, maybe a piece of pie,

and contemplate just what I do mean, seein' as how I'm not real sure myself. I'll be back in an hour or so."

Jack was puzzled by the direction the sheriff seemed headed.

Far as I know, there isn't any pie and coffee at the undertaker's.

The town's undertaker served not only to bury the dead, but also to build cabinets, chairs, and bookshelves for the businesses and homes in and around Apache Springs. He was finishing a nice table as the sheriff walked in. A bell above the door tinkled its announcement of a visitor. The undertaker had put it there so someone just stopping by to share a pleasantry didn't walk in on the gruesome sight of a corpse being readied for burial.

"Good morning, Sheriff."

Cotton nodded a response. "I came to ask a question."

"Happy to oblige. What would you like to know?"

"Was Bart Havens shot *before* or *after* he was strung up?"

"Before. Why?"

"You're sure?"

"When you've seen as many men as I have who've had their neck stretched, you wouldn't be asking that."

"So, someone shot him, then strung him up to make it look like he'd been hanged?"

"As I see it, that's exactly what happened. Not the first time I've seen such a thing. But there's a distinct difference between a death by hanging and one by gunshot. Havens was shot first. I'd stake my life on it. Don't seem to me to be important, though. He's still dead."

"Reckon he is at that."

"Anything else you want to know?"

"That about does it. Thanks for your time," Cotton said as he left. The bell tinkled at his departure just as it had on his arrival. He looked up to see Jack running toward him.

"What's the problem, Jack?"

"No problem, just my curiosity workin' up a sweat."

"Curiosity about what?"

"Mostly about the way you been actin'. I never knew the undertaker to serve pie and coffee. That and whatever else is eatin' at you needs to get said. Friends are the best place to start in that kinda situation."

Cotton squinted in the bright sunlight, giving Jack a quick questioning glance. "All right, Jack. We'll go to the hotel and I'll try to explain my *mysterious* ways," he said, shaking his head.

"You buyin'?"

A lady, in what had once been a white apron but which was now stained with splotches from various sources of kitchen detritus, came to their table. When she asked what they'd have, Jack said he'd just have coffee. Cotton told her he'd have coffee *and* a piece of blueberry pie. When she exhibited a surprised look at him knowing they had blueberry, which was not one of their regular menu items, he pointed to a distinctive blue stain on her apron. She left, laughing all the way to the kitchen.

"Comin' right up," she quipped from across the room just before disappearing through a curtained doorway.

"Okay, Jack, there are still *some* questions that need answerin'. And I reckon that could be part of what's got me twisted in a knot."

"Like what? The money's back, Havens is dead. The threat is behind us. What could possibly be botherin' you now?"

"I talked to the undertaker. He said Havens was strung up *after* he was shot. It was the bullet that killed him."

"He's dead. Him and every last one of his gang of cutthroats. What's the difference? Hell, let it be."

"That's right. He's outta our hair. But the results of his comin' here in the first place haven't been fully felt as of yet, at least in my opinion. Consider this. Havens paid each and every one of those gunslingin' hombres a thousand dollars to kill us, with the promise of more to come. Then he held 'em back until he was ready to eliminate you and me. Why? He made no secret that he hated me for gettin' him run outta Benbow Creek, Texas. Hatred was the kinda thing that seemed to get his day started off right. And, don't forget, he brought with him enough money to rent that building and hire carpenters to make the inside look like a bank. He spent a lot of money puttin' on his little performance. You with me so far?"

"Uh-huh."

"Didn't you wonder why he didn't turn Sleeve Jackson or Buck or one of the others to just blast us on sight? Maybe even back-shoot one of us from a darkened alley."

"Never thought about it."

"Havens was not stupid. He was cunning and clever. He never did anything without a well-thought-out reason. And that's what we've got here, pardner, a *reason*."

The waitress came with the coffee and pie. Accompanying them was a silly grin left over from Cotton's clever deduction as to the day's dessert. She did, however, have on a clean apron.

Chapter 53

"I reckon you got me, Cotton. I never gave none of that any thought."

"Yeah, well that's not all, not by a long shot." Cotton forked off a piece of pie, then slipped it into his mouth. He took a sip of coffee, dabbed at his lips, and leaned forward. "Consider this. You were with me when Thorn came ridin' into town with the money in those four satchels, right?"

"Yep."

"What was it he told us about seein' Havens take his buggy and head east?"

"Uh, he said he thought it curious for Havens to leave town so close to time for the bank to open, so, after finding the bank empty, he saddled up his horse and followed the buggy out of town. Caught up to him too late to save him from a crowd of angry men, though." Jack sipped his coffee with a frown.

"And when he came into town drivin' Havens's rig, where was Thorn's horse?"

The look on Jack's face was more than just surprise; it

was a mixture of realization that what had seemed so clear and simple had turned muddy and complex, along with a touch of self-recrimination for not making the connection himself.

"Damn!"

"Another thing, I looked the ground over real good where we found Havens, and there was no evidence of any gang of horsemen trackin' up the surrounds."

"So you're sayin' there were no vigilantes lookin' to even a score?"

"That's the way the signs read."

"Mrs. Blanchard's bunch of angry ranchers didn't take retribution on the thievin' banker?"

"Not the way I see it."

"That means Thorn had to have been the shooter," Jack said with a scowl. "I said it before, and I'll say it again, I never *did* trust that fella. But how'd he get out to where he shot Havens?"

"I figure he went out with Bart, or maybe made *him* go at gunpoint. Could have plugged him along the way."

"What about his horse?"

"Maybe he left it tied up just outside of town. I don't know. Doesn't really matter."

"So Thorn had a plan of his own from the beginning?"

"I'd say it happened about that way. That's probably why he wanted to get me aside early on and convince me he was a marshal disguised as a gunslinger. Likely he did that to keep one of us from shootin' him."

"Why would he think we'd shoot him?"

"He probably knew the others were like as not to explode at any moment, like a jug of nitroglycerin lyin' in the sun. Very unstable. He wanted to separate himself from the scum."

Jack stared at his plate for a moment, then took a sip of coffee. He wasn't through with his questions, and Cotton must have seen by the way he frowned over the top of his cup that he was mulling over something that didn't quite fit. Then, like a jackrabbit flushed from the brush by a coyote, Jack put his cup down and looked at Cotton with narrowed eyes.

"Since he brought the money back, what the hell did Thorn gain by his tomfoolery?"

"*Everything* he came here to get, he got." Cotton downed the last drops of coffee and scooted his chair back. He started to get up, when Jack took hold of his sleeve.

"Uh, and just what was that? That 'everything' stuff?"

"He came for *all* of *Havens's* money and a beautiful woman, to boot."

"Delilah?"

"Why don't you go up and ask her about him?"

Jack got up, put his hat on his head, and said, "I think I'll do just that."

Cotton went outside while Jack asked the desk clerk if Delilah was in. The sheriff had strolled halfway down the street when Jack came running after him.

"Damn! You knew, didn't you?"

"Yep."

"When did you figure it out?"

"When I saw her gettin' on the Silver City stage just before Thorn came back with the buggy."

Jack's face went ashen. He and Delilah went back a long way. In fact, at one time he was sure he was in love with her, thought marriage might even be in the works. Things hadn't worked out for them, but he still had deep feelings for her. He'd even shared her bed when Melody was gone. The spark was still there. For whatever reason, he was crushed by the revelation that she might have had something to do with Thorn McCann killing Havens and, perhaps, even played a part in getting away with Havens's money. Jack stood shaking his head. His eyebrows loomed dark over eyes that seemed to search for a more simplistic answer, but he was greeted by no such revelation. He didn't even want to consider the worst about the beautiful Delilah Jones. "Damn!" he muttered, again. "Then the satchels that Thorn brought to town weren't all of them?"

"That's the way I figure it. McCann got away with every penny of Havens's money, and nobody will ever be the wiser."

"What do you mean? Aren't we goin' after him? Make him pay for what he did?" Jack said, surprise on his face.

"Nope." Cotton continued on to the jail. Jack noticed his strides were more purposeful than before, his apparent resolve showing in his calm expression, and now likely his desire to push it all behind him would become uppermost in his mind.

"Why? If he's guilty, shouldn't he pay?"

"Yeah, I expect he should. But there are a few pieces of information missing that would make that impossible."

"Like what? We know he did it."

"Like how much money did Havens have? Where are *his* records? Did anybody see Thorn with other valises of money? If they had, did they know what was in them? Can we prove *one* thing I've just said?"

Jack sank onto the bench outside the jail. He seemed overwhelmed with the whole convoluted scheme. "Damn Havens for ever coming here," he growled. "And damn Thorn McCann, too."

"I agree with you, Jack, but there is not one single thing we can do about it. Looks to me like he's gotten away with *a perfect crime*."

"And maybe with a *perfect* woman, too," Jack said, sadly, glancing across the street to Melody's Golden Palace of Pleasure, just as she walked out on the porch, surveying the street. She gave him a slight wave, then went back inside. He wondered if he had ever loved Melody in the way he had once loved Delilah.

He had no answer for that.

"You're in charge, pardner; I'm ridin' out to tell Emily what's happened. She'll be relieved." Cotton had no more than gotten five steps out the door, than he heard his name being called. He turned to see Darnell Givins hurrying toward him. He had a fistful of greenbacks and he was waving them in the air.

"Sheriff, Sheriff! Look at what I found!"

"What is it, Darnell? Just looks like money to me. Since you're the bank president, I'd figure seeing greenbacks wouldn't come as any surprise to you."

"Well, it surely has this time."

"And why would that be?"

"Because it is all counterfeit!"

"What! All that money McCann brought back to town was phony?"

"Nope. What he brought back was fine, the genuine article. What this is came from the various businesses that accepted the bills tendered by Havens's gunslingers. They paid for drinks, clothing, ammunition, hotel rooms, whores—all of it in counterfeit paper. What do you think about that?"

"I think you've just completed the puzzle by supplying the last piece."

Jack stepped outside after hearing Darnell's explanation of what he'd found. "How does finding that some of Havens's money was fake prove anything new?"

"Don't you see, Jack? Bart didn't have the money everybody thought he had. He found someone to counterfeit enough to hire himself some pistoleros long enough to rape the town by offering no-interest loans to attract folks to put their money in his bank. That was his whole plan in the first place. He wanted to kill me and take his revenge. As soon as he had enough, he was going to take off. Problem was, you and I proved too tough for his gunslingers, so he had to depart ahead of schedule. He didn't figure on Comanche Dan turning out to be a ringer, either."

"Havens outsmarted himself and it cost him his life," Jack mused, rubbing his chin as a satisfied grin came across his face.

"Simple as that."

"You suppose McCann knew what was in those valises of Havens's?"

"Depends on whether Delilah knew. He'll figure it out one way or another, and I suspect it'll occur pretty soon. About the time he tries to buy something with some of it."

Three days later, as Cotton was cleaning his Colt, the telegraph operator burst into his office, out of breath.

"What's got you ready to explode?"

"Got this here telegram for you. Sounds important." The man leaned on the sheriff's desk, panting, waving his hat to cool himself off.

Cotton unfolded the paper and read it. A wry smile curled his lips. It read:

COME TO SILVER CITY. NEED HELP. GOING TO HANG.
THORN MCCANN

Cotton thanked the operator, shook his head, and continued cleaning his gun.

Praise for
PHIL DUNLAP

"Phil Dunlap's *Cotton's War* is a rip-roaring yarn that realizes the best traditions of the Western genre: strong, well-defined characters, the color of the West vivid and perfectly researched, and the writing entertaining and quick as a bronc set free to run wild. A surefire read for Western fiction fans." —Larry D. Sweazy, Spur Award–winning author

"*Cotton's War* is an old-fashioned, barn-burning, gut-wrenching Western story that moves at a gallop over dangerous territory. Phil Dunlap's sharp prose packs the punch of a Winchester rifle."

—Johnny D. Boggs, four-time Spur Award–winning author

"This is a well-crafted story with a good, clear writing style. It hits a good pace and keeps it up."

—John D. Nesbitt, Spur Award–winning author

"Dunlap uses his passion for history and the Old West to paint a realistic setting for his work. The prose is good without being heavy, and the story has a good pace that readers will enjoy. For those who share his love affair with gamblers, scalawags, and claim-jumpers with gold fever, this fun novel will keep you guessing."

—*The Indianapolis Star*

"With a raft of well-drawn, even indelible, characters, the novel also offers a compellingly involved, quite plausible, and tightly woven plot." —*Booklist*

"[Dunlap] appears to be poised to become a new star in the Western writing firmament." —*Roundup Magazine*

Berkley titles by Phil Dunlap

COTTON'S WAR
COTTON'S LAW